T0210041

THE BIG HURT

THE BIG HURT

A MONTREAL MURDER MYSTERY

JOHN CHARLES GIFFORD

iUniverse®

THE BIG HURT
A MONTREAL MURDER MYSTERY

iUniverse books may be ordered through booksellers or by contacting:

iUniverse
1663 Liberty Drive
Bloomington, IN 47403
www.iuniverse.com
844-349-9409

Because of the dynamic nature of the Internet, any web addresses or
links contained in this book may have changed since publication and
may no longer be valid. The views expressed in this work are solely those
of the author and do not necessarily reflect the views of the publisher,
and the publisher hereby disclaims any responsibility for them.

Any people depicted in stock imagery provided by Getty Images are
models, and such images are being used for illustrative purposes only.
Certain stock imagery © Getty Images.

ISBN: 978-1-6632-2750-8 (sc)
ISBN: 978-1-6632-2751-5 (e)

Library of Congress Control Number: 2021907246

Print information available on the last page.

iUniverse rev. date: 09/20/2021

Who is the third who walks always beside you?
When I count, there are only you and I together
But when I look ahead up the white road
There is always another one walking beside you.
—From "The Waste Land" by T. S. Eliot

Chapter 1

AN ENIGMA WITH RED LIPS
AND A WIDE-BRIM HAT

THE DOOR TO THE WADE DETECTIVE AGENCY burst open and banged against the wooden coatrack behind it, toppling it like an eastern white pine tumbling in the Quebec wilderness. The Venetian blind swayed back and forth with such force as to make a seaworthy chump screwy in the head if he stared at it long enough. Antoinette and Henri, a pair of felines curled on the couch, had been sleeping peacefully. Their heads popped up at the ruckus, ears pointing upward, eyes wide on high alert. Eddie Wade was sitting behind his Royal typewriter with a shot glass an inch from his lips—frozen in time. He blinked like a startled owl.

A high-heeled black patent leather shoe with a dazzling leg attached to it appeared in the doorway, and then another. The owner swung her face around to the right as she came in and locked eyes with Eddie. "Sorry, ducky. Sometimes I don't know my own strength." She was about five six and wore a tan trench coat. Perfume suddenly wafted throughout the office. *Ducky* inhaled it like a condemned man in a gas chamber.

He put the shot glass down in front of him beside the

typewriter, smiled for an indeterminate amount of time, and kept his yap shut. He was busy assessing the rest of her. There had to be a bombshell of a figure under that coat; he was going to be patient enough to find out.

He kept an uncomfortable wooden chair in front of his desk for potential clients. The woman pulled it back slightly, angled it, and then plopped down. "You're Edward Wade, I presume?" It was a question with all the trimmings of an accusation. Her blonde hair rolled off her shoulders like a wave teasing a shoreline. She had an oval face, small chin, and puckered lips that were painted red, capable of provoking the most loyal of husbands into infidelity in a heartbeat. Her skin was porcelain and flawless. She took care of herself—good care. She didn't want to break; Eddie could tell.

He'd been engrossed in typing out a final report to a client on a case he'd just finished, and it took a few seconds for his mind to adjust to the hubbub. When it did, he added up all the columns, made his calculations, went back and changed a few numbers, then spat out the results. The sum total barked trouble. He leaned back in his swivel chair, put his hands behind his head—fingers interlaced—and said dryly, "I might be. Why all the melodrama, sis?" The smile was still in place.

Her coat was open with the belt hanging down on either side, exposing a red dress, almost scarlet, under it. She wore a black wide-brim hat capable of hiding the upper part of her face if she had to. The morning sun shot through the plate glass window and the blinds behind it and lined her face. Her eyes could have been cobalt or brown or amber. They were raptor like—maybe an eagle or a hawk—able to hone in on their prey from a great distance, and as sharp as an obsidian knife. Eddie pegged her for early forties, but she could've passed for a decade younger. Some people look younger from a distance. When they come closer, you can see the lines and gray roots. Nothing like that with this broad. She crossed one elegant leg over the other and leaned back as much as the chair allowed her. Her eyes bore down on him. She said, "If you are, I want to hire you to find that no-good, skinny, rotten husband of mine."

She was used to getting want she wanted. Eddie could tell that too. He took a deep breath, the smile barely visible but there nonetheless, and asked, "How'd you get my name?"

"What difference does it make how I got your name when I'm willing to pay you cold, hard cash to find that son of a bitch? Do you want the job, or do I look elsewhere?" She angled her head at him. "It's a simple question that requires either a yes or no." The cats put their heads back down between their paws and closed their eyes, unimpressed. What did they know?

Eddie reached over and nudged the shot glass a little so she wouldn't see it behind the typewriter. He didn't want her thinking he was a drunk. People who started their drinking in the morning were automatically suspect. Bad for business. Could she smell his breath?

"I'm always interested in cold, hard cash, sis." He flashed her a smile again so that she wouldn't miss it and then added, "Whoever gave you my name was confused—mistaken. It's Bonifacio Edmondo Wade, like the window outside says. That's a mouthful, I know, so just call me Eddie." He grabbed his notebook that was lying on the desk and opened it to a clean page. "Before I can answer you, I need to know a few things—some facts ... details. You said you want me to find your husband. How long has he been missing?"

"I didn't misplace him," she snapped. "He's not missing. That no-good rat ran out on me. A week ago. I've waited this long to do something about it, hoping he'd come to his senses. He obviously doesn't have any."

He stared at her, trying his best to measure her up. People came into his office all the time with stories that they either made up to get back at someone who'd harmed them or elaborated on, distorting the truth. A broad like this wouldn't be beneath doing either one. Eddie learned early on in his career that if he could cut through the bullshit first, he would save time, money, and possibly pain.

"If he left you," he said as empathetically as possible, "that's unfortunate. You have my sympathy, but it's not a crime." It didn't have to be a crime for Eddie to take on the case, but a little voice inside him told him he'd be better off in the life he had yet to live if he avoided her.

She stared back at him and pursed her lips. Apparently, she didn't like being challenged. She narrowed her eyes at him and then adjusted the chair again, lifting herself up slightly while hanging onto it and turning it under her several degrees to the right. The adjustment was strategic and left him more accurately in her direct line of fire. He wondered whether he should duck for cover. Instead, he braced himself. *Fire in the hole!* he thought.

"Unfortunate my ass," she said. "And I don't need your sympathy. The bum ran out on me with ten thousand dollars in cash that belonged to me and all of my jewels, except what I happened to be wearing at the time." She pointed a finger at him, the nail the same color as her lips and deadly, and used it like a rivet gun, jerking it in his direction with each word: "Tell-me-that's-no-crime!"

In spite of her attempt to knock some sense into him, Eddie wasn't intimidated.

"The cash and jewels are yours free and clear and not held jointly?"

"Yes!" she said. The word came out as a hiss.

The little voice was telling him again to back away. Something didn't sound right to him. Thunder between husband and wife usually meant he'd be caught in a torrential downpour—eventually. He'd rather be hunting down a psychotic murderer than get involved in matrimonial disharmony, especially among the wealthy. An alternative— that was what he'd give her—an alternative.

"Then, yes, that's a crime." He paused for a moment to pick up his pipe he'd been smoking, struck a match, relit it, blew some smoke across the desk, and then said, "Indeed it is." Puff, puff. "Yes, indeed." Puff, puff. Then he leaned back, pulled the pipe out of his mouth, looked her in the eyes, and said strongly but diplomatically, "Maybe you should go to the police with this, sis. They won't bill you for their services."

"I pay my fair share of taxes to the city, so their services aren't entirely free. Besides, I want nothing to do with the police. They're incompetent, and I don't trust them. That's why I'm here." After a big sigh, she added, "Do you want the job or not?"

Eddie liked snooty broads who were direct. There was never a mistake about what they wanted from him. It almost always avoided hardships down the line. Those who hemmed and hawed, those who prefaced every little sentence out of their mouths with *ah* and *eh*, they were the ones with the big surprises. Eddie didn't much like surprises. They had the potential to shorten his life span. He preferred to sidestep them from the very beginning.

If he grabbed this case, he knew he wasn't going to resolve it in a few days. Not this kind of case. More like a few weeks. Maybe never. A case of a husband who skipped out on his wife and didn't want to be found was always fraught with surprises. There was always more to it than what was being said, directly or not—things that he'd discover along the way. That was what concerned him—those surprises. Even though she appeared to be direct, this broad looked as if she had a few up her sleeve. They could complicate the case and disrupt his universe. Ask the police about domestic disputes; they'd tell you. But the woman obviously had money, and clearly, she wanted to spend it. Why shouldn't he get some of it? He ignored the little voice. Several times during the next week or so, he'd wonder why he had.

"My fee is fifty dollars a day, plus expenses. That's standard for any client. I'll need an advance of four days for the fees. If I find your husband in less than four, I'll reimburse you the difference. I'll tack on my expenses at the end. If the case goes on beyond four days, I'll ask you for more money as I need it. All that is standard too; you'll see it in the contract I'll have you sign. But I'll tell you right now, this investigation could take considerable time if your husband's holed up somewhere. I'm not a magician, sis. I don't pick cute, little white bunnies out of a top hat. People like to think I do now and again, but I don't. If that's acceptable to you, you can sign a contract before you leave."

"I'll tell you what … Eddie? It is Eddie, isn't it? Yes, of course it is. I'll tell you what, Eddie. You find that bastard, and there'll be a lot more money in it for you." She opened her purse, peeled out ten fifty-dollar bills from her wallet, and laid them on the desk. "There," she said, patting them. "That should be enough to get you started."

The lady was on a mission.

He took a pen from his shirt pocket. "You didn't say your name."

"Chanel Steele, with an *e* on the end."

He wrote it down in his notebook, *e* and all.

"And your husband's?"

"You mean that skinny, thieving bastard? His name is Willis Steele."

"How long have you been married?"

"Apparently too long." She snarled, showing her teeth for the first time. They were gleaming. "Two months, give or take."

"Your address?"

She gave it to him.

"How much are the jewels worth?"

"Five thousand ... give or take."

"And ten grand in cash, you say, give or take?" he asked. "Do you usually keep that much money in your house?"

"I have expenses ... like you," she said defensively. "I don't like writing checks, and I don't like running to the bank all the time. They're never open when you need them." She sounded insulted by the question.

He glanced at his watch and then back at his notebook. "I've got an appointment downtown shortly and can't be late. Will you be available tonight around eight? I need to ask you a few more questions."

"I'm a busy person, but ... I'll make myself available to *you*."

Eddie looked up from his notebook at her inquisitively. For a professional transaction, the sudden sultry tone seemed out of place.

All business now: "I want you to get going on this right away, before the bastard decides to go to Timbuktu or some such place."

"Of course."

If the bastard did go to Timbuktu, Eddie could get a vacation out of it, with the expenses covering it. He reached in a side drawer in his desk and pulled out a contract. He needed her signature before he could take the money.

He put the contract in front of her, pointed at a line at the bottom, and gave her a pen. "Sign on the dotted line here, and we'll get the show on the road. When I come tonight, I'll need a current photo of your husband and a detailed description of the jewels. I'll fill out the contract in the meantime and give you a copy tonight. I'll also need the names and addresses of people your husband associated with. Close friends and extended family members will do just fine."

She leaned into the desk and signed the document. With

about as much grace, formality, and dignity as she'd had coming into his office, she went flying out, leaving the door half-open.

Eddie got up and closed the door. He picked up the coatrack, along with his jacket, overcoat, and hat that had been hanging on it. He separated two slats on the blind with his fingers and peered through them. She was crossing the street in front of his office, going toward her car. She had nice legs, he thought. What was the word? Dazzling? Yes, she had dazzling legs. And she probably had a nice behind under her trench coat. Eddie watched her get into a canary-yellow Caddy, open her purse, pull out a pair of sunglasses, and put them on. And then she drove away.

He went back to his desk, picked up the shot glass, and finished the whiskey. There was something gnawing at him. On the surface, she seemed to be a contradiction. She was a high-class gal with low-class morals, or so it seemed. Rough around the edges. That meant she hadn't been born into wealth. Her elegance ended when she opened her mouth. Had she come from money, those rough edges would have been smoothed out before she hit puberty and refined at finishing school, where she would have learned deportment and etiquette, those upper-class rites preparing young ladies for entry into cultured society. If she had attended charm school, she must have flunked out. But he didn't think so. She had been born into the working class (no matter how hard a person tried, the rough edges could never be fully educated away), and somewhere down the line, lightning struck, and everything had changed for her.

Eddie guessed that she must have come into money from either a previous marriage or by devious means. Perhaps both. Or maybe she was just a shrewd investor. Any way Eddie looked at it, her husband, Willis, wasn't the source of her good fortune. She'd been married to him for two months, which reeked to him. It wouldn't have been the first time something like that happened—marrying for money, getting a little of it, and then splitting. Of course, Eddie didn't have all the details yet, so he couldn't very well come to any conclusions. But he always liked to speculate and then see how close he'd come when the facts came stumbling in, one by one. Kept him on his toes.

Still, he was glad that he'd taken on the case. Chanel Steele was an enigma to him, and he liked enigmas—especially beautiful ones. In any event, he had more questions to ask her, and he'd do that tonight. In the meantime, he picked up the five-hundred smackers she'd given him, turned around in his chair, put it in the small safe on the floor, and spun the dial. The cash would assuage any doubts he might have for the time being.

He got up from behind his desk, fed the felines, and made certain they had enough water in their bowls. He put his jacket on and then his overcoat and hat. He walked back to his desk, picked out a pipe from the rack, put his hand inside his coat pocket to make sure he had his tobacco pouch and matches, and then opened the door. He locked up, wondering how the broad with red lips and a wide-brim hat had gotten his name. The fact that she hadn't wanted anything to do with the police bothered him. What was her angle? Everyone had one.

He had an appointment to keep, so he walked to the underground parking garage a half block away with an uneasy feeling in his gut.

———«◉»———

Chanel Steele hoofed it to her car opposite the Wade Detective Agency, her high heels unsteady on the road, her unbuttoned trench coat ballooning out around her. She stuck the key in the lock of her yellow Cadillac Eldorado convertible, jerked it angrily to the right, opened the door, and got in. Exasperated, she sighed. And then a thought occurred to her, and she grinned. She reached across the seat where she'd just thrown her purse seconds ago, grabbed it, and took out her sunglasses. She put them on and then adjusted them in the rearview mirror.

And grinned again.

She pulled out into light traffic on rue Saint-Urbain and headed south into town.

Chanel Steele was a very rich woman. Her wealth, however, was in a trust fund established by her former dead banker husband. She received a monthly disbursement, enough to keep her in the lifestyle she was accustomed to. She was set for life. However, she did not have access to the full amount, and that annoyed her greatly.

Chanel continued down rue Saint-Urbain until she reached Dorchester. She turned right and drove about a mile farther to rue de la Montagne and then made another right turn and found parking on the street in the middle of the block. She walked back toward Dorchester to the Jamaica Grill and went inside. The café wasn't busy yet, so she had little trouble finding him sitting at a small table in the back.

Luc Legrand looked up at her as she approached. "You're late, baby."

Chanel sat down, put her purse on the table, and placed her hands together under her chin. "Sorry, dear," she said, syrupy. "I had to see a private investigator about a little problem that happened last week. Willis left me and took a few things that didn't belong to him. I won't bore you with the details."

"Why don't you just divorce him?" Legrand asked. "You two are always having some sort of tiff."

"Do you know how much trouble that would be? It would take years. Besides, I'm not sure I believe in divorce. I just married him, after all. Only God knows why."

Legrand picked up the bottle of wine he'd ordered earlier and, pouring some in her glass, said, "I read somewhere that people who don't believe in divorce sometimes believe in other things." His eyes flicked up and caught hers. "Like murder."

Chanel looked at him for a moment, grinned, and then said, "Nuts to him."

They clicked glasses and sipped their wine. Chanel studied his face. He had gorgeous, dark eyes, thick eyebrows, black hair combed back, and shadowed cheeks and chin—the kind that needed to be scraped three times a day to look clean. He had an athletic body under the dark blue pin-striped suit. They had known each other for—what? Must be close to five years now. They'd first met one Saturday night at a dinner party at her home given by her then husband, Guy Dupont, who was now reposing peacefully in an expensive casket six feet underground, a recipient of a bullet to the back of his head. As a bigwig at the Royal Bank of Canada, Dupont's newest hire was Luc Legrand. "Darling, I'd like you to meet Luc Legrand. Luc, this is my lovely wife, Chanel. Luc here is going to head our investments department." That was how it had started—simply, with little fuss.

"I would say ... *poor baby*," Luc said, teasingly, "but you don't look very woebegone."

"Just between you and me and the doorjamb, I'm glad to see him gone. But he made off with something very precious to me."

"Let me guess," Luc said, and then he paused a moment, grinning. "Money!"

"It's not funny. He also stole my jewels."

"And you went to a *gumshoe*?" he asked, his face contorted as if he'd just bitten into a rotten egg. "Why not the police?"

"I have no regard for the police. Besides, you know I'm a private person. I don't want this plastered in the papers. If I went to the police, the story would be in all the latest editions of every damn paper in the city. They'd have a field day with it until something else seedy came along." She reached over and placed a hand over his. "Other things could get out as well. Private investigators have to keep things … private."

Chanel and Legrand had been immediately taken with each other at that party. They had engaged themselves in conversation the rest of the night, while her husband went from guest to guest, shaking hands, telling little jokes, throwing compliments at them here and there, making certain that everyone was enjoying themselves.

The party had been, by their standards, small—only about twenty-five guests, mostly employees from their branch and from the head office. The occasion was to welcome several new members into their fold, Legrand being one of them. There had been a luscious meal beforehand—Quebec cider-spiked duck (Dupont himself had shot several of them the week before) and apple cassoulet or freshly caught trout with spring potatoes. After the meal, the senior-most bank official stood up, a tall, emaciated-looking man with white, frizzy hair who had spent the evening staring at the women and ignoring the men. With a tired and bored expression, he gave his obligatory speech, which included the obligatory jokes, at which everyone laughed as if on cue. After the dessert and the Champagne and the table chitchat, the guests formed into little, tight-knit groups and stayed that way the rest of the night, avoiding at all costs those in other groups whom they considered morons.

While a quartet of string instruments played in the sunroom adjacent to the living room, Chanel and Legrand had wormed their way out of their respective groups and found each other by the fireplace. They chatted there for a time and then made their way to the kitchen, where they continued the conversation. From there, they strolled to the patio in the back of the house, and from there, to the living room again. Looking back at it, Chanel felt there had been a spark between them. Finally, with a few hours left before the party would break up, they found themselves in the guest room on the second floor, where the chatting ceased. Legrand suffered, and had since his middle-teen years, from satyriasis, which was fine and dandy with Chanel, because she had always considered herself a nymphomaniac.

Legrand looked at his Patek Philippe. "We should be going. I have an appointment at the bank in two hours."

"Huh?" She was staring into his eyes but thinking about something else, not really listening to him.

"I said we should be going."

"Oh, yes, of course we should." She cocked her head to the side. "Do you know what I like about you, Luc?"

"I believe I do, but tell me anyway," Legrand said, phlegmatically. He'd always been a stolid person, dispassionate even, some would say. Chanel believed he'd become that way as a result of years of working in the bank. He had that certain cold banker's look about him—accusatory. Just like her former dead husband. But Chanel was one of many women who knew another side of him.

"You're filthy rich and don't give a shit about me."

Legrand rubbed the side of his rough face and grinned at her.

"You have a solid grasp of the universe," he said flatly. "Good for you!"

Chanel leaned into the table and lowered her voice. "You know that one man can never satisfy me, and I know you want to screw me every chance you get. After all, you've been doing it for five years now."

"Is that it?" he said, chortling. "I thought you'd have a more profound summation, something slightly less crass."

"And I want you to know that the feeling is very mutual."

With that, they clicked their glasses in a toast and chuckled.

After they finished the remainder of the wine, Legrand took out his wallet and placed some bills on the table. Chanel picked up her purse, and they walked out of the café. It was a lovely day for mid-March. Spirited winds pushed the high, white, fleecy clouds along. In Quebec, however, that could change on a dime. Chanel decided to leave her car where it was parked, and together they walked to Dorchester, turned left, and continued on, passing Drummond and Stanley. When they were nearly to rue Peel, they stopped.

"Wait here," Chanel said. "Give me fifteen minutes and then come up. Same room—three oh four." She turned and waited for an opening in the traffic and then crossed Dorchester and went into the Laurentian Hotel. *Willis Steele. Gone? Gone for good?* She giggled.

Chanel knew that Legrand would stand there looking at his watch every minute, and then exactly fifteen minutes later, he'd cross the street and follow her scent like a bloodhound into the one-thousand-room Streamline Moderne hotel and up to the third floor.

Chapter 2
THE NOISE

EDDIE WADE FOUND A PARKING SPOT IN FRONT of London Life Insurance Company at the corner of Sherbrooke and Mansfield. Earlier that morning, he'd checked in with his answering service and found that the company had left a message concerning a claim they wanted him to investigate. It sounded like a routine job—easy money in the pocket.

The answering service was new; he was still getting used to it. Last summer, he had had a gal Friday to answer the phone. Tangerine was her name. He'd rescued her from a mob-connected, high-stakes gambling operation that offered its clients a little something extra on the side in the back bedrooms, especially to the losers, and didn't know what to do with her, so he put her to work in his office. She was good at the job; Eddie had gotten used to her and relied on her. Over the next few months, they'd formed a strong bond. For her safety from the mob, she slept in his bed in the back room, with him on the couch in his office. That fall when the heat was off, it ended when she left for her studies at McGill.

With Eddie's help, she'd straightened her life around, but it broke his heart not having her around. He'd been her beacon of light in a dark universe, protecting her from the

15

sophisticated savagery of standing and influence and other twisted cruelties and barbarism wrought by the unrestricted power and wealth of men without depth, without empathy, and without a code to guide them; or if they had a code, it was self-serving and destructive. Tangerine was gone, and for a time, he had been left alone with a heap of fragmented images, a withered stump of time, and the vastness of an endless ocean of space before him. He might have loved her, but that possibility, too, was gone.

Eddie pulled back the door to London Life and entered. The company was big enough to have the entire building to themselves. He passed the reception desk, waved at the cute, young redhead behind it, the one who had too much lipstick on, tipped the brim of his hat to a harried-looking guy behind a desk he knew only by reputation, and walked down a hallway, stopping at the third door on his right. He heard a voice on the other side of the door. He waited until it was quiet, and then he knuckled the door twice and walked in. Reginald Nithercott looked up at him over his glasses from his desk and then glanced at his watch. There was no one else in the office.

"Three minutes, twenty seconds early, Mr. Wade." He stated an undeniable fact. Facts were important to Nithercott. "Good for you. You know what they say about the early bird. However, had you been three hours and twenty minutes early, that would be an entirely different kettle of fish. Punctuality does have its limitations, you know."

Reginald Nithercott had worked in the claims department of London Life since Moses was a babe. He was a fastidious man in his late forties, average height, brown hair (graying at the temples), with a thick mustache that hid his upper lip. He always wore a vest under his suit jacket, which he never took off outside his home, even though he spent the majority of his time at work, alone in his office. One had to dress appropriately no matter the circumstances; you never knew who might pop in all of a sudden. He looked at the disordered world around him and spent his adult life (and a good chunk of his teen years) trying to figure out how to bring some semblance of order to it. The various items on the top of his desk—a stapler; a round, leather-covered pen and pencil holder; in and out trays; a leather-framed desk pad; and a Burroughs calculating machine—all had their places in the universe and on his desk. For Reginald Nithercott, black was black, and white was white. Gray was not in his immediate framework of reference. He was single because no woman in her right mind would have him. He was a serious man. Notwithstanding, he was not without humor, but he doled it out sparingly, as one might do with coins when passing beggars on a street corner. Eddie had known him since he had his private license and liked him.

Eddie sat down on the chair in front of Nithercott's desk. "I heard you talking, Reggie, and I thought someone was in here with you."

"Please, it's Reginald. I've gone over that with you before. What you heard was me thinking aloud. I do that often when I'm alone." He narrowed his eyes in mock suspicion. As if he had to justify himself, he added, "It's a free country, isn't it? Talking aloud to yourself when you're alone helps you clarify your thoughts. You should try it sometime, Mr. Wade."

"Just Eddie, Reggie."

"*Please* ... it's *Reginald*, as you very well know. That's the name I was born with, and that's the name I will die with." He folded his hands in front of himself, fingers interlaced, and angled his head. "How long have we known each other?"

"A long time, Reggie," Eddie said, chuckling a little. "What kind of claim do you want me to look into?"

Reginald Nithercott looked over his brown horn-rimmed glasses at Eddie and sighed. "Don't presume our friendship.

Your name is Bonifacio Edmondo Wade. Hell's bells, just how do you get *Eddie* out of—"

"OK, OK, you win this time. Just tell me what the job is."

"I thought that for the sake of simplicity, *Mr. Wade* would be easier ..."

And on and on he went. Eddie knew he'd have to wait patiently for Nithercott to unwind before he got to the reason why Eddie had been summoned there. Finally, Nithercott did.

Sort of.

"Let me preface this by saying that life is never as simple and tidy ..."

Eddie sat back and made himself comfortable. Reginald Nithercott always got to the point in their discussions, but he made certain to take a circuitous route. There was no other option for Eddie; he had to have patience.

"... as we would like it to be. There are always loose ends. When one tries to clean something up and bring a modicum of order to it, one always finds a few dirty spots here and there that have been missed." He paused a beat and then went on. "Plato once said that, and I quote, 'Human behavior flows from three main sources: desire, emotion, and knowledge.' And I quite agree that ..."

And on and on he went again.

"Listen, Reginald, just tell me what you want me to do."

"Fine, but I had much more to say on the subject." He leaned back in his chair, making a church steeple with his hands, and locked eyes with Eddie for a long, dramatic moment. Then he said, "I want you to assuage the executives upstairs on the fifth floor."

"And why would I want to do that?"

"I was just coming to that if you'd be patient." He adjusted his glasses and smoothed out his mustache with his fingertips. "A woman walked into our building recently and wanted to know how to file a claim. One Sylvie Boucher. Are you taking this down? Good. She's the beneficiary on a policy we hold on her husband. She maintains that he is deceased."

"Well, that should be easy enough to verify. The guy's either dead or he's not."

"Don't be so crass. The appropriate term in the industry is *deceased*. Nevertheless, that was the precise reason I was preparing you with my initial remarks that seemed to bore you to no end. Life is not simple and tidy, as I said, and I have reason to believe that this claim isn't as well. If you'd been paying attention to the papers recently, you'd remember that a body was fished out of the St. Lawrence recently. Dr. Becket at the coroner's office doesn't know how long it had been in there because the river was cold and icy. It's the middle of March, so we could expect as much. It could be anywhere from weeks to six months—probably not more than that. The face of the deceased was for the most part unrecognizable. But there was a wallet on the man, and in it was a driver's license with the name Martin Boucher. It was barely legible, but the police did verify the name, although it took some time. The height and weight of the corpse approximated that of Boucher. There were no pictures at all. The police used the address on the license and went to the house to notify the family. Sylvie Boucher was the wife of the man in question; there are no children. The police wanted to know why she hadn't filed a missing person's report. She told them that her husband had gone to Toronto to look for work. That's where she thought he was."

"What makes you think her story's not true?"

"The police have one bit of information that they haven't released to the public. It seems that the body had one little bullet hole to the heart."

"I see. What's the angle?"

"Her story might very well be true. But we aren't especially thrilled about paying out twenty thousand dollars when the policy holder's body can't be definitely identified. We have only the license to go by."

"Could Dr. Becket get prints off the corpse?"

"He's working on that, but there's no guarantee. In the meantime, we need to move forward on this."

"So where do I come in?"

"Two things. I'd like you to interview Sylvie Boucher and verify all the paperwork. We actually did that already. What I'd really like you to do is get a sense of the woman. Does she seem nervous? Evasive? That sort of thing. I think the term you people would use is *pump*. I'd like you to pump her for information and note carefully her physical and emotional reactions. You're good at that. See whether something surfaces that's out of place. This also serves another purpose: it puts her on notice that the claim is being investigated. It might encourage her to do or say something that we'd be interested in. Which bring me to the second thing I'd like you to do." He paused and harrumphed. When he finished adjusting himself in his chair, he continued: "Plato also said, and I quote, 'You can discover more about a person in an hour of play than in a year of conversation.' I'd like you to put a surveillance on her to ascertain her behavior after your visit. See what kind of games she plays, if any."

"There's no problem doing both, but I do have another case I'm working on, so I'll have to juggle both at the same time."

"Do your best, Mr. Wade. I don't know whether anything will come of this, but at least your final report should allay the concerns of upper management—the fifth-floor people, you know. You've worked on and off for us for quite some time. They have respect and confidence in your abilities and opinions. I might tell you that I do as well, if I thought your head wouldn't swell to the size of a watermelon." Nithercott's humor was trickling out. Eddie thought he saw his lips pull back in a smile, but he wouldn't stake his life on it.

Eddie rose from the chair. "I'm heading out for lunch. Care to join me?"

Nithercott reached into the side drawer of his desk and pulled out a brown paper sack. "I brought a sandwich today. I'd be willing to share half of it with you. It's made with sour cream, fresh dill weed, boneless and skinless sardines, capers, and red onions. I got the recipe from ..."

Eddie collected the paperwork from him as well as Sylvie Boucher's address and started to leave. At the door, he stopped and said, "See you around ... Reggie!"

Reginald Nithercott sighed.

"There's no accounting for taste," he said.

Eddie retraced his steps down the hallway, gave another wave at the redhead at the reception desk, and as he pushed his way out of the front doors of the building, he almost ran into an old man—a bum, the skid row type. His overcoat was dirty and torn in places, and his hat was crumbled and shabby. He had a beaten look about him. And he reeked. He stared at Eddie with basset hound eyes, but he didn't say anything. His hands were deep in his pockets, and his shoulders were slumped. He didn't look threatening—he was too old and haggard for that—just sad.

There were hundreds of bums living on the streets and alleyways of Montreal. Eddie knew his share of them. They were down-and-outs, drunks, and dope addicts. Some were violent, while others were harmless. Some had been in the war and couldn't cope with life any longer, the war still raging inside of them. They all had a story to tell. Eddie wondered what this bum's was. He was going to reach into his pocket for his wallet for a few dollars but decided not to.

"My name's Eddie Wade. You look a bit hungry. How about joining me for lunch?"

━━━━●━━━━

The announcer on the radio that morning in Eddie's office had been in high spirits as he told his listeners that today was going to be one of those rare March days in Montreal: no snow, no rain, no winds to speak of—only blues skies and moderate temperatures. So, Eddie decided to leave his car parked at London Life and, together with the bum he'd just met, walked the few blocks to Bens De Luxe Delicatessen. ("Bens never had an apostrophe, and it will *never* have an apostrophe!" the owner once pontificated to a young cub reporter who had brought up the mistake during an interview.) They strode west on Sherbrooke to Metcalfe, turned left, and continued on for another block to Maisonneuve, to the three-story brown brick building with a rounded front corner, green awnings over large bay windows, and a large, illuminated, wraparound sign displaying *Bens*—without the apostrophe.

Once inside, Eddie ordered for both of them. The waiter had a wedge-shaped head and a long, pointy nose that dwarfed his other features. His eyes were dark and recessed. He wore the standard uniform of Bens: black bow tie, white buttoned-down shirt, black dress pants, black shoes, and a white-waisted apron. His overall appearance was ominous, but he was friendly enough. Before he left with the orders, Eddie noticed that he inched his head toward the bum furtively and used his pointy nose to sniff. His eyes fluttered several times, and off he went, head held high with as much dignity as he was able to muster.

In less than five minutes, their meals were on the table.

Eddie had tried making small talk on their way there, but the bum had said nothing. Now, as they ate their smoked meat sandwiches, no words were exchanged. There was no indication that the bum could even speak. Eddie considered for a moment that he might be mute.

The restaurant was packed with noontime customers, but it was large enough to hold many more. Eddie always made a point of eating here whenever he was downtown. Bens was a showhouse of colors that always cheered him up whenever he was in the dumps. The floor-to-ceiling columns and the walls themselves were painted in shades of bright greens and yellows with chrome edgings. The chairs were bright yellow, orange, and green. The long counter was edged in stainless steel, the stools were all chrome, and the floor was finished in red and tan terrazzo. On the west wall was "Bens Wall of Fame," covered with photographs of celebrities—mostly Canadian politicians and Hollywood movie stars—who had dined at the restaurant.

Eddie took a bite of his sandwich, chewed, and then said, "Good, huh?"

The bum looked up and nodded. He might have been mute, but there was nothing wrong with his hearing.

Eddie didn't want to stare at him, but he did take quick glances every so often. Of course, he knew nothing about him and had never seen him before, yet the man had a past. Life could only be understood backward. What people are today are the results of what they were yesterday. Eddie wondered what this man had been yesterday, last month, twenty years ago. He could speculate until hell froze over, but it wouldn't do him any good. Suddenly, his mind drifted to Alexander Kingston.

Alex had also been a bum. He'd been an alcoholic and heroin addict. He'd lived in a rat-infested alley. His sole purpose of existence had been to escape from himself. Some people might have said that Alex had had no clear view of reality. But they'd be wrong. His view of reality was all too clear. Eddie had known him before Alex made his descent into the pit.

He had grown up in Westmount and led a privileged life. When Eddie first met him, he had graduated from McGill and was enrolled in law school. He had everything going for him: looks, brains, and ambition. Slowly over time, he had sunk into the mire of his past that nearly devoured him. Like Eddie, Alex had served in the army during World War II. He'd been in the D-Day landings with the Third Canadian Infantry and stormed Juno Beach with his unit. Several days after the landing, his squad had been wiped out by the Krauts, and he was the sole survivor. Eventually, the war had ended, and he returned to Westmount, resumed life, and went to school. But the war was still inside of him, gnawing at his innards, little by little, until he couldn't take it any longer. Then things fell apart, and he ended up in skid row, a shell of his former self.

Those who knew him, but not his past, had only seen a drunken bum. But he was more than that. He had been living with the terrible guilt of surviving when his fellow soldiers were slaughtered by the Germans. "Why me?" he would ask Eddie. Eddie had gotten him the help he needed at Saint Ann's Hospital, which worked with veterans. Eventually, he became clean, resumed law school, and found a job with a large firm. A success story, yes, but it could have easily been different.

As they sat finishing up their meal, Eddie couldn't help but wonder what this bum's past was. He had one.

We all do.

———«⊙»———

During their time of fornication in a room on the third floor of the Laurentian Hotel, the skies had changed. Low, dark clouds now covered Montreal, cloaking the city in terrible gray.

What was that noise?

"It's going to start pissing soon," Chanel said over her shoulder to Luc, who was still in bed, lying naked. She looked at the sky through an opening in the thick drapes. There was a dark, formless layer of clouds—thick, opaque, and featureless. She was naked as well. She was always amazed by how things changed so fast. When she had entered the hotel two hours before, the sky was blue. Now it looked as if Zeus, or one of his henchmen, had thrown a pall over it—out of boredom perhaps. There was a better than average chance that it would rain. If it did, it would be down for the next few days. She knew her Quebec skies. And the wind? It had picked up so much that she could see paper, other debris, and remembrances of things past swirling about the sidewalks like little tornados.

"We didn't bring our umbrellas." A few moments later, she added, "I suppose we could buy a couple of them downstairs in the gift shop." She sounded half-interested.

What is that noise, now? I can hear it. What is the wind doing?

What does the wind ever do?

She took one more peek out the window, looking up for any signs of God or Satan. She thought she saw one, but she didn't know from which one it had come or what it meant. She shrugged her shoulders and returned to the bed. She lay crosswise on her stomach; Luc's back was buttressed against the headboard. She twisted sideways, supporting her head with the palm of a hand, her arm resting on balled-up sheets. She stared at Luc, who was sitting upright with his eyes closed.

"You're going to be late for your appointment," she said.

Only one lamp in the room was on, the one on the nightstand, nearest her side of the bed. Luc had thrown a towel over it before their lovemaking. Shadows cast shadows of their own. Semidarkness passed for light; good and evil wore the same face.

"I like to keep my clients waiting," Luc said dryly, opening his eyes but not really looking at her. "That way, I have the upper hand."

"Are you going to shower? You should shower. Your client might smell sex on you."

"That's fine if he does. Actually, I'm counting on it. A little afternoon spark would probably impress him. Animal masculinity impresses the male of the species as well as the female."

That noise again. Is it the wind or something else?

Chanel hated his arrogance, but she could never resist his obsession with sex. Not that she wanted to. She had little regard for him as a person and knew he felt the same about her. Yet those assignations during the last five years only bound them together more tightly. Luc was reckless, compulsive, and bold in his private life. One woman was never enough. She could never love him; but why would she want to? One day, some floosy would come along and want him for her own. He might even become infatuated with her; he'd done it before, but it never lasted. Quietly, stealthily, shyly, she would attempt to harness him in, little by little, by leading him to Freud or Jesus. And when she couldn't, she'd discover the real goat god, the Satyr with hoofs and hairy ears and a permanent stiffy. When she did, she'd find herself on the bottom of his long list of past receptacles. However, Chanel knew that she was no better than him. The only difference between them was that at times she felt a small pang of guilt. That was all she could afford—a small pang—because she harbored much greater guilt for Guy Dupont and now for Willis Steele. She didn't have room inside herself for much more.

More times than not, Luc would do his best to belittle her. And he would do it politely and with a smile. He saved the rough stuff for the sex. The sarcasm would weave itself through his nice words like a filthy thread weaves itself through a white, laced handkerchief. At times, her feelings would be hurt—he had that power—but it was always temporary. She would fortify her defenses and come at him with her own arsenal of insults, readjusting herself to fit her own requirements. They'd always laugh afterward. It had been a game of sorts but never deadly.

Overall, she found their relationship as incomprehensible as Auschwitz.

Perhaps one day she'd have to do something about that.

"Well, if you're not going to take a goddamn shower, I am," she said, getting up and cat-footing to the bathroom.

Twenty minutes later, she was towelling herself off and replacing her face. She took one last look into the mirror, checking her makeup, wondering whether her image would leave a trace of recriminations for past sins.

They dressed in silence; neither had much to say until their next coupling.

"You can leave first. Your client is probably wondering where you are."

Luc stared a her for a moment, no smile, no expression to speak of.

"Tell me, Chanel. Did you kill Willis? Mum's the word if you did. It'll be our little secret."

There was dead silence in the room for a moment.

"Don't be daft," she said, nudging him toward the door, hoping he hadn't seen the shocked look on her face.

With that, they both said *Darling* at the same time, kissing each other's cheeks, first on one side and then the other, and then Luc was out the door.

Chanel walked a few feet and plopped down on the edge of the bed with her hands folded on her lap, contemplating humanity. It was, she concluded as always—in one fashion or another, whether taken as a whole or in the little pieces, whether it was overt or concealed—rotten to the core.

That noise—I can still hear it. It's not the wind; it's something else. But what?

With her former murdered husband and now Willis on her mind, she believed that things never worked out by themselves; they never just stayed put.

They always needed a little help.

Chapter 3
SECRETS

MILE END, A FEW MILES EAST OF THE DOWNTOWN
area, was a network and refuge for first- and second-
generation European immigrants—Irish, Jews, Italians, and
Greeks. Working class mostly, with sizable families. A quiet
area generally, with storefronts scattered here and there:
the local grocer, the local druggist, the local barber, the local
watering hole, and of course, the local private investigator.
The people who lived there had a special name for where rue
Saint-Viateur intersected with rue Saint-Urbain. They called it
the Holy Corner. It was the heart and soul of Mile End; it was
the heart and soul of Eddie Wade.

At the southeast corner was the Lion's Den, the
neighborhood gin joint. Kitty-corner from the Den was a
behemoth towering over the urban landscape, capable of
swallowing up fourteen hundred sinners with one gulp. St.
Michael's Catholic Church had been built in 1915 and modeled
after Hagia Sophia in Istanbul. It was Byzantine by design.
It had a dome, and along the side facing Saint-Urbain, there
was a minaret-styled tower. The roofs had a bluish-green
patina of oxidized copper, forming a pleasant contrast with
the brown brick and white ornamental trim. Outsiders who

came into the area cast bets as to whether the structure was a synagogue, church, or mosque. St. Michael's provided many services to the community, not the least of which was a convenient location for sinners who drank at the Den. They would wobble out of the bar, cross the intersection, go up the stairs, open the massive doors, and confess their sins away before they went home to the wives.

Eddie parked his car on Saint-Urbain outside his office and walked the twenty feet or so to the Den. The bar was more crowded than usual this late afternoon. There was a murmur of voices laced now and again with the fiery spittle of profanity in English, along with its counterpart in French. Eddie heard snippets of conversations as he made his way to the bar.

"The son of a bitch should never have been there!"

"Tabarnak!"

"He disrespects Richard, he disrespects us!"

"He's the president of the league. He had a right to be there!"

"Esti d'épais à marde!"

Eddie sidled up to the bar. He knew exactly what they were talking about.

The previous night, the Canadians hockey team had played Detroit at the Forum on Sainte-Catherine. The Canadians' star player, Maurice Richard, had been suspended for the rest of the season four days earlier for punching an official. The man who suspended Richard, Clarence Campbell, president of the league, had attended the Detroit game, and the Montreal fans were not pleased. After the first period, someone threw a tear gas bomb near to where Campbell had been sitting. The officials ended the game minutes later, and Detroit was declared the winner 4–1. The fans peeled themselves out of their seats, coughing, spitting, and rubbing their eyes, then left the building, enraged at the officials, at Campbell, and at the way Montreal had been treated. They were met outside by thousands of other fans who had not attended the game but had been gathering in Cabot Square opposite the Forum and up and down Sainte-Catherine to protest Campbell for the suspension of their god-hero Richard. Then the gates of Hades opened, and the hounds of wrath and destruction were released. As the saying goes—all hell broke loose!

The fans rioted and chanted slogans in French and English: *À bas Campbell! Down with Campbell! Vive Richard!* Windows were smashed, bystanders were attacked, newsstands went up in flames, cars were overturned, stores were looted and vandalized, and police and civilians were injured. Rue Sainte-Catherine lay in shambles.

The drinkers at the Den were beginning to break up and started to leave, going home to wives and dinner. Bruno came over to Eddie, shaking his head.

"A special broadcast," he said, thumbing the radio behind him. "Maurice was telling people to cool it. No more rioting, he said; enough's enough. We drew a crowd in to listen to him."

"Tell me about it," Eddie said. "I was at the game. Almost got hit with a flying beer bottle."

Bruno shook his head again. "It's all politics, Eddie. All politics."

That was Bruno's pat answer to everything that went wrong in the world, from a husband beating his wife to a typhoon in the south Pacific. *It's all politics!*

Bruno was the owner of the Den. He was also Eddie's landlord. He had the stature of a professional wrestler and the demeaner of either a Mafia hitman or a "puddy tat," depending on his mood. He bore a remarkable resemblance to heavyweight boxing brawler Two Ton Tony Galento in his younger days, and like Galento, he could settle an argument with a wicked straight right to the jaw. Now, pushing sixty, he had mellowed. But he could still hold a tray of drinks in one hand and throw a drunk out with the other without so much as spilling a drop.

He liked telling the story of how he came up with the name of the bar. Not the least a religious man, he would point at chapter 6 of the book of Daniel in the Bible, explaining how Daniel had been saved by God from the lions in their den. Paraphrasing the great book, he'd tell whoever would listen, "I was found blameless before God." Besides being landlord and tenant, Bruno and Eddie were also good friends. More than that, Bruno was Eddie's father confessor.

Eddie ordered a Molson, and by the time Bruno brought it over, there were only a few patrons left in the bar. They probably had no wives to go home to and would likely sit until closing.

"So, what kind of case are you working on now, Eddie?" Bruno asked as he wedged the cardboard beermat under the glass.

"Matrimonial discord," Eddie said. He hoisted the glass, winked at Bruno, and then sipped.

"Oh, jeez …" Bruno grimaced. "Didn't I tell you to stay away from those cases? It'll be the death of you one of these days. I'd rather go a round or two with Marciano than get between a husband and wife hellbent on destroying each other."

"Husband's a runner. Took off with her cash and jewels."

"You need to see a shrink. Sometimes I think you're suicidal."

"The wife's got money."

"Not enough for that kind of discord." He threw his hands in the air. "But I guess that's what you do for a living."

Eddie told him the bare bones of the case, because that's all he had at that point. Bruno stared at the far wall in front of him for a few moments while considering what he'd just been told. He narrowed his eyes. There was a slight tick on the right side of his face. That was his way of focusing. Soon his face relaxed. He turned to Eddie.

"Sumptin' stinks." He thought for a moment and then added, "Like rotten fish. The broad ain't tellin' you everything."

"That's what I figured. I'm going to her house soon for round two of my interview with her."

"She's holding something back. You should be worried about that. I'd give her the dough back and tell her to find someone else. You don't need that kind of headache."

"You're right, but she threw cash at me like she had too much of it. Anyway, like you said, it's my job. That's what I do."

Bruno shook his head. "It's all politics, Eddie." He stabbed a thick finger at him. "And you can take that to the bank."

They talked for an hour, mostly about last night's game and the riot. Eddie drank his beer, smoked his pipe, and then left. As he closed the door of the Den behind him, he noticed someone sitting on the steps of the church kitty-corner from him. The sun, which had been peeking out briefly, was now retreating behind the buildings and houses, and darkness was beginning to throw a blanket over Mile End, but there was enough light for Eddie to see across the intersection. *Well, I'll be damned!* he thought. It was the same guy, the bum, whom he had bought lunch for that afternoon at Bens. His forearms rested on his knees, and his head hung down. No doubt about it. It was the same guy.

Eddie's first thought was that the bum had followed him to Mile End. But how? The guy couldn't have had a car, and Eddie was sure he didn't have money for a taxi. He could have walked here or maybe taken a tram. But how did he know where Eddie was going? He considered for a moment going over to him. The guy hadn't said a word to him earlier and was unlikely to be chatty now. Still, Eddie was curious. Perhaps he would have gone over, but he had a few important errands to do before his appointment with Chanel Steele at eight. He walked back to his car, started it, and then drove slowly through the intersection, staring at him.

The old guy lifted his head and stared back.

⎯⎯➤«⦿»⎯⎯

The two-storied, brown brick Victorian house was perched on a small hill set back on a 12,000-square-foot lot on avenue Mount-Pleasant in Westmount. A centered-sweeping wooden arch trimmed in white loomed over the entrance. Above the arch was a balcony with a wrought iron balustrade. On either side of the entrance were castle-like, hexagon-shaped towers with three windows on each level. The long front lawn was framed by eight-foot-high privacy hedges that bordered the property; two enormous ancient sugar maples stood naked on either side of the house like guards protecting it from intrusion from the outside world. In the fall, the leaves would turn into fiery red and orange torches. The brooding structure had been designed long ago to keep secrets in and humanity out.

As Eddie Wade made his way up the cement path, he mumbled something to himself about not being able to afford the heating bill of a house like that for even a month. Maybe he was in the wrong business. He thumbed the buzzer, and a few moments later, he was greeted by a woman in a black dress with a white collar and trim. A stout woman who looked as if she could endure pain and hardship without complaining, she wore her hair tight against her head with a bun in the back. After Eddie told her his name, she said, "Bonsoir, monsieur. The mistress is expecting you." She led him through two sets of doors and into the house.

The foyer was spacious, with highly polished wood wainscoting on three of the walls. Straight ahead, a semicircular staircase led to the second floor. Next to it on the right and recessed into the wall was a replica of the armless Venus de Milo, displayed in all her glory on a rosewood plinth. Eddie walked over to it and examined it for a moment, figuring he may never get to Paris to see the original. It stood six feet tall and was made of plaster. The maid waited patiently by a door across the foyer, as still as the statue. Unable to understand what all the fuss was about Venus, Eddie returned to the maid, who opened the door for him.

The room was small and cozy with a fireplace off to the right. The furnishings were expensive looking, as he had anticipated. Pierced fanback mahogany chairs with rich golden fabrics were scattered here and there, probably early twentieth century. A small table likely used for intimate dining was pushed off the right. A bar of considerable size bordered one wall. A long davenport set back, which could seat five people, faced the fireplace. Directly facing Eddie was a matching love seat, upon which sat Chanel Steele. She wore a long, silk Japanese robe. It was dark purple with green and white floral patterns, dotted here and there with red flowers. The sleeves were wide and came three-quarters the way down her arms. If she had been standing, the length would have covered her feet. The top was open enough for Eddie to see more cleavage than what was expected for an interview. She had one leg crossed over the other, with the robe spread back on either side, fully displaying the dazzling legs he'd only glimpsed earlier that morning. One hand held a cigarette holder. She took a short puff and blew smoke in his direction.

"You look tired, ducky," she said. "Take off your overcoat and hat. Come sit by me." She patted the cushion gently with her hand. "Don't be frightened. The lady doesn't bite."

Eddie crossed the room, draped his coat on the back of the love seat, put his hat on the top of it, and sat down. "No? But I might," he said jokingly. As an afterthought, he added, "Mrs. Steele."

"Please call me Chanel." She paused a moment, her eyes racing around his face, and then asked, "Do you bite, Eddie?"

"I've been known to on occasion, but I never draw blood."

"That sounds naughty, Eddie. Are you a naughty boy, ducky dear?"

She was the same woman who came bursting into his office that morning—physically, that is. But her whole demeanor had changed. Even the tone of her voice. She was no longer the crass broad who used foul language. Maybe he'd misjudged her. Maybe she was something entirely different. Now, she was drunk with her own desirability. Why was she suddenly wearing a mask? What was she after? How many more masks did she have?

On the coffee table in front of them, a candle burned brightly, its flame long and fluttering like the tongue of some mythological beast.

Eddie blinked his eyes as if coming out of a trance some enchantress had placed on him.

"Listen, Chanel," he said, "I'm here because you hired me to find your husband, who stole from you. I need more details to help me find him."

"Oh, don't be a party pooper, Eddie. Business is so boring. Get me a drink, will you? Pour yourself one while you're at it. Scotch, two ice cubes." She took a puff of the cigarette and motioned with her hand.

Eddie got up, fixed the drinks, and returned. They clicked glasses. He took a sip, glancing down at her leg, which was slowly moving up and down at the knee.

"You're a handsome man, ducks. What do you do for kicks around town?"

"I work, pay my bills, and feed my cats."

"A guy like you? How bourgeois. Do you know what I think, Eddie?"

He took another sip of his drink, thought a moment, and then asked, "No, what do you think, Chanel?"

She was trying to seduce him, that much was clear to him, but he couldn't figure out her game, her angle. She must be after something. He wasn't averse to being seduced; however, the worst thing he could do was get involved with a client who was paying his bills.

She leaned to the side and put her mouth to his ear, their flesh touching. She whispered, "I think underneath all those clothes is a wild animal."

He slowly turned his head, and they were face-to-face, inches apart. Eddie felt her warm breath on him. The top of her robe had spread apart even more when she changed position. One breast was nearly exposed. He couldn't say anything at the moment. He wanted to respond with some clever repartee, but wit eluded him. All words eluded him.

She persisted like a she-cat on the hunt for a mate: "Are you a wild animal, Eddie?" Her voice was soft and hushed. She answered before he could say anything. "I think you are."

Eddie felt as if he were being led into a trap, but he couldn't understand why. Chanel was gorgeous, and she was using her beauty as a weapon against him. But to what end? He couldn't allow that to happen. He was about to get up when she suddenly threw a naked leg over his lap, pinning him to the love seat.

"I think you are," she repeated.

He could taste her hot breath on his mouth. She lifted his free hand and ran it up and down her leg. Then she moved her face another inch toward his and traced his lips with her tongue. When she finished, she whispered, "You're wild, Eddie, and I'm going to be wild with you."

In the back of every human brain was something sexual, too dark and primitive for civilized consideration, which tried at propitious moments to work itself to the forebrain.

It was such a driving force that the most strong-willed person was but a child in its wake. The results were often exhilarating and ecstatic beyond normal human experience and tolerance, but it was also poisonous because it bore deeply into places of the soul that were rarely explored. At times, it was ... deadly.

Eddie was about to surrender to the force when his eyes picked up movement from across the room. Someone had opened the door a crack but hadn't come into the room. The maid? It was enough to break the spell. He squirmed out of her grasp and stood up.

"Chanel, you hired me for a job, and I think we should talk about that."

"Oh, you're no fun," she said flippantly and only slightly annoyed. Apparently, she was unaware that the door had been opened, or if she was, she didn't care. "I suppose you're right. But being right is sometimes boring." She gathered herself together, pulled her robe closer around her, and straightened herself up in the love seat. "OK, have it your way, if you must. What do you want to know?"

Eddie sat down again and got out his leather-covered notebook and a pen. He marvelled at her ability of seduction and at how fast she had gone to work on him. She was good; she had performed magnificently. Maybe she had had a lot of practice. He couldn't help but wonder why she had come after him. He was also curious about how he had responded to her. Eddie was no moralist, but he was cautious by nature and profession. He was disturbed by how easily he had fallen into her trap. He reminded himself that a trap was a device to catch and retain an animal. He had walked into it with his eyes wide open! As it turned out, he had no more self-restraint than the next schmuck.

"Tell me about Willis. You said you've been married for two months. How long have you known him?"

"I'd rather whisper in your ear and put my tongue in your mouth, but if you insist. But just so you know, I had been undressing you this morning in your office. You were sitting there naked in front of me. Do you know how difficult it was for me to restrain myself from reaching across that desk and grabbing your—"

"About Willis," he said, interrupting her.

"About Willis ... let's see. Willis ... you mean that good-for-nothing asshole? Of course, you do." She paused to sigh; it was long, deep, and audible. "Willis and I have known each other since we were in diapers. We grew up in the same neighborhood and went to the same schools together. He was the first person I played show-and-tell with, in the shed in his backyard on a warm summer's day, while his mother was in the house listening to a soap opera on the radio." She laughed. "I guess we had our own little soap opera going on." She sighed again, but this time as if it was an expression of a fond memory. "At thirteen, we went beyond show-and-tell. In the same shed. I'll spare you the gory details. At fifteen, we declared our love for each other." She thought for a moment. "I think we were sincere. Anyway, at nineteen, I set my sights higher. We both had come from working-class families, but I couldn't see myself living life by the clock. Having a half dozen little ones and a husband who worked eight to five was repulsive to me. I think I sort of loved him, but if we married, I knew the kind of life I'd have. I would have spent the rest of my life in want ... from the finer things in life, if you catch my drift. I wanted nothing to do with it. At twenty-one, I met Guy Dupont. He was twenty years my senior, a banker, and came from a wealthy family. I decided I would love *him* instead. Willis faded away."

"What happened to Dupont? Divorce?"

"God, no. I would never have divorced Guy. He was murdered one night in town. Shot in the back of the head.

The police never found out who did it. That's why I have no regard for them. They're incompetent. That was five years ago, give or take.

"About three months ago, Willis and I ran into each other on Crescent. We started seeing each other—you know, movies, restaurants, all that. Those old feelings started to surface again, in both of us, and finally he asked me to marry him. Which is what we did. Just us two at city hall. Us and a couple of witnesses. He moved in after the little ceremony. I insisted he stop working. He drove a truck, you see. I couldn't have him doing that. He had to change because he now had a different status. He really didn't have to work at all. He complained that he had nothing to do. It wasn't like he was a lawyer or doctor. He was a truck driver, for God's sake. I couldn't be married to an ordinary workman. I guess that was when the marriage started to go downhill. He couldn't adapt to this lifestyle. All he did was mope around and complain. Then a week ago, he must have decided to call it quits; he took off with my cash and jewelry, as if they were souvenirs."

"Where were they kept?"

"In the safe behind that picture," she said, pointing above the fireplace.

"He had the combination?"

"Yes."

"Anyone else have it beside you two?"

"Just Percy."

"Who's Percy?"

"He's my son by Guy."

"How old is he?"

"Twenty-three. He's a nice boy."

"How did Willis and Percy get along?"

"They got along fine. They enjoyed playing chess together."

"Did Willis ever use violence against you when you had disagreements, like about him having to quit his job?"

"Oh no. Willis may have been a lot of things, but he never hurt me, if that's where you're going with this."

"Did he have any enemies?

"Enemies?" She thought about it. "Are you suggesting something happened to him?"

"I look at a case from all angles, Chanel. I'm not suggesting that anything happened to him, but I have to keep an open mind until I collect enough evidence. Right now, I take it at face value that he left you on his own volition. But I wouldn't be doing my job very well if I closed the door on other possibilities. Everything is on the table at the moment."

"Generally, he was a nice guy to us and other people. I don't know whether he had enemies. I hadn't kept him on a leash, but I don't think he did."

"Fair enough," he said. "I'll need a description of the missing jewelry. Also, I need a list of his closest friends and family members."

"I have all of that ready for you, ducky, like a nice little girl." She got up and walked over to a small table behind them and pulled out a drawer. She walked back and handed him a large envelope. "There are pictures of my jewels with what they're worth on the back. The insurance company insisted I have them. There's also a list of people who were closest to Willis: names, addresses, and phone numbers. Didn't I do well, ducky?" She made little clicking sounds in the back of her mouth and winked at him. "You probably thought I was traipsing around all day in town, going from bar to bar, picking up men."

Just then, a young man entered the room.

"Oh," he said, slightly startled. "I'm sorry, Mother. I didn't know you had a guest."

He was a gangling youth with long blond hair that swept over his eyes. He looked unsure of himself, as if he questioned his place in the universe. He wore brown corduroy pants and a dark orange jumper. A white collar stuck out from under his neck. His eyes were deeply set, which gave him a brooding look, but his complexion was rosy, healthy even. In the right light, you could see a trace of down on his cheeks. He could pass for fifteen.

"That's quite all right, Percy. I want you to meet the man who's going to find Willis for us. This is Mr. Wade. Mr. Wade, my son, Percy—Percy Dupont."

The two shook hands. "Glad to meet you, Mr. Wade. I suppose Mother has been telling you all our dark family secrets."

"Only the ones I need to know," Eddie said, putting on his overcoat and hat. Looking at Chanel, he said, "I'll be in touch. If you think of anything else I should know, call my answering service and leave a message." He reached into his coat pocket for his contract with her. "This is your copy with all the details laid out as we discussed." Then he turned the side of his head slightly toward the windows as if listening. "I thought I heard someone shouting outside." They all stopped a moment to listen.

"That sounds like our neighborhood drunk, out to save the world," Chanel said, annoyed. "Actually, he's not from the area, God help us. Some derelict from skid row, I suppose. Once a fortnight, he rambles through the neighborhood to inform us that we're all going to hell. Someone calls the police, they pick him up, put him in the dry tank or whatever you call that thing. They release him after a few days. Two weeks later, the whole cycle begins again. We affectionally call him the Madman of Westmount. I suppose it's my turn to call the paddy wagon."

Chanel and Percy walked Eddie to the front door and out onto the steps. "Have a listen, Eddie," Chanel said. "He could save your life!"

The derelict, who appeared to be anywhere from thirty to

eighty, wearing a ragged, filthy overcoat a couple of sizes too large, was walking slowly past the front between the hedges.

"Repent, sinners and fornicators! The Lord is coming. Repent ye now. The day of judgment is near. Gather ye rosebuds while ye may. The day of judgment is upon thee! Repent ye now, repent ye now, sinners and fornicators! The day of ..."

They said their goodbyes on the steps.

"Nice to have met you, Percy," Eddie said, smiling.

"Yessiree Bob, Mr. Wade. It was my pleasure."

With that, Eddie made his way down the long pathway to his car, "sinners and fornicators" still ringing in his ears.

Upon reentering the house, Chanel made her obligatory call to the police, much as she despised them—for the good of the neighborhood. Then she and Percy returned to the sitting room.

"Mother, could I ask you a question?"

"Certainly, Percy. What is it?"

"I hope I'm not being too personal, and please tell me if I am, but why did you marry Willis?"

"I wanted to have a male figure in the house for you to look up to. Oh, I know you're not two years old anymore, but just the same. I thought it would be good for you to have another male for you to talk to—you know, man to man, things that you can't talk to me about."

"I thought we could talk about anything, you and me."

"We can, dear, but sometimes there are certain things that men like to talk to other men about. Didn't you like Willis?"

"Certainly. He and I always got on OK." He paused a moment and then said, "Did he love you?"

"I suppose in his own way. Not the way your father did but in his own way. At least I thought he did. Considering what he did, I'm not so sure now."

"Have you considered that he might have married you for your money?"

"Oh, Percy, I'm not sure of anything anymore," she said, sounding slightly deflated. "Maybe I rushed into the marriage."

"I hope I didn't make you feel sad, Mother."

"You could never do that, Percy," she said. She gave him a hug and kissed his cheek.

"I'm going to bed now," Percy declared cheerfully. "See you in the morning. Good night, Mother."

"Sleep tight, Percy."

With that, Percy left the room.

He walked up the semicircular staircase and to his bedroom. He sat down at his desk and folded his hands in front of him, looking out the window into the dark night, contemplating the world around him. He could hear the muffled words below from the man who would save the world of its sins. For some strange reason that Percy could not comprehend, he felt an affinity toward him—a kinship, so to speak. He looked forward to the man's return.

At times, he felt he had a good grasp on things. The little pieces seemed to fit nicely together. Other times, it was nothing but darkness and disorder, as when he had listened at the door downstairs to his mother and Mr. Wade. He had wanted to act to save her from herself; however, all he was able to do was open the door slightly to stop them. It had worked.

He tried to recall certain things in his past, but his memory, which had once been a vast, well-lighted fortress on a mountaintop, was now a small, unlit dirt hut in a shadowy and isolated marshland. There are those who might throw hope away because they have an abundance of it. Percy would never do that, for he had been shackled to it all of his life. Even though he had his jumper on, he was chilled. His skin was speckled with goose bumps that seemed to burrow their way deeper into him. Who would blame him when he felt the occasional need to disassociate himself from the harsh realities of the world?

He picked up a letter opener from the desk and went to his closet opposite his bed. Pushing several large boxes aside, along with his shoes, a tennis racket, and several tennis balls, he began to pry loose the false wall. Once it was loose enough, he grabbed either side, jerked it free, and then set it down. He then reached inside and retrieved a gun. He held the grip in one hand and with the other ran his fingertips along the barrel, feeling the cold, hard steel.

═══◉═══

The first day ended with a thud.

Chapter 4
HIERONYMO'S GONE
MAD AGAIN

THE FLAT, HAZY LAYERS OF DARK GRAY STRATUS
clouds lay low over the city. The gods were at it again.
Through boredom, or simply to be spiteful this time, they
cheated Saturday morning of sunshine, and in doing so, they
stole from Montrealers what otherwise would have been
rightfully theirs. A fine, misty fog lingered, swallowing up
building tops. Later, the sun would emerge—and with it, a
certain reprieve—and the gods' warm breath would make
the steamy vapors suspended in the atmosphere disappear
like magic. Now you see them; now you don't.

Eddie Wade turned left off of Dorchester onto Cathédrale,
drove for two blocks and hooked another left onto Saint-
Antoine, then parked his car across the street from the
Montreal Gazette. Above the building, the Canadian Red
Ensign rippled and snapped in the occasional gusts.

Eddie cursed himself mostly in English, but he used a
few choice French words as well. Chanel Steele had been on
his mind all morning. He was appalled by his behavior the
previous night. He thought he had acted, well, appallingly.

Beautiful women were, and had always been, a weakness for him; they were his Achilles' heel. But he'd entertained the idea—falsely, as it turned out—that he had made some progress in rectifying the matter.

There wasn't one particular type of woman who could stir him into becoming a glassy-eyed, drooling adolescent. If it were only one type, he'd be better equipped to avoid the power they had over him. He could easily spot them, formulate an immediate strategy of escape, and then run like hell in the opposite direction. No, there were many types, and they always spelled trouble for him.

It mattered not the color of their hair or eyes or the measurement of their waist or whether they were tall or short. If asked, Eddie wouldn't be able to describe them. The most he could say was that he was mesmerized by certain types. The *she* of the species; that certain *she*; that enchanted *she.* Once spied, once engaged, he turned into a helpless schmuck, a marionette. They could then pull his strings and make him hop or jump or dance to their melody. Once the realization set in of what had happened, it was always too late.

It had happened again last night, and the *she* this time was Chanel Steele herself.

With distance now, he reflected. If the door hadn't opened a crack, he was certain they would have spent the night making the beast with two backs. There was no doubt about that. One of his main tenets in life was to never mix business with pleasure. But that was exactly what he'd done. Chanel was a gorgeous woman. He made no attempt to rationalize his behavior. "Oh! I just couldn't help myself." No, there was none of that. He'd broken an important precept. If he were so inclined, he might have gone to confession, because he considered it a professional sin. But he wasn't so inclined, so he had to be satisfied with simply being appalled with himself. He cursed himself again. *Tabarnak!*

He climbed the stairs to the third-floor photo lab. He'd phoned earlier and explained to Sid Herschel that he needed a half dozen copies made of the photos of Chanel's jewelry and also of Willis Steele, her thieving, runaway husband. Sid had a little business on the side when things were slow at the paper. He'd told Eddie that if he could get them to him that morning, he could have them done if he was willing to wait an hour or so. Eddie dropped them off with him, and to kill a bit of time, he climbed the stairs again to the fourth-floor newsroom.

He swung the doors open and was accosted by a steady ruckus of noise. To his left, three operators sat at a switchboard, talking into horn-shaped speakers that hung around their necks with headphones covering their ears. They were all jabbering away at the same time, plugging in and pulling out jack plugs in front of them that connected the calls. Small lights lit up on the back panel, and the operators pushed the plugs into the corresponding sockets, flipping the panel switches to the up position. "Montreal Gazette. Whom do you wish to speak to? Thank you. One moment please. I'll connect you." Then they placed the plugs into the associated sockets and pushed the switches down to ring the called parties. All this happening at the same time could give Eddie a headache if he lingered too long to chat up his sweethearts. Instead, he stopped briefly to wave at them. The motion of his hand caught their eyes, but their heads remained straight. They smiled and flashed him a cheerful wave. Then he proceeded through another set of doors.

The newsroom looked like a gutted-out warehouse with wooden desks shoved side to side in three rows and two aisles between them. Reporters, heads down, pecked out their stories. Lamps goosenecked over the typewriters because the windows were too grimy and smeared with soot to illuminate their masterpieces. Notebooks, pens, and pencils were scattered about. The edges of the desks were trimmed with decades of cigarette burns. There was a constant buzz of voices. Someone yelled, "Copy boy! Copy boy!" A haze of tobacco smoke hung in the air. The teleprinters droned away in the background. Several beat reporters were standing off to the side, drinking coffee, smoking cigarettes and pipes, telling jokes, and laughing, waiting for the one assignment that would make their names a household word.

Jake Asher sat manning the police desk. He was leaning back in a swivelled chair, a dead cigar in his mouth, feet resting on a drawer that had been pulled out, his eyes closed tightly. Eddie rapped on his shoe with his fingertips as if knocking on a door. Asher's eyes flashed open.

"I thought you might be sleeping," Eddie said.

Asher was a seasoned crime reporter whom Eddie had known since he opened the Wade Detective Agency. There were few criminals in the city he didn't know. The ones he didn't know weren't worth knowing. He was short, fat, and bald, but he could sprint after a story faster than a gold medalist winning the hundred-yard dash. His mind was an encyclopedia of facts and statistics of Montreal crime.

"With this racket? Believe me, I've tried! I was thinking about how I was going to open a story. I'm sick of the who, what, where, when, and why bullshit. Lately, I've been working on how to engage readers so they'll want to read to the very end of the story. You know, space out the juicy stuff. If you tell everything there is to know in the first paragraph, why read to the end? My copy editor was pleased with the last three stories I wrote and gave me the green light. So, I'm green-lighting it." He took his legs down and shoved another chair away from the desk with his shoe. "Sit down. Fancy seeing you here." After a pause, he pointed a chubby finger at him. "You want something, don't you? You always do when you look at me like that." A huge grin appeared on his face. "You want coffee, help yourself over there. It's mud by now."

Eddie sat down and told him he was waiting for Sid to make copies of the photos he'd brought to him, and then he explained the photos and the case to Asher.

"Chanel Steele from Westmount?" Jake asked. "Let me see ... let me see now. That name sounds familiar. Wasn't she Chanel Dupont at one time?"

"She was."

"A super-duper-looking broad, as I remember. A little rough around the edges but definitely someone you don't disremember."

"So, what do you remember about her, besides her physical attributes?"

"Isn't that enough? Actually, I remember her old man. Someone put a bullet in his head. A beat cop found him between two buildings downtown; can't recall where just now. I'd have to look it up. Guy Dupont was his name—a hotshot banker. He worked at the Royal Bank."

"A hotshot banker with an enemy."

"Yeah, you're right. I wrote several stories about the murder at the time, and something didn't sound right. Bankers do make enemies from time to time, but they ain't usually murdered. However, if a banker is crooked, all bets are off. I remember looking into his background and couldn't find anything on him. By all accounts, Guy Dupont had been as straight as an arrow. The one person who had the most to gain from his murder was his wife. Besides her legs and bazookas, that's why I remember her. She would not only inherit his estate—which she did—but she'd get her freedom back—which she also did."

"Did she want her freedom back?"

"If I remember correctly, the marriage wasn't all that good. I looked into that angle. There were twenty or so years between them, and I did hear rumors that he cheated on her, although I couldn't verify that at the time. I tried though. You know, the *Gazette* is no tabloid. We're in the era of responsible journalism. I couldn't very well report on that with no evidence. So, I dropped it because another story broke, but I still had a gut feeling that his wife had something to do with his murder. If I had the time, I would definitely do some more nosing around. But you see, Montreal is like all other big cities—there are no lack of things happening. There's always something hanging in the air to go after. Who wants to read about something that happened five years ago when there's last night's murder and mayhem to report on? The readers who sit in their cozy little dwellings feel closer to all the blood and gore."

Eddie considered his meeting with Chanel the previous night. She'd gone after him without any encouragement on his part. No half-innocent, half-contrived games of flirtation that invited misinterpretation. She'd gone for his jugular from the onset. "Maybe she'd done some cheating on her part," he said.

"Maybe. Maybe they were both doing their fair share of cheating. All the more reason for her to end the marriage. Motive—God, she had plenty of it. With the kind of money the Duponts had, she'd have had no problem finding someone to pull the trigger."

"Did the police find a weapon?"

"No, but they found a shell casing by the body, and they have the bullet. But they had nothing to match it to."

"Copy boy! Goddammit, copy boy!" the same voice shouted in the background.

"Anyway," Eddie said, "that's not my concern. I was hired to find Chanel's current husband. One Willis Steele."

"Yeah, well, good luck with that. Runaway husbands don't usually want to be found. He's probably spending her money in one of the casinos in Vegas."

"Maybe Timbuktu."

"What?" Asher said, taking the cigar out of his mouth. "They have casinos there?"

"Never mind."

"Or maybe he's sitting around the corner drinking a Molson as we speak. Like I said, good luck."

Sid Herschel walked down the aisle with a large envelope in one hand and the index finger of the other poking the middle of the glasses that kept sliding down his nose. He stood all of six four with wide shoulders and big hands. His jaw was long, and his mouth was in a permanent smile. He handed the envelope to Eddie, then put a hand on each of their shoulders—Jake's and Eddie's—as he stood between them, grinning like Blunderbore deciding which one to eat first. *Fee-fi-fo-fum!*

"Hey, how 'bout we three gents scoot over to Mother Martin's for a Birdbath or two? I'm buying. I'm using Eddie's money."

A "Birdbath" was a double martini served in an oversized martini glass.

"You must think we're on the night shift, Sid," Jake said. "We'll be missed. I'm out. Nix on that."

"I've got an interview coming up, Sid, or I'd be glad to go," Eddie said. "How much do I owe you?"

"Gee, what's the world coming to when grown men turn down a free Birdbath? I'll send you a frickin' invoice so I can write it off my taxes."

———«●»———

He paid the old geezer at the newsstand across the street from the Laurentian Hotel for a copy of the *Daily Herald*. Then he walked a few steps to his right and leaned against a building. He had gotten little sleep last night, and his eyes were glassy, but he had a clear view of the hotel's entrance. He opened the paper to no particular section and held it up as if reading it. The paper covered his upper body, but he could see over the top of it when he needed to. The misty air held stubbornly like an undertaker's grip.

And then he waited.

Goddammit, he'd wait all day if necessary. He didn't think he'd need to though. He'd been through this before—many times. Too many times. He should have acted long before now—a month ago, maybe even two months ago. Hell, he should have acted last year. It was torture—a form of self-abuse. He hadn't thought he was a masochist, but maybe he'd have to rethink that.

He was right; he didn't have to wait long. Ten minutes later, a yellow Cadillac pulled into the side lot next to the hotel. He watched Chanel Steele get out of the car and walk to the entrance. She briefly looked around, as if somehow her past were following her, and then entered. He made a mental note of the time and place.

He shook the paper out in front of him again, keeping his eyes on the hotel entrance. Cars passed by on Dorchester from both directions. And then a tram. The street bore no traces of spent liquor bottles, greasy papers reeking of fish, butt ends, dirty ticket stubs, candy wrappers, or other testimonies of activities of the living. Twelve and a half minutes later, he saw Luc Legrand approach the hotel and enter it. He noted that time as well.

He folded the newspaper and put it under his arm. Then he took out a small notebook and flipped through the other entries. Times and places. Other hotels. Numerous entries. He took a pencil from his pocket and added to them. His little notebook gave him a feeling of satisfaction and justification.

But nothing of his madness.

The feeling was short-lived, replaced by a sense of determination. He knew life could turn on a dime. With every second of the clock, there was the possibility of change; with every second of the clock, there was an opportunity.

He turned and walked down Dorchester with a youthful, jaunty step achieved only by someone who was not afflicted with a soul. He passed a waste bin along the sidewalk and flung the newspaper inside. At his back, in a cold blast of wind, he heard a warm, moist voice whispering in his ear. "Soon, soon!" it said, and a grin spread from ear to ear.

Hieronymo's gone mad again.

———◉———

Zebulon Whitehead did not have a headful of white hair. It was black. And straight. And parted in the middle. He was in his mid-forties, and there were no signs of gray in it, although some would argue, and rightfully so, that because of his lifestyle, his hair should have been white, if not fully gray. His name and the color of his hair had always been a source of amusement for his fellow students throughout his younger years. "Whitehead—what the fuck? You should be called Blackhead!" He'd heard that from the time he'd entered school until he got sick of it one day in his early teens and busted the nose of a boy with a two-by-four on the school lot. The word got around fast. Those who knew him now would never have been tempted to tease him, because Zebulon Whitehead had a mean-looking face and a meaner disposition.

Eddie Wade sat at the kitchen table in Whitehead's dump on rue Visitation off of Sherbrooke, across from La Fontaine Park.

"Zeb," Eddie said, "I need a big favor from you."

"What's in it for me?"

"The usual percentage if you get me a lead. Nothing if you don't."

Whitehead made a face and then said, "Fuck, fine wit me. Whattaya lookin' for? The Holy Grail?"

Eddie took a copy of each picture and spread them out on the table. "This is the husband, Willis Steele. I'm looking for him," he said, pointing at his picture. "And this is what he stole from my client, his wife."

Whitehead was one of the major movers in the city. He could move stolen goods faster than Determine could run the Kentucky Derby. If Willis Steele was looking for a fence, Whitehead would be high on the list.

"These are real purty, real purty. They'll fetch a tidy sum if it's done right."

"Contact the other fences so they'll be on the lookout. Show them these pictures. Call me if you get a lead."

"Don't tell me my business, Wade. You think I was born yesterday? I know how it's done better than you do. Now get the fuck outta here. I got things to do." As an afterthought, he added in a softer tone, "How're yer cats? You want a beer before you leave?"

Chapter 5
THE TWO OF THEM

THE FLAMINGO WAS ONE OF THOSE RARE BIRDS in Montreal that wasn't busy on Sunday nights. Located on Drummond above Dorchester, it was in the heart of the city, so it should have been busy, but it wasn't. Its pink and blue plumage that framed the windows painted a steady neon glow in the club. Tranquil it was, without the long neck and legs. That was what Eddie wanted—peace and quiet.

Whenever he could, Eddie set Sundays aside to catch up on paperwork or to do nothing. Most of the time, he felt guilty about leaving his two cats, Antoinette and Henri, alone during the week, so he made sure to overwhelm them with his attention on that day. He was out of the office a lot working on cases, in his car or pounding the cement, doing the necessary legwork. That was his job. Maybe he shouldn't have cats if he couldn't give them the attention they deserved. But it wasn't as if he were neglecting them; he wasn't. Besides, they slept nearly eighteen hours a day. Maybe they didn't miss him at all. Anyway, he was attached to them, so they weren't going anywhere. On this particular Sunday night, when the cats had had enough of his attention and curled up on the couch, he grabbed his pipe, got in his car, and drove into town to the Flamingo.

He sat at the bar and knocked back the last of his whiskey. "Pierre!" he said, holding up his shot glass.

The barman looked over the edge of yesterday's edition of *La Presse* and nodded. He got up from his stool at the end of the bar, grabbed a bottle of Canadian Club, and waddled over to Eddie, all three hundred pounds of him. His white apron covered him from just below the neck down to his ankles, traveling a mountainous terrain. The neon lights reflected off the apron, turning him a pinkish blue. Eddie liked him for a lot of reasons but mostly because he took pride in maintaining a professional distance from his customers: far enough to leave them alone when they wanted to be, but close enough to talk if they were chatty.

Pierre poured Eddie's whiskey and said, "Fine night, eh?" and waddled back to his stool.

Eddie nodded.

Conversation would be thin that night.

He puffed on his pipe a few times, then got up, walked over to the Wurlitzer, and dropped a quarter into the slot. He pressed D-4 three times and walked back to the bar. By the time he got there, "I Need You Now" was playing. He liked Eddie Fisher.

He made a point of not thinking about cases on Sunday nights. He liked to clear his head of work and start fresh on Monday mornings. Right now, though, he couldn't help but think about the bum he'd had lunch with at Bens last Friday afternoon and how he had magically appeared on the steps of St. Michael's Church later in the evening, kitty-corner from the Lion's Den in Mile End. There was quite a distance between Bens downtown and the church in Mile End. Eddie didn't believe in magic; there was always some trick behind it. It was no coincidence that he had been sitting on the steps of the church, as if waiting for Eddie to come out of the Den. How had the bum gotten there? How had he even known where

Eddie might be? Eddie now wished he'd taken the time and gone over to hm. Maybe he'd have the answers now.

He had no idea how old the bum was. His hands had been dirty, gnarly, and rough, as you'd expect from someone living on the streets, but they weren't a young man's hands. His face had had deep creases in it brought about by age, and his eyes confirmed it. Eddie remembered looking into them and seeing decades of a troubled past. It was difficult to determine the age of someone living on the streets, but that one looked old enough to have served in the military during the Great War. Eddie's own father would have been, too, if he were still alive. The heartbreaking truth of the matter was that Eddie knew little about his father

He reached in his back pocket and pulled out his wallet. He opened it and took out a photo that was folded in half. He flattened it out on the bar and stared at it. There were three people in it, standing in front of an old brownstone building in Brooklyn. He was nine years old at the time the picture was taken. His parents looked so young. He stood between them, their arms around him, smiles as wide as an ocean. It had been another time, another life. Although he carried the picture with him, he seldom looked at it. He couldn't remember the last time he had taken it out of the wallet.

But he remembered that day. How could he forget? They had been walking home from a Chinese restaurant. He couldn't remember what his parents had to eat, but he'd had egg foo young. As they approached their apartment building, they saw that one of his father's friends had been waiting there. Eddie had seen the man before but never knew his name. He stood there with his hands in his coat pockets and his fedora low on his forehead. He didn't say anything; he just stood there staring at Eddie's father. He hadn't been happy, or sad, or angry; the stare was sort of vacant. Eddie always thought he looked like a gangster out of the movies. Eddie's father ran up the stairs and into the apartment building; over his shoulder, he told everyone that he'd be right back. When he returned a few minutes later, he had a Brownie box camera in his hand. He asked his friend to take a family picture. That had seemed strange to Eddie, because his father was never one for having their pictures taken. The man took his hands out of his pockets, looked through the viewfinder while they gathered in front of the stoop, and snapped the picture. His father took the camera and then gave it to his wife and told her and Eddie to go up to the apartment, and that he'd be back in fifteen minutes. "I need to buy a pack of cigs." So as Eddie and his mother climbed up the stoop to the entrance of the brownstone, Eddie looked over this shoulder at his father and his father's friend as they made their way down the sidewalk.

That was the last time Eddie had ever seen him—the back of him, strolling down Quincy Street with a man who looked like a gangster. "I need to buy a pack of cigs." Those words were the last Eddie would ever hear his father say.

Eddie's mother tried to file a missing person report at the local precinct the next day but was told she'd have to wait for three days before she could. "If your husband's out on a bender, he'll be back in a day or two. Don't worry too much, lady. He'll be back when he runs outta dough. I seen it a lot, lady, so don't worry. He'll be back." But he wasn't. She returned on the morning of the fourth day to file the report. And then she waited. Weeks went by, and then a month, without a word, without hope. She returned to the precinct and left the address and phone number of her best friend in Quebec. She could be contacted there should they have any further information on her husband's whereabouts. Then she went to their apartment and packed all their belongings that she could squeeze into two suitcases. She and Eddie took the train north to Montreal, the city of her birth. Both of them, mother and son, had had the world kicked out from under them. Two lost souls in an uncertain and frightening world. It would have been better had her husband been found in an alley or in the Hudson, dead. Their souls would have eventually healed. In limbo, the pain continued forever.

Lincoln Wade had never been seen or heard from again.

That was twenty-nine years ago. Ever since that time, Eddie had been plagued by uncertainty. *Where did he go? Who was the man with him?*

His father had rarely held a steady job. The money he did make often went toward gambling and drinking. But they'd been together as a family. That had been important to Eddie, even at the age of nine. Because of that, there had been the promise of something better. He'd seen it in his father—when he was working and dried out. There had been special times when everyone was happy. But for the last twenty-nine years, his father's legacy beset him with those two questions: *Where did he go? Who was the man with him?* They lingered in the air like the smell of the rotting corpses on the battlefields of Europe.

It was during the end of the war that Eddie had learned about his mother's death. Agostina De Luca Wade had been hit and killed by a car on rue Saint-Denis on March 11, 1945. The papers had her age at forty-eight—a misprint. She was fifty-eight. In spite of the hard life she'd had without a husband, she looked much younger than she actually was. She had a spirit and a determination that had provided both her and Eddie a decent life in a rough neighborhood in Montreal.

If Eddie's father were still alive today, he'd be sixty-eight years old. His mother's death was his father's fault. If he hadn't abandoned them (was that what he had done?), perhaps they'd still be in Brooklyn. She wouldn't have died at that particular time and in that particular place. Maybe she'd still be alive today.

He folded the photo and returned it to his wallet. The second he did, the bum flashed in his head again.

The one who had been sitting on the church steps wasn't the same one he'd had lunch with at Bens, he reasoned. He couldn't be. After all, it was difficult from a distance to tell one from another. Many of them wore similar oversized coats and hats pulled down below their ears in cold weather. That was a much more reasonable explanation. He just wasn't the same guy; he couldn't be.

Eddie raised his shot glass to the barman again.

"How 'bout one for the road, Pierre?"

—————«o»—————

When there should have been only him and her together (he would stop to count: one, two), a third would always appear. There was always another by her side. It was supposed to be only the two of them. He'd been faithful to her beyond expectation (no one could truthfully say otherwise), yet there was always a third.

Yesterday, it happened again. He'd watched them enter the Laurentian Hotel, twelve minutes and thirty seconds apart. They were trying to be discreet about their rendezvous, but he knew what they were going to do in there. It was shameful for a mother, not to mention a married woman, to behave like that. Now he would have to act.

Again.

Would it never end? He was becoming weary but not despondent; wasn't that a testimony of his faithfulness? Evidence of his commitment? Was it not proof of his unrelenting endurance all those years? Did she not realize that? Would she ever realize that? He had acted before—for her, for them—but there was always another beside her.

He picked up his revolver.

Soon, he thought.

It had to be the right time.

His resolve was steadfast.

When he acted, when he was done with this one, the third, then there would be only the two of them.

Him and her.

Again.

As it should be.

Chapter 6
THE BRUTE

WITH THE SUN IN HIS REARVIEW MIRROR, EDDIE drove southwest to Lachine from Mile End early Monday morning, taking Notre-Dame to Victoria and then turning right at Sixteenth just past Lasalle Park to Provost. The radio was on, and he listened to the announcer informing Montrealers that the Soviet Union and seven of its Eastern Bloc allies were preparing to sign the Warsaw Pact in Poland in the coming months—a strategic move in the Cold War environment. Canada had been pals with them once, drinking buddies even. Oh, they had their little tiffs now and again, and they didn't much trust each other, but this time they were putting on the gloves for real. It was us versus them—NATO versus the communist bastards. The bell for round one had sounded six years before. No one knew which round they were in now or how long the fight would last. They both had good trainers in their corners, and the cut men would always stop the bleeding from round to round, but were either of them capable of going the distance?

Eddie turned the radio off. He could see the large white sign with bold black lettering on the top of a dirty brown brick building long before he pulled into the parking area:

Quebec Transport Company. The concrete lot was huge and situated in front of the building. Twenty or so trucks were parked in rows with military precision. They were mostly GMCs and Macks, some rigid trucks and some tractor units with semitrailers with fifth-wheel hitches or gooseneck ball mounts, with two and three axles for heavy-duty hauling—the big rigs. There were a half dozen smaller trucks for the local hauling. Eddie arrived just before the workday began. He swung his car around to the left where the cars were parked and found a spot between two sedans. He locked the car and walked to the door with a sign perched above it, directing visitors to the office.

The office was large, with five or six desks scattered about. Paperwork, files, and dirty coffee cups sat on most of them. Truckers in their gray company uniforms were milling about, talking and laughing, smoking cigarettes and drinking coffee, waiting for the clock to hit eight so they could get on the road. Eddie asked one of the drivers for a Mr. Nadeau. The man pointed to the back of the office without saying anything.

Nadeau had frizzy red hair, a short goatee, and wire-rimmed spectacles. He sat at a desk, engrossed in paperwork. Eddie walked over to him. He had an intelligent look about him, the professorial type. Late forties, maybe early fifties.

"Eddie Wade. Private investigator. I left a message yesterday about Willis Steele."

Mr. Nadeau looked up, blinked his eyes several times, and then rubbed his nose with an index finger. "Yes, yes. Sit down. You mentioned something about Steele being missing."

Eddie pulled out a chair and sat down. "He's a little more than missing. He split on his wife, taking some valuables that didn't belong to him. I'm trying to find him."

"You gotta be shitting me," he said, blinking his eyes again. "Willis Steele? Are we talking about the same guy here?" The sleeves of his white shirt were rolled up on his forearms. He pushed them up farther to his elbows.

"If he's been employed by you for the last eight years, we are." Eddie tipped his hat back a little on his head.

"Yeah, he's worked here that long, up until a few months ago. And then he quit when he got married. To some rich dame, I heard. He came to me personally. Most guys just don't show up when they quit. Said he was really sorry." He angled his head at Eddie and blinked twice. The sides of his face jumped up and down. "You say he skipped out on her?"

"With some things that didn't belong to him."

"That doesn't sound like Willis at all. Not the Willis I know."

"Life is full of little surprises."

One of the drivers was sitting within earshot of them, with his feet up on a chair, drinking coffee and smoking a cigarette. He had his back toward them. Eddie lowered his voice a notch.

"Tell me about the Willis you know."

"He was one of my best drivers. Always on time. Always willing to go above and beyond. He'd fill in for anyone out sick or who quit without notice. Worked overtime without complaining."

"You're saying he was trustworthy then."

"Hell, yes, he was trustworthy. I had plans on bringing him inside, you know, into the management end of things. I have to tell you that I was shocked when he told me he was quitting. Out of the clear blue sky. Said it wasn't his idea. Said the woman he was marrying didn't want him working anymore. Helluva thing, but what could I do?"

"So, he never stole anything out of one of his trucks or from the office."

"Never. And I can't believe he stole anything from his wife either. Maybe she misplaced whatever she thinks he stole."

He fingered his nose again. "I find it hard to believe he just up and left her. It isn't in his nature." He looked at Eddie askance. "Maybe something happened to him. Did you look at that angle?" Without waiting for an answer, he said, "No, I bet you didn't. It looks like you just want to pin a rap on him. You cops are all the same. You go for the jugular from the get-go."

"His wife's jewels and ten Gs went missing when he did. They were in a safe that wasn't broken into. He knew the combination. It looks pretty bad for him. And I'm not a cop. His wife hired me to find him. I just want to hear his side of things."

Nadeau didn't say anything.

"You said something could have happened to him. Like what?"

"How in the hell would I know? Listen, Willis is one of the good guys. He'd bend over backwards to help anyone out of a pickle." He shook his head and went back to his paperwork. "You better leave, Mr. Wade."

Eddie left the building feeling satisfied with the interview. Nadeau painted a different picture of Willis Steele from the "skinny, thieving bastard" that Chanel had told him about. Eddie, however, had been an investigator long enough to understand that some people had dual personalities, often hiding a dark side from the people closest to them. The world was full of those people. They led normal lives until the right opportunity appeared, and then they killed or embezzled or stole. Their wives, or husbands, or bosses would scratch their heads. These types were the last ones they could ever imagine doing something so terrible.

As Eddie was walking through the parking lot, he noticed a tall hulk of a man leaning against his car. His hair was cut short, and his face had a day's growth on it. He wore the company's gray uniform. It was the same guy who had been sitting a short distance away from Nadeau's desk with his back toward Eddie. He had an unlit cigarette in his mouth. Eddie stopped short of him.

"I saw you in the office a while ago," Eddie said. "Do you know Willis Steele?"

The man jerked himself away from the car, turned, and faced Eddie, legs apart, weight evenly distributed, hands on his hips. "My name is Branch York. I want you to remember that. I don't like private dicks in general, and I don't like you in particular."

Eddie was slightly shorter than York and weighed maybe twenty pounds less, but he wasn't intimidated. If it came down to fists, Eddie Wade could take care of himself. He'd spent the years before the war as a professional prize fighter.

"I'll take that as a yes; you do know Willis Steele. How well?"

"I think maybe you're trying to frame Willis for something. I'm his best friend, and I don't like that."

"I'm investigating a case that involves him, and I really don't care what you like. Where is he? Hiding out somewhere? If you know and won't tell, you could be tapped as an accomplice if he's arrested and the case goes to court." Eddie didn't know that for certain, but he decided to throw it into the mix for good measure—see whether York would open up. "You could be looking at a stretch in Bordeaux."

York had small, dark eyes, and when he narrowed them, they looked dangerous. "You know, I don't think I'd mind hurting you right now."

Eddie noticed York's body stiffening up. If York was going to pick a fight, he did the wrong thing. His body should be ready but relaxed. The guy was a brute, but Eddie didn't think he'd be much of a fighter. However, he learned long ago never to underestimate anyone who was getting ready to break a few bones. They sometimes had ways and means you'd never expect.

Eddie stood his ground. He turned sideways. His arms hung loose at his sides, his hands ready to form into fists that he'd used in more than fifty professional fights. "I bet you would. I bet you'd like to hurt me bad." It was a taunt but only a little one, to show he wasn't backing down.

"Yeah, real bad. I'd maybe like to put a big hurt on you that you ain't gonna walk away from." He began fisting his big hands.

Common, mutual, civilized discourse, however, was always Eddie's first line of defense to avoid engaging in the ancient ritual of fisticuffs handed down to us from our Neanderthal ancestors. He hoped that York was the type of fellow who would respond to reason.

"Before you decide to do something you'd be sorry for, you should know that I haven't come to any conclusions about Willis yet. I don't know whether he's missing by choice or whether he had a little help."

York's hands relaxed. "I've known Willis since we were kids, and I can tell you that he'd never run out on his old lady. And he'd never steal from her either. I think you want to pin a rap on him; that's what I think, and that makes me mad. If I thought I wouldn't get into trouble with the boss, I'd show you just how mad I am." He moved past Eddie, bumping into his shoulder, knocking him off balance slightly.

"Branch York is it?" Eddie said, looking at him as he was walking away. "I'll remember that."

"Yeah, you do that, and you should maybe want to start looking over your shoulder from now on. You never know who could be behind you."

"Thanks for the warning, Branch. Have a nice day."

York walked to a truck with a semitrailer hitched to it. A long-haul driver. On the door of the cab was written *Cannonball York.*

————»«●»«————

From Lachine, Eddie drove east across the island, stopping once to fill up his tank. He put the receipt in the glove compartment and would retrieve it later when he added up his expenses. They could balloon fast on a case. He pulled up to a modest-looking, pale yellow clapboard house on rue Blondin in Rosemont and parked in front of it. The neighborhood was made up of other modest-looking clapboard houses that were probably all constructed at the same time twenty or so years earlier. No doctors or lawyers or corporate accountants lived in this neighborhood. The people who did had mediocre but steady jobs with modest incomes. They paid their bills on time, minded their own business, and took their vacations within a hundred-mile radius from their homes. You'd find no vagrants here, or drug dealers, or criminals of any stripes. Life on rue Blondin was a pleasant affair, if not uninspiring, for all who lived there.

Eddie didn't like surprises, so he hoped that Sylvie Boucher didn't either. That was why he hadn't phoned ahead of time. Surprise visits to people he interviewed more times than not yielded surprising results. He knuckled the door several times and waited. After a minute, the door was pulled back.

"Yes?" the woman who answered the door said. "Can I help you with something?"

"Mrs. Boucher?" Eddie asked. "Mrs. Sylvie Boucher?" Eddie's appearance and demeanor suggested to most people he encountered for the first time that he engaged in either law enforcement activities or criminal activities. Or both.

"Yes," she said again, drawing the word out cautiously. "Do I know you?"

"No, you don't, ma'am. My name is Eddie Wade, and I represent the London Life Insurance Company. I'm here to help you with your claim. I need to verify some of the paperwork so the company can process it. Do you mind if I step in? It won't take that long."

She stared at him, wringing her hands, befuddled. "I thought that was all taken care of. They said I would be receiving a check this week."

"Yes, you're correct, but I just have to go over a few details, and then the check will be released."

Mrs. Sylvie Boucher stepped aside for him. She stood five feet two, weighed 102 pounds, had mussy, short brown hair, and wore a haggard, mournful look on her face. Her black dress was wrinkled. No makeup; no jewelry. She showed him into the living room. Eddie sat on the couch, and she took an armchair. She offered no refreshments. She didn't seem to be the kind who would.

"First of all, I want to say how sorry I am for the recent death of your husband. It must have come as a terrible shock to you."

"It was," Sylvie said. After a few moments, she added, "It still is." Tears began welling up in her eyes.

Eddie laid a folder on his lap and opened it. He skimmed the first and second pages. "Let's see now. The report says that your husband, Martin"—he used the French pronunciation—"was found by a police constable on the shore of the St. Lawrence near the warehouse district on the morning of March 10. That would have been on a Thursday." He looked up at her. "Is the correct, ma'am?"

"It is."

"Good. Later that day, they contacted you with the news because they found his wallet in his trousers with his driver's license in it. Is that also correct, Mrs. Boucher?"

"Yes," she said. When Eddie didn't say anything right away, she added, "That is correct."

"Good then." He frowned for just a split second, hoping she'd see it.

"Is there something wrong?"

"No, no. Everything's fine, Mrs. Boucher." He coughed into

his fist and then said, "Now then, when was the last time you saw your husband alive, if I may ask?"

"About two weeks before that."

"Why hadn't you contacted the police then ... if I may ask?"

"Because he wasn't missing. He'd gone to Toronto to see about a job."

"Toronto," he repeated. "I see. Had he gotten there? Had he called you while he was in Toronto?"

"I told the police all this last week. I also told the nice man at the insurance company too."

"Yes, ma'am, I understand. I'm just here to verify all that so they can move forward with your claim. This is pretty standard."

"I see," she said. After a long moment, she added, "He never calls me when he's away. He says ... he said that—I shouldn't tell you this because it's rather personal."

"Mrs. Boucher, I've been an investigator for quite some time now. There's little that I haven't heard. What you tell me remains private. Besides, it could help speed up your claim."

"If you're sure that it will remain private. And that it could help. I suppose I could tell you, now that he's no longer with us." Mrs. Sylvie Boucher swallowed once and ran her hand across her forehead. "Martin never calls me when he's away because ... well, because he says that his desire for me grows stronger when he returns ... that way. You see."

"I see," Eddie said. "Was he away often, Mrs. Boucher?"

"No, not often. Sometimes when he went hunting up north."

"Had he gone to Toronto before that time?"

"Not for years, and then we'd gone together."

"So, he must have returned to Montreal, but you didn't know he had."

"Yes, I suppose that's right."

"Or maybe he hadn't gotten there."

"Yes, maybe."

"I see." Eddie shuffled some papers and then said, "And the next day, Friday, March 11, you went to London Life when they opened the doors at nine in the morning to file a claim as the beneficiary of the decedent—that is, Martin. Is that correct?"

She twisted in the armchair and then placed her hands on her knees. Her tone changed. "You make it seem like I committed a crime. Yes, I did. I was his wife. I *am* the beneficiary, you know. I have that right."

"I hope I didn't offend you, Mrs. Boucher. That was not my intent. I'm only verifying the information on this report."

"I'm sorry."

"No need to be."

"Would you like coffee?"

"Thank you, ma'am, that's very kind of you, but no."

"I don't have any made just now, but I could make some."

"No, that's fine. Thank you though."

"Then is there anything else you'd like to know?"

"Just a few more questions, and I'll leave you in peace, ma'am. I'm afraid the next few questions might be sensitive, but I have to ask them anyway. You know ... to move the claim along." Eddie licked his lips. "Did you and your husband—the last time you saw him alive—part on friendly terms?"

"Mr. Wade, I really think you're going too far. How dare you imply—"

"Mrs. Boucher, I'm not implying anything. I just want to know the mental state of Martin when you last saw him. If he was upset, I need to know just how upset he was and why."

"If you're suggesting he was suicidal, then I can tell you no, he was not. We have ... we had a good marriage. He was very happy when he left. Very. He said he was going to miss me while he was away. He was looking forward to the trip— the prospects of a new job. That's what he said. Mr. Boucher always had a pleasant disposition."

"Are you aware of any enemies he might have had? Anyone who might want to harm him?"

"My husband was a well-liked man. Everyone who knew him would tell you that. A pleasant disposition is what he had. A pleasant disposition. Why would anyone want to harm him?"

That was a good question. But someone had, with a bullet to the heart. Of course, Eddie couldn't tell her that, at least not right now.

The interview was over. Eddie offered her his condolences again and then showed himself out the front door. He decided to sit in his car for the next thirty minutes. He was on London Life's clock, not his own. He figured that the grieving widow would stand at the window and wonder what he was doing out there. Which she did.

Nothing that she'd said specifically had caught his attention. For all intents and purposes, the interview had gone as he had expected it. Mrs. Boucher had said all the right things; her facial expressions and bodily gestures had been consistent with that of a recent widow, allowing for individual differences. She'd become unsettled by some of his questions as one might expect she would. Yet ... Eddie had left with a sour taste in his mouth. There was something indeterminate, either in word or gesture, that Eddie had picked up on that was eluding him; he just couldn't quite pinpoint it. Notwithstanding, he was certain about one thing though.

Mrs. Sylvie Boucher of 48 rue Blondin had been lying to him through her teeth.

———— ◉ ————

At eleven thirty that night, Eddie sat behind his Royal eating a bagel with cream cheese, tomato, and lox that he had picked up earlier at the Fairmount Bakery and finishing up his notes on his two cases. The Four Aces were singing "Three Coins in the Fountain" on the radio. It was a clear night, a little chilly, but nice. He'd left the blinds open; his office was small, and by doing so, it seemed less claustrophobic. Out of the corner of his eye, he could see the occasional car passing by on Saint-Urbain. He was about to get up and file his notes when he looked down and saw Antoinette, who was pure black, and Henri, who was mostly white, sitting on their haunches, looking up at him. *Pathetic*, he thought. He'd fed them earlier, but felines had a keen sense of smell, and he'd been eating lox after all. He opened the bagel and peeled a layer of the fish off, pulling it apart into two pieces and setting them down in front of them. Mademoiselle and monsieur were delighted with themselves.

He filed the cases in his cabinet, got his notebook, and sat down again. He had to plan out the next few days of interviews. London Life wasn't in a mad rush about the Boucher case (Sylvie Boucher wasn't going to get her check until they were damn well ready to give it to her), so Chanel Steele became the priority. One of the interviews he was looking forward to tomorrow was Helen Steele, Willis's sister. He was hoping to get some kind of lead from her on the whereabouts of her brother if she was cooperative.

A car raced by in front of his office, loud music playing, yelling and screaming. He could hear the hubbub even with the windows closed. Teenagers—a night of drinking and hellraising. He hoped they'd make it home in one piece.

It was getting late, and he'd been up early that morning. He opened the bottom drawer of his desk for the bottle of Canadian Club and poured some into his coffee cup. Whenever he was on a particularly difficult case, like Chanel Steele's, his mind would always go into overdrive, keeping him up until the wee hours. A little whiskey before bed helped him fall asleep and stay that way. He gulped down half of it.

The Four Aces gave way to Patti Page singing, "Cross over the Bridge."

He remembered Branch York this morning, wanting to put the big hurt on him. He chuckled to himself. He'd had enough hurt put on him during the war and as a private dick. One more time wasn't going to matter much. Maybe he was pressing his luck though. Maybe he should get out of the detective business, find something else to peddle besides his services. At times, he had to lie and cheat just like the criminals he chased down to get at the truth. At times, he'd been on the end of a rope, hanging off a cliff. How much more luck did he have?

"Cross over the bridge, cross over the bridge," Patti sang. "Change your reckless way of living, cross over the bridge."

He took one last swallow of whiskey. It was smooth going down, with only a hint of fire in his throat. He should sleep well tonight. As he reached over to the radio to turn it off, his eyes caught movement in the window. Through the slats of the Venetian blinds, he could see a dark figure with what appeared to be an arm extended outward toward the window. It took him a second or two to realize that a gun was pointing at him. He dropped to the floor just before three shots rang out. The window imploded, and shards of glass rained down on him like broken pieces of his youth, slicing into his skin, capable of leaving scars as deep as his soul.

Chapter 7

FAIR IS FOUL, AND
FOUL IS FAIR

THE ALARM CLOCK BEGAN BLASTING AWAY AT six o'clock the next morning. Eddie hadn't gotten much sleep after last night's fireworks. But there was a person he wanted to see before eight, so he had to get up early enough to make the drive. He reached over to the nightstand, turned the alarm off, peeled himself out of bed, and put on his robe and slippers. He shuffled into his office, made a cup of coffee, sat down on the couch, and thought about the close call he had had the previous night.

The gunshots had awoken Bruno next door in his apartment over the Lion's Den. He'd rushed over to Eddie's office wielding a baseball bat. The window had been shattered, and Eddie was on the floor. "Saints and sinners! What the hell?" He used Eddie's phone to call the Old Vic for an ambulance, and then he called the police. He had still been in his pajamas and slippers, so he carefully walked around the glass to have a look at Eddie. When the shots had been fired, Eddie had just gotten down by the edge of his desk by mere seconds, with his hands covering his head, so the shards of glass were confined to just the tops of his hands, the desk protecting him from more serious wounds.

The ambulance had taken twenty minutes to get to the office, and the doctor looked at Eddie as soon as he stepped into the office. He'd wanted to take Eddie to the emergency room, but Eddie said no. Outside of his hands, there was nothing wrong with him. Reluctantly, the doctor worked on Eddie there. He'd taken a tweezers out of his medical case and proceeded to carefully pull the bits of glass out of the tops of Eddie's hands. Luckily, there hadn't been many, and they weren't deep. While he was doing that, Bruno had gone back to the Den and returned with his toolbox and a large sheet of plywood. He knocked the remaining glass out of the frame with a hammer, swept the glass off the floor and desk, and then nailed the piece of wood onto the window frame. That would do until Eddie had time to call a glass company to replace the window. At one point while he was working, Bruno had said over his shoulder, "Didn't I tell you to stay away from cases involving matrimonial disharmony?"

After the ambulance had gone and Bruno finished nailing up the plywood and returned to his own apartment, Detective Jack Macalister sat down on the couch with Eddie. Macalister had come with a uniformed constable who was outside the office with a flashlight, shining it around the front of the building.

"So, who wants to put you away this time?" Macalister had asked. "He did a pretty messy job of it."

"Yeah, with any luck, he'll do better next time. Practice makes perfect; that's what I always say." He paused a moment, a half-joking, half-serious expression on his face. "I don't know who it was; it could be any one of several dozen people. You want some names? I keep a current list, adding and removing names as they're either killed or go to prison."

"Goddamn it, Eddie, cut with the wisecracks. The guy was

a little sloppy, but it could have turned out worse. It doesn't look professional, or I wouldn't be talking to you now."

Jack Macalister and Eddie had served in the American Army together. Toward the end of the war, they had run into a nest of Germans on high ground, and all hell broke loose. Macalister had been shot, and Eddie, exposing himself to machine-gun fire, rushed to him and helped him down the hill to cover. For his trouble, Eddie's knee was grazed by a bullet. Eddie had saved his life, and Macalister never forgot it. He owed Eddie his life.

"I didn't see the shooter, only his silhouette and the gun pointing at me. I ducked in time."

"That's obvious," Macalister said. "I'll work the case myself until I get the bastard, but you'll have to give me something more to go on."

"When I find something, I'll let you know."

That hadn't sounded convincing, even to Eddie.

While they'd been talking, the uniformed constable had come in and was digging around the wall opposite the window. When he finished, he walked over to Macalister.

"I found the shell casings outside and pulled the bullets out of that wall," he said, pointing. "Now all we need is a gun to match it to."

After they left, Eddie's first thought had been the truck driver he had had a run-in with that morning—the one who had threatened him: Cannonball Branch York. If it was him, he didn't want to give York a second opportunity. He had to confront the bastard—see what happened, see where that would lead.

So now, as he sat on the couch drinking a cup of coffee at six fifteen in the morning, he wondered whether his looking for Willis Steele was motive enough for Branch York to take several shots at him. Trying to kill him was an extreme way to show his discontent. It didn't seem reasonable, but then again, neither did York.

An hour later, Eddie was in his Ford, moving westward toward the Quebec Transport Company in Lachine, hoping to catch Branch York there before he pulled out in his rig. He had an interview this morning with Helen Steele, Willis's sister. That would have to wait. He'd reschedule it for tomorrow, if she was available.

———— «●» ————

Branch York was drinking coffee and smoking a cigarette in the trucking office, waiting for his shift to begin. It was crowded, with other drivers doing the same thing. The radio was on, and Tony Bennett was singing "Rags to Riches." Branch liked that song, liked it a lot. But before that, the morning news had been on. There'd been a news flash—a shooting at Mile End last night! There were few details, but no one had been hit. The corner of York's mouth had curled as he'd listened to it. Someone had shot three rounds into the window of Wade Detective Agency, narrowly missing private investigator Eddie Wade, who sat behind his desk.

That lucky son of a bitch, York had thought. *Three bullets. You'd figure one would have hit him. What were the odds?*

Branch York knew why he didn't like Wade; he had a big nose and stuck it where it didn't belong. But there was something beyond that, something that burrowed deep inside of him, maybe too deep for him to ever know. In the meantime, he'd have to be content with not liking Wade, because Wade was searching for Willis Steele, and that just had to stop.

At a few minutes before eight, York stubbed out his cigarette in the ashtray, finished his coffee, and made his way outside. As he reached up to open the door of his truck, he heard a voice behind him.

"Too bad you missed me last night. Very amateurish, if you ask me."

He turned around and saw Eddie Wade standing with his hands in his pockets.

"It's you again. What the hell do you want?"

"I said it's too bad that you missed me last night."

"Whaddaya takin' about? Speak English or French. You're not coming through; I don't understand you."

"Oh, I think you understand me all right, Cannonball."

"Is that Chinese? Funny, you don't look like a Chinaman."

"You're a real comedian, Branch—a load of laughs."

"Listen, you got something to say, say it. I ain't got all fucking day."

York stood with his hands on his hips. He was tall and powerful. He narrowed those small eyes at Wade again.

"Someone tried to put me in the ground last night with three bullets, but he only managed to shatter my front window and ruin a wall. I'm trying to find that person to give him an invoice for the damages. I think that someone is you."

"You gotta be fucking kidding me. Now, why would I want to do something like that?"

"Because you're a hotheaded asshole and a friend of Willis Steele."

York felt his face flush. Wade was right; he did have a temper. He took a few steps toward the son of a bitch but stopped. He had a mean look on his face, and he was fisting his hands.

"If I wanted to knock you off, sonny boy, I wouldn't have missed."

Eddie didn't say anything to that; he shifted his body slightly, readying himself for an attack. But York turned around again and opened the door of his truck.

"Beat it, chump. You come here again, I'll file a police report for harassment."

He climbed up to the seat but didn't close the door.

"You're a piece of work, Wade," he said. "You can't find

Willis, and you can't find the bum who shot at you, so you accuse an innocent man because it's the easy thing to do. Easy Eddie. That's what people should call you. Maybe you should find another line of work."

"Oh, I found the bum all right, and I'm telling you that next time it won't go well for you."

Branch started the rig and let it idle for a minute. He closed the door and rolled down the window.

"Next time, eh?" York said with a grin. "Well, maybe next time the bum might be a little luckier."

He put the rig into gear and drove off, leaving Eddie standing in the parking area with his hands in his pockets.

———«●»———

That night, Eddie went to Willis Steele's favorite watering hole—that is, his favorite since before marrying Chanel Steele. At that point, Chanel had insisted he stopped going there because it wouldn't be fitting for someone who lived in Westmount to be seen at such a place. She had her standards, and she made sure that Willis was going to abide by them. This she told Eddie when she gave him the list of places he frequented along with the names of relatives and friends. It was only last night, after the shooting, when he looked at the list closer that he realized Branch York's name was on it.

The "Merrimaker" was down by the port, surrounded by an army of cold storage warehouses. Millions of tons of merchandise moved through this area annually, supplying the rest of Canada. The sign above the door was washed out and weather-beaten. The brown bricks on either side of the entrance had graffiti painted on them. When Eddie opened the door, he was struck by the smells of stale beer, cigarette smoke, and others of undetermined origins. The dive was long and narrow. The bar was off to the left; opposite that, along the wall to the right, were small, round wooden tables and chairs that ran from the front to the rear. A pool table sat about five feet directly from the bar in the back. The green felt was faded and torn in places, repaired with thick, army-green industrial tape, a survivor from the last war. It wasn't crowded, but there were enough patrons to warrant a waitress. The men who were there looked like down-and-outs taken out of cold storage, whose better days were distant memories. There was a constant drone of voices; no one looked particularly merry.

Eddie walked down the aisle and took a stool at the middle of the bar, where the barman stood reading the late edition of the *Gazette*. Farther down, a middle-aged woman was washing pint glasses in a sink. Eddie pulled his pipe and tobacco pouch from his coat pocket and set them on the bar. He looked around him and wondered why Willis Steele, a relatively young man, would choose this dump to frequent.

The barman turned the page of the paper he was reading and without looking up said, "You want something to drink, or are you going to shake the place down?"

Eddie took out his wallet, flipped it open to his private license, and showed it to him.

"I'm not a cop if that's what you're asking. I'm looking for someone, but you can give me a half pint of Molson in the meantime."

The barman poured the beer from the tap and set it in front of Eddie. It had a nice head on it. He knew what he was doing.

"Everyone in this goddamn city seems to be looking for someone. The paper's full of missing people. Look here," he said, ruffling the paper and pointing. "It says in the Personals, 'If you see Jacques, tell him to come home. His kids are hungry.' Now I ask you, can you beat that?"

Eddie nodded in agreement and filled his pipe. He set a match to the bowl and took some short puffs to get it going. "You got that right about missing people," he added, as if the nod wasn't enough. He reached into his pocket again for a nail and used the head to tamp down the ash. After relighting the pipe, he said, "The one I'm looking for is called Steele, Willis Steele, with an *e* on the end. Heard he likes to drink here."

The barman looked at Eddie askance. He was in his mid to late fifties with thinning gray hair, a broken nose that had healed crooked, and scar tissue above his eyes. Eddie thought the guy had been around the block a few times.

"What did he do?" he asked.

"He was a bad boy. His wife's looking for him."

"The cops too?"

"Not at the moment, but that could change."

"Sure, I know him." The barman stopped and changed directions. "Don't I know you from somewhere? The name on your license said Wade. You wouldn't be Eddie Wade, the fighter, would you?"

"Former fighter."

"I used to watch you fight at the Forum before the war. Then you disappeared. I noticed your nose. It's been broken a few times, like mine. I fought around the city myself, but that was before your time. You had a wicked left hook, as I remember it." He reached over the bar with an extended hand. "Marceau Arceneault. Glad to meet you, but I went by the name of Kid Arson—a play on my real name my manager came up with. My punches were supposed to be like fire when hitting an opponent."

"I remember the name from when I was a kid."

"Lived like a dog those days. Saved enough money and got out early with my noodles intact. Used it to buy this joint."

"Good for you. A lot of fighters ended up on the skids."

"Yeah, I guess we're the lucky ones. I see you done OK for yourself." Arceneault stopped to pour himself a beer. He took a swig, ran his palm over his mouth, and said, "OK, Eddie, come clean. What did Willis do?"

"He married a rich, good-looking broad and ran out on her two months later with her jewels and a lot of cash. She hired me to find him."

"The last time he was in here, he said he was getting married the next week. He didn't seem too pleased about it. He said she was trying to control his life. She wanted him to quit his job at the trucking company and stop coming in here. He wasn't a very happy man for someone who was getting hitched up."

"How well did you know him?"

"He'd been coming in for years. He was one of the few truly nice guys who come in here. I asked him one time—why here with all these bums twice his age? He said because no one bothers him. He can drink in peace and quiet. The last time he was in, I asked him why he was getting married if the broad wanted to control him. You know what he said? He said because he loved her. Can you beat that one? He let himself be controlled by a broad outta love. Jesus almighty Christ."

"Do you think he was capable of stealing from her and then doing a disappearing act?"

"Hey, Eddie, that's a loaded question. Everyone's capable of stealing, given the right frame of mind. When opportunity knocks, you'd be surprised just who opens the door. Sometimes it's little stuff, and sometimes not so little. Maybe you should ask Trixie here," he said, thumbing toward the waitress. "She knows him far better than me. Trixie, come over here, will yah?"

Trixie wiped her hands on her apron and walked over to them. Her hair was too blonde, her eyeliner was too brown, and her lips were too red. She looked as if she could have been a hot tomato twenty years before, but a middle-age spread was starting to show, and there were no signs that it would stop. The former pugilist turned barman filled her in on the conversation.

"It doesn't sound like Willis, but who can tell these days? I've known him since before high school, but we weren't that close. He was always one for playing jokes and getting into trouble. My folks wouldn't let me hang out with him. Anyway, I was a little older than him, and he already had a tart. Lost track of him after high school, until he walked in here one day." She turned to the barman. "Jeez, Kid, what was it? Gotta be five, six years ago?" Then to Eddie: "Two months ago, he comes in, says he's getting married, and we haven't seen him since." A moment later, she added, "After all those years, like we don't exist anymore—like we're not good enough for him now. The nerve ..."

"So, you think he was capable of doing what his wife is accusing him of?"

From behind them on the other side of the bar, someone shouted, "Hey, Trixie! How 'bout a game of pool? Loser buys a round."

"Listen, I gotta go and entertain the troops. You'd think they had better things to do but sit all night and spend their pensions." She leaned into Eddie. "But if I were Willis's wife, if I caught him, I'd hang him up by his balls!"

Eddie left after finishing his beer. The fetid air inside was starting to give him a headache. He took a deep breath of fresh, cool air. He thought it was a fair exchange. It was. He felt better. He swung right and walked down to his car. The port off to his left was as quiet as the city morgue not far away. He thought about what Kid Arson had said; everyone was capable of stealing given the right frame of mind. Eddie had to agree. But Willis's ex-boss and his best friend, Branch York, had said otherwise, and they knew him better. But maybe they hadn't known him as well as they thought. Maybe the right opportunity had knocked on Willis's door, and he had opened it. Eddie had to dig a few more holes to find out. He'd have to be careful, though, of York while he was digging.

As he stuck his key into the car door, he glanced over his shoulder to the right. Someone was standing near a building down from the Merrimaker. He squinted to get a better look. Was he that bum again he'd taken to lunch and who then popped up that night at the church? He wasn't certain. He got into the car, made a U-turn, and drove to where he saw him. He stopped. The guy disappeared. There was nothing there but redbrick and shadows under the streetlight.

He could have been that bum all right; or maybe it was a different bum named Branch York.

Chapter 8
PLANNING IS EVERYTHING

ON WEDNESDAY MORNING, EDDIE DROVE EAST from Mile End to Saint-Leonard for an interview he had set up the previous day. Helen Steele was her name, the no-good, skinny bastard's kid sister. She wasn't a kid any longer, and if her voice was any indication of the rest of her, he was looking forward to meeting her. Sensual, moist, and appealing—that was what her voice had sounded like over the phone. Eddie reminded himself that it was a cardinal sin to become romantically involved with anyone associated with an active case he was working. That didn't, however, preclude him from appreciating a little window dressing now and again. Moreover, the sad fact was that it wasn't beneath him to break his own rules. Chanel had been a case in point, saved only by someone opening a door rather than by his own willpower. Notwithstanding, he was in his mid-thirties, good looking, and healthy. If he did decide to break the rules, the circumstances would have to be extraordinary—and the broad, shockingly sensational. Helen Steele's voice suggested he was on the right track. With his tongue hanging out and drool running down his chin, he anticipated the rest of her just might meet his criterion.

He pulled up to a ratty-looking brown-brick apartment building built sometime in the last century. It sat in the right neighborhood, because all the other buildings looked the same. They were derelict, neglected for decades—ramshackle with crumbling pieces of brick lying on the ground beside them. Their owners probably lived in the countryside and showed up only to collect the rent once a month. He opened the door, and inside, all the buzzers had been taped over. He opened the inner door, which was unlocked, walked up three flights of stairs, and knocked on 301 at the landing. On the second knock, Helen Steele opened the door.

It wasn't as if he'd put all of his money in the pot, laid his cards on the table, and hoped for the best. If wasn't as if he'd gambled his life on one last shake and then rolled the dice. No, it was neither of those things. All he'd done was phone Helen Steele yesterday for an interview, listen to her warm, magnificent, luscious, beautiful female voice, and had high expectations.

"You must be ... Eddie."

There it was again—that voice.

"Miss Steele?" he asked incredulously. "Miss Helen Steele?"

"Come in, and we'll have that little chat you wanted."

Helen Steele turned her body sideways so that Eddie could squeeze through the doorway.

"Just move some of the stuff on the couch and sit down. Get the weight of your feet."

Eddie sat down, and Helen took the armchair opposite him.

The apartment looked like a rat's nest and reeked of last night's grease and fried fish. Piles of clothes lying on the floor dotted the living room. Ashtrays overflowing with dead cigarette butts were on each of the end tables. Empty beer cans were scattered about. Helen Steele sat smiling at Eddie with her hands folded on her lap. If she had attempted to clean up before the guest arrived, she missed the mark.

Eddie smiled back at her in disbelief. The voice didn't match the body—not even close. Helen was a rotund lady in her early forties. She wore a long, woolen pink bathrobe with matching slippers, and her hair was in curlers. She had three large moles on the most conspicuous places of her face. With her last name the same as her brother's, she was probably unmarried. Eddie always believed that there was someone for everyone to love in this hard, cruel world, but there were exceptions to every rule. He guessed he wasn't the only one she'd fooled with that voice of hers.

"Now," Helen said, unfolding her hands and patting her lap. "What sort of information were you looking for? I think I mentioned to you on the phone that I haven't seen Willis in years."

"I understand that," Eddie said. "I just want to get the sense of what kind of person Willis is. Are your parents still in the city?"

"They moved to California more than a decade ago. It hadn't gone well for them, and they ended up getting a divorce—American style. As far as I know, they're still in San Francisco with a lot of distance between them. Good luck if you're going to try and find them."

"What was Willis like growing up?"

"He was two years older than me and very protective. He was nice to his friends, but he had the devil in him, if you know what I mean. He liked to get into trouble. Chanel had a good influence on him, but even that only went so far. They had been friends and hung around together ever since I could remember. They were like two peas in a pod. I suppose if Chanel hadn't been in his life in those days, Willis would have gotten into worse trouble than he did."

"What sort of trouble?"

"Nothing too serious. His favorite pastime was hiding behind bushes and throwing tomatoes he'd stolen from gardens at cars passing by. Strictly kid's stuff. It could have been a lot worse though, but Chanel hadn't liked what he was doing and told him so, so Willis pulled back. When they were in their teens, she threatened to stop seeing him when he started to steal cars to go on joyrides. He stopped."

"So, Chanel could control him."

"That's right. Willis really liked her, and I guess he didn't want to ruin that. She was gorgeous even then. They stayed together until after high school. Chanel's parents had never really been thrilled with Willis from day one, so I guess they must have been glad when she dumped him for that rich guy. I guess she must have gotten fed up with him, and who's to blame her? I was floored when you said Willis and Chanel were married."

"Did Willis ever get into trouble after high school?"

"Only once that I know of. About ten years ago, he stole some money from the company he worked for. He drove for a milk company, you know, delivered milk from house to house. I don't know all the details, but he did a year and a half in Bordeaux for that. When he got out, he began driving a truck. Mostly in Montreal, but sometimes over-the-road too. He told me that he was going straight, that he learned his lesson. Apparently, he hadn't if he stole from Chanel."

"That's what I'm looking into, but I've got to find him first. Any ideas where he might be?"

"We kind of drifted apart. I haven't talked to him in a few years. Your guess is as good as mine. Say, forgive my manners. Would you like a drink, Eddie?"

Eddie didn't want a drink. He had enough information and wanted to just get the hell out of there. The smell of old, fried fish, cigarette ash, and stale beer was making him woozy.

Outside in his car, he thought that maybe with that much cash and jewels in the house, the temptation was just too great for Willis. Opportunity knocked on his door. Maybe his old ways had come back, in spite of what others had said about him.

———«◉»———

Later that night, Luc Legrand pulled up to a warehouse near the port in his black Lincoln Capri. He locked up his car, entered the building, walked through a storage area, and knocked on a door in the back; he opened it before anyone could say anything. An ox in his sixties sat behind a desk in a nondescript office.

"Vitto," Legrand said, looking sharp and fit in his pin-striped suit. "How they hanging?"

"At my age, the fact that they're hanging at all—it's a good sign. Sit."

Legrand dragged a chair from the back wall to the front of the desk, wiped the seat off with a handkerchief, and then sat down.

"Every time I see you, you look like you just finished a photo shoot for *Esquire*. Don't you ever wear blue jeans and a T-shirt?" He relit his half-smoked cigar and sent a cloud of smoke in the room.

"Only in the confines of my home, and then only when I don't have guests. Bankers have their standards, you know."

"I thought as much. Anyway, I just wanted to check with you on how everything's going with the business. Smoothly, I hope."

Vitto was Vittorio Coppoletta, the longtime Mafia don who controlled most of the illegal activities in Montreal and a great deal of the legal ones as well. Sometime early in his illustrious career, someone who didn't much like him had referred to him behind his back as the "Egg" because of his bald head. He'd found out about it, liked the nickname, and started using it himself. A week later, he'd sent a case of eggs to the guy as a gesture of his appreciation. A week after that, he'd had his boys measure him for cement shoes and dumped him in the Saint Lawrence.

"Things couldn't be better," Legrand said. "The operation is running as smoothly as a baby's behind. You're receiving your weekly cut, so that should tell you something."

"Yeah, I know, I know, but we hadn't talked in a while. I don't like it when we don't talk for a while." Several more puffs; another cloud of smoke.

"You know, there's this new invention. It's called the telephone."

"Goddamnit," he said, slapping the top of his desk, "that was a humdinger! A real lollapalooza! I gotta use that sometime. Come on, Luc, you know I don't like to talk on the phone. You never know who might be listening. Anyway, I'm a-happy with the news. Any changes, you be sure to let me know."

"Like always, Vitto, like always."

"Why fix something when it ain't broke, eh?"

"That's what I always say."

"Heard rumors you're still giving it to that Dupont dame. Sounds like it's serious."

"It's Steele now, and yes, I'm still seeing her, but I'm about as serious with her as I am with all the others."

"Maybe you hadda something to do with her new husband disappearing, no?"

"How do you know about that?" The surprised look on his face was genuine.

"Come on, Luc, you know there ain't much in this city I don't know about. That's why everything runs so smoothly." He paused a moment and then said, "Maybe you want to step into the action permanently with the broad?"

"I had nothing to do with that skinny shrimp taking off. Besides, I don't particularly like the broad. She's too pushy for me, but she's got a helluva body. We just have a mutual agreement, she and I. Know what I mean?"

"Yeah, I know what you mean. Just play it easy is all I'm saying. You don't want any complications. Bad for your business, bad for mine. Keep your head down. A rich broad who thinks she's been wronged can destroy a man. And then what happens to the business? She destroys that too! I've seen it done before."

"Naw, it's nothing like that, Vitto. It's strictly sex. No strings attached."

"Sex? No strings attached? Now that is really a humdinger! A real lollapalooza!"

Luc never called Coppoletta "Egg." He thought it was undignified. He would always call him Vitto. On his way home that night, he called him a son of bitch. He didn't like the son of a bitch interfering in his personal life. But just how personal was it when Coppoletta knew everything about it? He wished he could do something about it, but he knew it was useless. Coppoletta was just too powerful. That made Luc feel emasculated. He hated that feeling; he wasn't used to it.

His business arrangement with him—that was something different. He didn't mind the son of a bitch checking on things. Coppoletta had that right. Business was business, and they both had a financial stake in it. But he had no business telling him who he could or couldn't see.

Maybe he could do something about it after all. He'd have to think about it.

He checked his watch. It was late, and he was tired. It had been a long day. Oh, well, in a few minutes, he'd be home. After a hot shower and a whiskey, he'd be sleeping in his bed, cozy and warm, the day ending and his dreams just beginning.

=☰◍☰=

Legrand should be home soon.

At least he hoped he would.

He stood behind a large maple tree directly across the street from Legrand's house. The clouds blocked the moon—darkness, except for a dim streetlight overhead. He couldn't have picked a better night.

He'd been in the neighborhood a few nights ago, scouting the area out. At this time of night, people were inside their houses, minding their own business or sleeping. That was good. That had given him the opportunity to check in between the houses and alleyways without some busybody screwing things up. He knew exactly where he'd run, where he'd go, but to be on the safe side, he also had an alternative route. Planning was everything. He'd read that somewhere, but he couldn't remember which book. The author, of course, had been writing about something else, but it certainly applied to him. It had made sense, and he never forgot it.

Except once.

That damned private investigator, Wade. He really botched that one. He'd rushed it; that was it. Well, that wouldn't happen again. Next time, he'd plan it out better. Like tonight.

A car had just turned the corner and was now driving down the street. All he could see were the headlights. He edged himself around the tree so that he couldn't be seen and then carefully peeked around it. The car was going faster than it should have been if the driver was going to pull into Legrand's driveway. It didn't, and as it passed him, he edged himself back around the tree, keeping his body close to it. Wrong car. That was fine with him. He had all the time in the world.

But Legrand didn't.

As he waited, he couldn't help but think how many more times he would have to get rid of the *third*. Every time he thought it was just him and her, someone new would appear in her life, and he'd have to take care of it. He shrugged. *As many times as necessary,* he thought.

His thoughts were interrupted by another car, this one driving more slowly. Again, he edged himself around the tree. The car slowed down even more and then turned into the correct driveway. It was a black Lincoln; it had to be Legrand. The engine died, and a second later, so did the headlights. The door swung open, and the driver got out; it was Luc Legrand all right.

Legrand took a few steps away from the car, and when he was parallel with the front end, the killer emerged from behind the tree and crossed the street. He was calm, but his steps were spirited. When he was approximately ten feet away, Legrand looked up.

The two men were facing each other from a distance.

The killer kept walking toward him; there was an almost joyous, youthful rhythm to his pace. Legrand had a confused looked on his face. The killer could plainly see it under the dim streetlight, which made him smile from ear to ear. Legrand's expression changed abruptly to fear when he saw the killer raise his arm and point a gun at him. He fired two shots directly into the middle of Legrand's chest. Luc Legrand collapsed onto the cold, hard cement—like a sack of Manitoba potatoes.

The killer turned and ran back across the street and in between two houses, then disappeared into the night.

Chapter 9
MORE THAN JUST INTERESTING

EDDIE HAD WOKEN UP ON THURSDAY MORNING feeling as if he'd just completed a twenty-five-mile forced march with full military field gear on an empty tank; he could eat a cow—bones, guts, everything. His usual breakfast of toast and coffee wouldn't cut it this morning.

He'd hightailed it down Saint-Urbain to Mont-Royal and had a hardy meal at Beauty's while chatting with the owner, Hymie, who was working nonstop behind the counter. The restaurant was small and crowded with locals. With the continuous hum of voices, the smells of bacon, eggs, pancakes, coffee, and maple syrup mingled with those of cigarette and cigar smoke. Some sat with their heads down, shoveling food into their mouths. It reminded Eddie of his time in basic training in the army, when everyone wolfed down their morning chow as if it was going to be their last meal. As they finished, they lit a cigarette or relit a cigar, finished their coffee, and talked about politics or the weather. When the conversations died out and Eddie was on his third refill of coffee, he unfolded the early-morning edition of the *Gazette* to the front page. He had an interview scheduled in Outremont, which was only a five-minute drive away, and he needed to kill another half hour.

The two-word headline could not be misinterpreted by anyone: "Banker Murdered." The byline was Jake Asher, and the article was short. Eddie read it with interest. Most of it was filler; Eddie figured Jake hadn't had a lot of information about the actual killing, and the police were being closemouthed. The entire article could have been written in one sentence: an executive at the Royal Bank of Canada, Luc Legrand, was shot dead outside his home last night. Jake ended the article by saying that the police were stymied.

Interesting, he thought. *Royal Bank of Canada.*

That was where Chanel Steele's former husband, Guy Dupont, had worked. He'd been murdered five years earlier; found shot in the back of the head downtown somewhere. Maybe the bank should start providing its employees with hazardous-duty pay. After his initial interview with Chanel, Dupont's murder had piqued Eddie's interest so much so that he'd scheduled an appointment to see Dupont's elderly parents in Outremont. He folded the paper, paid Hymie for his breakfast, got into his car, and drove to Mr. and Mrs. Dupont's house.

Outremont.

It could hardly be called a city, but that's what it was. It was more like a village surrounded by Montreal. If you were strolling down a particular sidewalk in Montreal and didn't know where the boundaries converged, you could be in and out of Outremont in a minute by crossing several streets. It had been named after someone's elegant house last century and lay on the northwestern side of Mount Royal. Outremont meant "beyond the mountain" in French. It was an enclave for the French aristocracy. Eddie usually stayed clear of it. He had nothing against the French, of course, or the aristocracy for that matter. But he was against anyone trying to kill him. Last year, a blue-eyed beauty from Outremont did her best to reduce the world's population by one when she and an accomplice had tried to murder him and nearly succeeded. Since then, about as close to Outremont as he would go was Beauty's. But here he was again. Whether or not he had a death wish did cross his mind as he pulled up to the Duponts' house on Dunlop across from Pratt Park.

A maid or a nurse answered the door and showed Eddie into the drawing room, where the aged Duponts sat drinking their tea in front of the fireplace. Everything in the house looked new, if it was the middle of the nineteenth century, but it was clean and well cared for.

"Thank you for seeing me on short notice," Eddie said, sitting down in an armchair at an angle to the davenport where the Duponts were sitting.

"We had to rearrange some appointments to squeeze you in, Mr. Wade," Mr. Dupont said. "Our schedule these days are enough to turn the hair of a young man white." His voice was slow, gravelly, and hesitant.

The Duponts had to be in their nineties. They were small and frail, and both had white hair. They sunk into the davenport as if being enveloped by a tomb as their final resting place.

"Sorry about the inconvenience, Mr. Dupont."

"Save the apology, Mr. Wade. I was just jerking your chain. We haven't had a guest in the house in a month. It's a pleasure to see some young new blood here. Our friends, when they do manage to hobble over for the rare visit, all look as if they've been preparing for their own funeral. And please call me Arnaud. This is my wife, Hortense." She nodded at Eddie. "I'm afraid I'll have to do the talking for the both of us. You see, she had a stroke after our son was murdered. She actually recovered quite well, except for her speech."

"Sorry to hear that," Eddie said, nodding back at Mrs. Dupont with a sympathetic smile.

"You said on the phone that you wanted some information about Guy." He pointed at the tray in from of him. "Pour yourself some tea, if you'd like. It's still very hot."

"I've been drinking coffee all morning, so I'll pass on that. Thanks." Eddie kept his notebook in his coat. He wanted this to be more of a conversation than an interview. "I've read pretty much all that had been written in the papers about your son's murder, and I wondered if you had any information that hadn't been included."

"May I ask why you're interested in the case now? The police investigated it at the time and didn't come up with anything. His murder remains a mystery to this day."

He explained about being hired by their former daughter-in-law to find Willis Steele. He didn't mention anything about the stolen money and jewels.

"So, you think there's a connection between the two cases?"

"No, I don't, but I do want to cover every possible angle."

"Unfortunately, I really can't say any more than what's already been written in the papers and in the police report."

Eddie noticed that Arnaud's wife reached over and nudged his arm with her hand.

"The police were quite thorough, and the papers reported everything they had on the case," he continued.

Hortense cleared her throat and nudged him again.

Eddie looked at Arnaud and then Hortense and then back at Arnaud.

"But?" Eddie said.

Arnaud sipped his tea, his hand shaking, and then glanced quickly at his wife. He set the teacup on the tray. His hair flared outward around his ears, giving him an unkept look that belied the rest of him.

He pursed his lips twice and then said, "We have no evidence for what I'm going to tell you. We didn't even share our concerns with the police. However ... we believe—"

He stopped abruptly as if he were finished. Hortense immediately swatted him lightly on the arm.

"If you're going to look into this case, we'd suggest you start with Chanel."

"Why do you say that?" Eddie wasn't entirely surprised.

"As I said, we have no evidence. But we were very close to our son. He told us everything. We had frank talks about his life frequently. I know for a fact that he had no enemies. He would have told us; we're quite certain about that. Killing someone is an extreme act—and a very final one. So there has to be something in it for the killer to make it worth the risk." He stopped to cough into his fist for a moment, and then he picked up his cup again and sipped his tea. Setting the cup back on the tray and clearing his throat, he said, "Are you familiar with the Latin phrase cui bono? It's a question."

"I am. It means *Who benefits?*"

"That's right, Mr. Wade. Who benefits? Well, I'll tell you who benefitted from my son's death. There's only one person on God's green earth, and her name is Chanel."

"That's a pretty strong accusation to make without any evidence."

"I know it is, young man. That's why we didn't tell the police our concerns."

"So, what are your concerns?"

"We never liked her. She's always been coarse and vulgar. Oh, she learned to cover that up over the years because she had to, considering the position she married into, but she was still abrasive and uncouth to the bones, because it was in her nature to be so. You can't hide something like that forever. We always thought Guy had married down. Excuse me if you don't like that, but that's the way we felt. It had nothing to do with money and everything to do with character. Her lack of personal wealth had never been an issue with us, but her character was. We saw through her the first time Guy brought her here to meet us; unfortunately, he never did."

"That doesn't necessarily lead to murder."

"Of course, it doesn't, young man. We may be old, but we're not stupid. But I ask you again, cui bono? And again, there's only one person."

Eddie couldn't say that he hadn't entertained the idea himself.

"Do you have other concerns?"

Both husband and wife looked at each other and then back at Eddie.

"Does the name Thornton Hill mean anything to you?" Arnaud asked.

"I'm afraid it doesn't."

"Of course not. Why would it? He'd been engaged to be married to Chanel. Our grandson told us all about it. Then maybe four or five months ago—I can't remember exactly when—he went missing. Disappeared, just like your Willis Steele. Never to be seen again."

Eddie couldn't believe what he was hearing. Three men in Chanel's life—one murdered and two disappeared. He took out his notebook and wrote the name down.

"Interesting," was all Eddie could say.

Arnaud leaned forward and said, "Son, it's a helluva lot more than just interesting." He sat back again and readjusted himself. "It's worth at least another look. Of course, this happened years after our son's murder."

"Did you know Willis Steele?"

"Met him once or twice when he dropped Percy off for a visit."

"What did you think of him?"

"He was always polite and gracious to us, but if you're

asking why he married a widow with a grown son, a widow rich with our son's money, I could only speculate. I wouldn't want to besmirch a man's good name." He seemed to want to say more, but he paused a moment, his eyes fixated on Eddie's chest. "Could I be so bold as to ask you a personal question, Mr. Wade?"

"Of course." Eddie didn't have a clue as to what the personal question could be.

"That tie you're wearing—is it the fashion with young men these days?"

Eddie looked down and then back up at Mr. Dupont.

"It was a gift I got from someone years ago. I feel obligated to wear it once in a while." He chuckled.

"It's quite … colorful."

"That's one of the kindest things people have said about it."

"I see. I don't mean to be—"

"No, that's fine," he said, waving him off. "It gets all sorts of reactions from people. I'm used to it. So, you've been able to maintain contact with your grandson."

"Percy was the only reason we tolerated Chanel. For his sake. We had to talk our son into establishing a trust fund so Chanel wouldn't have access to all of his money at one time, in case something happened to him. Which it did, and we're glad that we did it. There's a clause in the trust fund. If something happens to Chanel, the fund and the estate then go to Percy." He paused a moment to glance at his wife and then back at Eddie. "I'm afraid Hortense is getting a little sleepy."

Eddie decided to cut the interview short.

"Of course. Thank you for seeing me. I'll see myself out."

The Duponts had given him plenty, so he thanked the old couple again and went out to his car.

He was furious. Chanel had failed to mention Thornton Hill. She'd been engaged to him last September or October, and then he disappeared. Months later, she married Willis, and two months after that, he disappeared. Why wouldn't she think to tell him about that? He turned the key, stepped on the starter, put the shift into gear, and pushed the gas pedal down.

He was off to Westmount to find out.

———«◉»———

Percy sat on a chair in his bedroom with his feet on the edge of the bed, wondering about his future. He didn't do this often, but when he did, it was never a pleasant task. He despised the future, and he couldn't very well avoid the present. It was the past that really mattered. All that aside, his future arose in him this morning like bad food, and he was forced to contend with it.

What would his life be like in ten years? Twenty years? If it was just he and his mother, alone, there would be some predictability he could count on. He'd know his place in the world. He'd have a sense of comfort and stability, which he would find reassuring. Wasn't that how most people felt? He wasn't sure, because he didn't know a lot of people, and the ones he did know, he couldn't say. However, what he could say for certain was that he would find it immeasurably gratifying to know that his life would continue on just the way it was right now, with just his mother and him alone in this big house. Today would be just like yesterday, and tomorrow would be just like today, both rooted in the past. Nothing would change. That's what he wanted—a world that he could manage from one day to the next. Dammit, was that asking too much?

He didn't think so.

The first time he'd realized what he wanted was after his father had been murdered. It had been an unintended consequence but real nonetheless. It had been so peaceful and predictable, just he and his mother together. Each day had been like the previous one. And as the years passed, he'd realized that that was what he wanted forever.

But then another man had entered his mother's life, and his world had spun around and was flushed down the toilet. It was as if his father had returned from the dead. Almost but not quite. He was right back to where he had been. Those had been dark days. His world had been thrown off-kilter; he was nearly suicidal. But as luck would have it—luck or fate—that was short-lived because the man had gone missing. He was in control again. He had regained his composure, straightened out his world—as one might straighten his hat on his head while looking into a mirror—and was very pleased with himself. He and his mother had been alone again in the big house.

But then, as if some relentless jokester hadn't had enough laughs at his expense, his world exploded a third time when his mother—didn't she know what she was doing to him?—brought home Willis Steele. He had gotten a taste of what his world could be like with just his mother and him twice before, and because of that, that third time had had a terrible effect on him. It was as if someone had yanked a tablecloth off a table set with dinnerware—plates, glassware, and cutlery—expecting them to remain in place. Instead, everything had gone crashing to the floor. This time, he nearly put a bullet in his head. But luck had been with him again (at this point, he began to think it was fate) because Willis had gone missing just like the one before him. And for the last few weeks, he had been in control of his world again.

How long would it last this time? He knew that his mother had often made poor decisions, as when she hired Mr. Wade. And it had become clear to him that his mother had been unaware just how her poor decisions affected him. Mr. Wade could very well nudge his world off its axis again. He couldn't let that happen; no sirree, not on his life. He couldn't very well let that happen again.

He had to do something about it.

He took the letter opener from his desk and went into his closet. He shoved aside his shoes and tennis racket, pried the false wall loose, and retrieved his gun. He went back to his bed and sat down. He ran his fingertips over the gun as one might do with a woman's body (not that he had any direct knowledge of that); then he grasped the grip with one hand. It felt good. He dropped the magazine and then pushed it up again expertly—he'd practiced doing that a lot recently—until it clicked into place. He pointed it at his reflection in the mirror of his dresser. *Bam!* That was all it would take to set his world right again.

Bam!

Chapter 10
THROWING A HARNESS
ON EDDIE

EDDIE WADE STOOD WITH HIS HAT TILTED BACK and his arms akimbo—his overcoat spread out on either side of him, exposing a surrealistic, multicolored tie that his girlfriend at the time had given him for his birthday two years before. It beggared all description. Salvador Dali would have given him a wink and a nod.

"I want a straight answer, and I want it right now." His voice was firm. He was angry but in control of himself—for now. "Why didn't you tell me about him?"

"Sit down, Eddie. Relax. You're getting your knickers in a twist over nothing."

He was in Chanel's kitchen. She was preparing tea for herself. The kitchen had been designed primarily for food preparation, so there wasn't a lot of space to move around in. The table was nothing more than a chopping block with two chairs on either end. Eddie took up a third of the available space. It would be difficult for him to maneuver about. On the other hand, it was the same for Chanel. There was nowhere she could hide.

"I don't want to sit down. Answer the goddamn question."

"Testy, aren't we?"

"Answer the question."

"What I want right now is a cup of tea. Join me?"

She opened a cupboard door above the pots and pans and retrieved two cups, and then she picked up the tea pot and filled them. She was calm, and her movements were smooth and deliberate. Her blonde hair flowed over her shoulders like cascading liquid. It bounced a little when she moved. She was one cool chick.

"Milk and sugar?" she asked, turning around. She lowered her eyes to his chest. "Jeez, that's an awful tie you're wearing."

"Enough with the games, Chanel." His voice was a few decibels higher than what it should have been for polite conversation. He realized it and brought the volume down a notch or two. "You were engaged to Thornton Hill sometime last fall. He goes missing, and a few months later you married Steele. Now he's missing, and you never thought to tell me about Hill." He wasn't certain whether that came out as a question or an accusation. Maybe it was both.

"What possible reason would Thornton Hill be relevant to why I hired you? He had nothing to do with Willis stealing my money and jewels." After a brief moment, she said, "Should I assume you take your tea plain?"

Eddie felt himself getting ready to explode. She was trying to manipulate him just as she had tried last week, albeit for another reason. She'd nearly succeeded then, but tonight she wouldn't.

"Then let me spell it out for you, sister. You had one husband murdered, one fiancé goes missing, and another husband takes off on you. For all intents and purposes, he's missing too. And you're telling me that you can't see any possible connections to all three?" He paused briefly, and then jacking up the volume again, he asked, "Is that what you're telling me?"

Maybe he intended to rattle her pots and pans; maybe not. But that was what happened.

She stared at him with her hands on her hips. She was still stunning, her face much younger than what it should have been, even without all the makeup. But this time, her eyes were fiery red instead of blue.

"I don't like the tone of your voice. Are you accusing me of something?"

"Should I be accusing you of something?"

For a long moment, there was nothing but silence in the kitchen. The tea was still very hot, with no sign of it cooling. Then there was a massive explosion. Debris rained down on him like the London blitz.

"Get out of my house right now!" she shouted. "You're fired!"

"That's the best thing I've heard all week, sis. I'll send you a bill for my expenses."

"You do that—now get out!" She pointed in the general direction of the door as if by the odd chance he might have forgotten where it was.

Eddie turned, walked out of the kitchen, and went down the hallway, with Chanel taking up the rear. As he was opening the front door, another hail of words lambasted him from behind.

"And that goddamn tie of yours is as ugly as sin!"

———«◉»———

Chanel locked the door and returned to the kitchen. She sat down at the end of the table with her tea. She took three deep breaths to help her calm down. They didn't do much. Then she sipped her tea. *Damn that man*, she thought.

She should have known better than to hire that son of a bitch. Private investigators had a reputation for poking their noses into other people's business where they don't belong. But that was an asset, wasn't it? How could she have known that that nose would be pointing in her direction? He had to have been investigating her own background to have found out about Hill. Few people had known about the engagement. *Dammit!* The blame belonged to her though; after all, she had been the one who sought out his services. Oh well, it was done with; she'd fired him.

Then a horrible thought occurred to her: *What if he goes to the police? This could all get out. The police might even start their own snooping.* This was more than just serious; it was catastrophic. It wasn't just her reputation that was at stake; it was—. She couldn't finish the thought. Maybe she was too hasty in firing him. She had to spend more time on this— think things through.

The morning paper sat folded on the table. She reached for it and then spread it out in front of her for the umpteenth time. She wouldn't read it again. There was no need to. The story wasn't going to change. Luc wasn't going to magically appear out of nowhere to screw her again. That was done with. *Get used to it.* She looked at his picture. It was one of his better ones; the reporter probably got it from the bank. He looked as if he could do with a shave, but he always looked that way. She marvelled at the speed of how things changed. Not long before, she had a husband and a lover, and now she had neither. But she had to look on the bright side of life: she did have her freedom again. And she wasn't any less well off financially. That was something!

Wasn't it?

She sipped her tea and wondered what to do about Eddie Wade. Clearly, she had to do something about him—and soon! She just couldn't let him run free with the knowledge he had. Just then, the kitchen door swung open.

"Mother," her son, Percy, said, "are you all right? I heard shouting."

"I'm fine, Percy. I just had a disagreement with Mr. Wade is all. There's some tea on the counter for you. Drink it up before it goes cold."

"Thank you, Mother. I should like a cup. I was on my way down to make some when I heard the shouting, so I stopped. Did Mr. Wade upset you? I heard some harsh words exchanged. Of course, I couldn't hear what was being said, but the tone was rather severe." He picked up the cup of tea from the countertop and sat down at the other end of the table, facing his mother. "Were your feelings hurt, Mother? Was he abrasive toward you?"

"Oh, it's nothing like that. We just had a difference of opinion on something. Nothing to worry about. Anyway, I fired him."

Percy nearly spilled his tea. After he regained his composure, he said, "Can I tell you a little secret, Mother?"

"Of course."

"From the time I first met him, I never liked him."

"Why was that?"

"I don't know exactly, but I'm sure it had to do with his mannerisms. He just didn't look right to me. I think he was uncouth. Was I being unfair?"

Chanel remembered when Eddie had come to the house for the interview. They'd been in the sitting room, on the love seat, when the door opened. She'd noticed it but hadn't said anything. Had Percy been listening at the door? If so, he'd gotten an earful. Maybe that was the reason he didn't like Eddie. He'd always been a little protective of her. And she was, after all, still married.

"It doesn't matter, Percy. He's fired and won't be coming back." But she did have to do something about him. She couldn't have him running to the police.

"I think that was a good decision, Mother."

Chanel made more tea, and for the next hour, they had a pleasant discussion, partly reminiscing about the vacations they had taken alone, just the two of them, because Guy Dupont always seemed to be too busy with work to go with them. When Percy was nine or ten, Chanel used to take him to the Laurentians and rent a cabin. There she would lie out in the sun while Percy chased the squirrels around. And then for a change of scenery, she'd cross the border into the Adirondacks in upper New York and go on boat rides on Lake George. Percy had loved this the most. They had spent much time exploring the wilderness around the lake as well as the neighboring towns of Queensbury and Glens Falls. Percy always looked forward to their next trip, year after year. When Chanel would forget and suggest they go somewhere else, Percy always talked her into returning to the Adirondacks. They had had such wonderful times there—a lifetime ago.

When Percy was older, in his teens, she would take him to Paris, and there they would explore the touristy sights as well as all the museums. She'd take him to the Louvre, Notre Dame, the avant-garde art galleries bordering the Seine, the Eiffel Tower and the Arc de Triomphe, the medieval Latin Quarter and the bohemian village atmosphere of Montmartre. She wanted to expose him to as much culture and sophistication as she could. God knows Chanel had lacked that in her own upbringing; she would make sure Percy didn't. During those times, their bond had strengthened to a remarkable degree. Now, all these years later, Chanel sat drinking tea with her handsome, young son, having fun indulging themselves in the past.

However, when Chanel changed the subject and started talking about his future, Percy became reticent. He always became extremely uncomfortable whenever the topic came up. She pushed and prodded him though because he was at the age that he should start making a life for himself. Granted, he had no particular skills to speak of, and he never showed any interest in attending university to acquire any. Could the reason be that he would never have to worry about money? She had enough for both of them. Nevertheless, he should start making his way in the world. He could start by finding a girl. He had never dated in the past, so now would be a good time to start. She'd have to prod him into doing that as well, she guessed, or she might have him living with her into old age.

During their conversation, part of Chanel's brain had been working on how to throw a harness on Eddie Wade.

"OK, young man," Chanel said, patting his hands, "it's time for bed."

"Yes, Mother. I do feel sleepy."

Percy got up, kissed his mother on the cheek, and then left.

When she was certain that he was upstairs in his bedroom—the house was old, after all, so she could plainly hear his footsteps ascending—Chanel went to the counter near the icebox and picked up Eddie Wade's card with the phone number to his answering service on it. Then she went into the hallway where the downstairs phone sat on a small mahogany table with a vase of silk buttercup ranunculus (she loved those flowers, she did—lovely yellow ones!) and picked up the receiver.

Then she dialed the number.

Chapter 11
A SEA CHANGE

DAMMIT TO HELL, EDDIE THOUGHT.

From Chantel Steele's house in Westmount, he had driven straight down Dorchester for twelve minutes to the Flamingo in town and ordered a Boilermaker. He was still steaming and needed to decompress, so he started by cursing himself—using a clever mixture of French and English expletives—which wasn't an altogether inappropriate starting place. He hadn't handled the situation with Chantel well at all. It was amateurish. He knew better. He let her get under his skin, and because of that, he became aggressive. What a dope. In all fairness to him, though, she was as hotheaded as he was. But you know the old saw about two wrongs. In this case, the two wrongs resulted in a lost opportunity for him to make a nice chunk of cash.

You're an idiot, Wade! he thought.

Notwithstanding, his concern was legitimate. He still wondered why she hadn't mentioned Thornton Hill to him. It was obvious to him; why wasn't it obvious to her? Unless it was, and she had tried hiding it from him. That was a possibility. When he stood back and looked at the big picture, she had one murdered husband, a fiancé gone missing, and a second husband gone missing—all in a five-year period. Something was rotten to the core, and the stench could knock a shmuck off his feet as far away as Demark. Yet Chanel hadn't found it important enough to mention Thornton Hill. If it were just the murdered husband, and then five years later, that no-good, skinny, thieving bastard took off on her, he could see it as an unfortunate occurrence. It wouldn't have aroused the interest of any private dick in North America, or any cop for that matter. But if you threw Hill into the mix, now you had something. Of all people, this should have been apparent to Chanel; yet she kept her trap shut.

The question was, "Why?"

Eddie couldn't really say he didn't care—because he did. By firing him, Chanel had taken something important from him. Cases like this really stirred him up, kept him awake at night. He loved them. They kept his adrenalin flowing, his senses on high alert.

Cases like this came closest to replicating the feelings he had had in combat during the war. They made him feel alive more than he had ever felt before. In the heat of battle, he could reach out and touch the face of Lucifer, and if lucky enough—let no one tell you otherwise; it was all luck—live to tell the story.

But those feelings were contradictory. In the midst of danger, facing the possibility of death, with his adrenalin rushing, he wished to be anywhere other than where he was. It was a balancing act. He sought out life-destroying danger, but once found, he then prayed for peace and security. Once his prayers were answered, the cycle would start over again. Danger was addictive; they upped the ante in life. And it was always luck that saw him through.

Water under the bridge. He'd been fired, so the case was no longer his concern. It was no longer his business.

He ordered another Boilermaker, and when Pierre brought

it over, he poured the shot of whiskey into the beer, swished it around, and took a long chug from it. *Dammit to hell,* he thought again. The case could have gone on for another week or two. Maybe longer. That would have brought in a lot of dough; Chanel had it and wasn't shy about spending it.

Forget it, he thought. *Stop feeling sorry for yourself.*

He blew it, plain and simple.

He walked over to the Wurlitzer and dropped a nickel into the slot. By the time he got back to his stool, Billie Holiday was singing "Gloomy Sunday." If anyone could soothe his soul, it was Billie. It was Thursday but as gloomy as any gloomy Sunday had ever been. He took another swig from his drink and remembered one of them last year, right here at the Flamingo. A woman sitting directly behind where he now sat had been eyeing him for a good while through his reflection in the mirror behind the bar. She hadn't been particularly beautiful, but there was something that drew him to her. After a time, a well-dressed punk in a vested suit had walked in, and the two began to squabble, making a public nuisance of themselves. The guy had gotten a little rough with the broad, which Eddie couldn't tolerate, so he got up, and the two of them exchanged words. The guy ended up on his back, knocked out cold. Eddie had escorted the broad out and gave her his card. If he could be of any help to her, call him. A few days later, the police had found the broad with a dagger shoved up between her ribcage, the end of which was in her heart. He had been no help to her at all. What a rotten way to make a living.

Gloomy ... that was what it was.

The neon lights on the window were flashing steadily when he thought he saw someone looking in the window. He looked closer; no one was there.

He asked the barman, Pierre, to use the phone. The ever-reticent Pierre flashed him the OK sign. Eddie got up and walked to the end of the bar. He dialed his answering service. He had one message: Chanel Steele wanted to see him tonight at her home, no matter how late. He pressed the disconnect but kept the receiver to his ear.

What in the hell could she want?

He hung up the receiver, paid Pierre for his drinks, and left the Flamingo. Outside, he caught movement to his right. A man was walking down the sidewalk a half block or so away. He wore a raggedy overcoat too large for him and a crushed felt hat. Was he the same guy he'd been seeing—the one he had lunch with? The bum? He turned right and disappeared around the corner. Eddie had too much on his mind to go after him, so he jumped in his car, pointed it to Westmount, and hit the accelerator.

—◉—

Same house, same hallway, same kitchen where a few hours earlier Chanel had parted company with him in hostile circumstances.

Déjà vu, baby, he thought.

"Eddie, all I can say is that I'm sorry," Chanel said. "I was completely out of line. You asked a legitimate question, and instead of answering you, my mouth got the best of me. If you could find it in your heart to forgive me, I'd like you to stay on the case. I need you to find my husband. That's all that matters to me right now."

What in the hell happened to the brassy Chanel Steele he'd been dealing with for the last week? She sounded like one of those battleaxes who uses her husband as a punching bag and then throws him out in the street, and the next day, she wants him back again, promising him the moon and the stars. For a second, he felt sorry for her and wanted to apologize to her for overreacting and raising his voice. *Not on your ever-lovin' life, baby!* The thought left him as fast as it came.

"Apology accepted. Now tell me about Thornton Hill. And give it to me straight."

They were standing in the kitchen. Eddie kept his hat and coat on. His hands were in his pockets. Her hands were cupped in front of her. She was wearing a robe and slippers. Her hair was tied back in a ponytail. Eddie would have liked to think she looked desirable. Maybe under different circumstances, she would have been. Now, she simply looked pathetic. A strong person always did when acquiescing to a stronger one.

"There really isn't much to it. Thornton and I met last summer at a nightclub. We were mutually attracted to one another. We started seeing each other pretty regularly whenever he was in town, and after a while, he proposed. We became engaged but hadn't set the date. When the fall came, I became antsy because he hadn't brought up the subject, so I began pressing him for us to set the date. Then one day, he was gone."

"Did you inform the police?"

"No, because I thought he had just gotten cold feet. I still think so."

"Did you try to find him?"

"Of course. I went to his apartment, called numerous times, but nothing. I began to think he left the city for good—relocated."

"What did he do for a living?"

"He was a salesman. You know, he used his car."

"You mean an over-the-road salesman?"

"That's it. He sold auto parts. He was usually gone three or four days out of the week. He covered a pretty big territory in the province. At first, I thought that's where he was, you know, on the road, but when he hadn't shown up for a couple of weeks, I began to think he'd gotten cold feet. I really don't think this has anything to do with Willis disappearing. That's why I hadn't mentioned it."

"Maybe," Eddie said. "Is there anything else I should know? You hold back on me, it makes my job more difficult. I need you to understand that. We're after the same thing."

"I do, Eddie. I just can't think of anything else."

"There's just one more little detail."

"What's that, Eddie?"

"My fees. You paid enough upfront to last another day. After that, I'll need another four days. That's two hundred bucks. I did tell you that it might take some time. Don't worry about the expenses until the case is closed or you fire me again."

She chuckled. "That won't happen again. I'm so sorry about that."

She looked up at him with those gorgeous blue eyes of hers. He could easily envelop her in his strong arms, hold her tightly against his body, tell her "That's OK, baby. Everything is going to be just fine," and pat the top of her head with his big paw.

But he didn't.

"Don't be sorry. You're the one paying the bills. You do the hiring; you can also do the firing."

"Well, that won't happen. It was unfair of me."

"I'll be in touch."

Before he got into his car, he scanned the area around him. Had that bum followed him here? He wasn't becoming paranoid; that much he knew. The guy kept popping up in places where he shouldn't be. The first time was outside London Life, then again outside of the Lion's Den. He'd been sitting on the steps of the church. And he was certain that was him tonight outside the Flamingo, walking down the sidewalk as Eddie came out. What was he up to? What did he want? Maybe he wasn't really a bum. Maybe he was wearing a disguise. But for what purpose? Eddie had enemies—plenty of them going back years. He had seen the guy up close when they had lunch together. He hadn't looked familiar, but that didn't mean much. People's faces changed over time. Maybe he'd gotten the goods on someone early on in his career that put him in prison. Maybe the guy had just gotten out and wanted to settle the score. It had happened before. *Shit*, he thought. He was going to have to be more careful now. He didn't relish the idea of having to look over his shoulder every time he walked down the street or left a building. But that was what he might have to do.

On his way back to Mile End, he couldn't help but marvel at the sea change that had come over Chanel Steele.

What's her angle? he thought. *She has to have one.*

Chapter 12
MY FAIR LADY

SHE HAD TO HAVE ONE.

An angle, that is. No one changes her personality that fast without a reason. Gone were the little quips and the sarcastic one-liners. There hadn't even been a hint of a suggestive innuendo or a trace of flirtation. Chanel had been on her best behavior, polite to a fault, bordering on being obsequious. Of course, on the surface, Eddie knew precisely what she was up to: she wanted him back on the case. She'd done what she had to do. And she succeeded. Notwithstanding, he was certain there was something buried underneath all that: her angle. She was hiding it from him. He hated when clients did that to him—and a lot of them had. Could it somehow involve her former fiancé Thornton Hill? Her sad little story about how they met seemed reasonable enough—maybe too reasonable. But she'd left something out, something important, something she didn't want the world to know, especially the police. By her own admission, she didn't trust them. He was certain that she had deliberately lied to him, and he was going to find out why. And he was going to do it on her dime, now that he had been reemployed by her.

That was what had been on his mind when he woke up on Friday morning.

Before he even dressed, he had gotten out the telephone directory and made a series of calls, looking for someone related to Thornton Hill. There weren't many Hills listed, and he found one on the third call: Thornton's mother. And she was willing to talk to him.

Bingo!

After he had had his usual coffee and toast at the local greasy spoon, he drove to the municipality of Anjou, east of Mile End. He was there in twenty-five minutes, having left after the rush hour traffic. Mrs. Hill lived in a moderately respectable apartment building tucked away under some huge maple trees. Two large arborvitaes stood guard on either side of the entrance. You didn't have to be rich to live there, but you did need a steady cash flow.

"Thanks for seeing me on such short notice, Mrs. Hill," Eddie said, sitting down on an armchair in the living room.

"Think nothing of it, young man. And please call me Florence. Better yet, just call me Flo. It'll save you from saying an extra syllable."

Eddie gave her one of his goofy grins. *Flo? OK, Flo it is!* It was a good start. Whenever the person he was interviewing volunteered a diminutive, it usually meant he wouldn't have to pull or prod information out of her.

She was possibly in her mid-sixties—maybe a little younger, maybe a little older. Short and plump, she wore a gray and black dress with a floral pattern. Her gray hair was combed back into a bun. She looked neither rich nor poor and had an unmistakable aura of respectability about her. Eddie was drawn to her immediately. She sat on the davenport opposite him with a fluffy, odd-eyed white angora feline on her lap. One eye was blue, and the other was brown.

"And this is Marjorie. Three syllables, I'm afraid. I hope you don't mind cats, Eddie."

"I have two of them myself."

That was all that was needed. For the next ten minutes, they exchanged cat tales.

After Eddie had told her that Antoinette helped him type up his reports (she giggled at that), she offered to make him some coffee. He wouldn't have minded another cup, but he declined. He wasn't going to be there very long, and the whole process seemed as if it might take her some time. Besides, she looked too comfortable sitting on the couch with Marjorie on her lap.

"You said you wanted to talk to me about my son. Do you have any information on where he is?"

"I wish I did, Flo, but I don't. I'm working on another case, and your son's name came up."

"Oh," she said, surprised. "May I ask you who this involves?"

Eddie thought about it for a moment. He couldn't really give her any information on the case, but he didn't want her to shut down either. She seemed pretty open to having this discussion. A wrong move, and the whole thing could go into the trash bin.

"Chanel Steele. I believe you might know her."

"Oh, yes, Chanel. Actually, I know of her. I really never met her."

That was strange. Her son had been engaged to Chanel, and she never met her. He asked her about that.

"Well, it's a long story. You see, my son has his demons. Don't get me wrong now. He's a lovely man. There's a picture of him on the mantelpiece."

Eddie glanced at it but didn't get up.

"Unfortunately, he took after his father in many ways. Thornton liked his drink. When he wasn't drinking, he was kind and generous, but when he drank, well, he could be quite unpredictable."

"Unpredictable how?"

"He's a salesman, you see. His territory included southern Quebec and eastern Ontario. He would be gone for about two or three days a week. But at times, I wouldn't hear from him for weeks on end. And then one day, he'd just show up. He'd tell me that he'd stayed in his hotel room with a couple of bottles. He would always confide in me—always had since he was a little boy. He felt ashamed at his behavior, but he said he couldn't control it."

"Did he confide in you about his relationship with Chanel?"

"I'm afraid he did. He told me that they loved each other very much. But when he was drinking, he would ... let's say he wouldn't be very nice to her. He said he never left marks on her, but I know the poor dear had scars on the inside, if you know what I mean. Sometimes he would even beat her in front of her son. What was his name now? Let me see ..."

"Percy."

"Yes, that's it. Percy, poor boy." She stopped to clear her throat. "Whenever that happened, he would come to me the next day and cry and cry and cry. He never intended to hurt Chanel, but he said once he started drinking, it seemed as if the devil himself got into him, and he couldn't stop himself. But I know it wasn't the devil, Eddie, at least not the one he was thinking of."

"How's that, Flo?"

"He was his father's son. Thornton grew up watching his father do the same thing to me. The man is dead now. Cirrhosis took him. When he wasn't drinking, he was charming and gentle; and when he drank, he turned into a beast. I had to live like that for decades. Thornton might have believed that that was how men treated their women. I'm sure he never introduced me to Chanel because he feared I'd have a talk with her." She thought for a moment and then added, "I believe I would have too. I suppose I could have phoned Chanel, but I didn't want to go behind Thornton's back."

Eddie couldn't imagine anyone harming this nice little old lady.

"Do you have any idea where Thornton could have gone?"

"Well, the police asked me that same question when I filed a missing person's report. The company he'd worked for said he just didn't show one day. Before he became engaged to Chanel, he always talked about going to live somewhere down south. He mentioned California and a few other states out west where work was plentiful. Maybe that was where he went."

"Is it strange that he never tried to contact you?"

"Yes, Eddie. It's very strange."

———«◉»———

Eddie felt nauseated driving into town. The very thought of someone like Flo Hill being used as a punching bag was depressing to him. He gripped the steering wheel tightly with both hands. He wanted to smash someone's face. At the moment, anyone's would do.

Dammit! he thought. Chanel was still holding back on him. She hadn't told him about the beatings. Maybe out of embarrassment. Maybe not. What more she was hiding from him?

Then a wild thought occurred to him.

Eddie was sure Chanel hadn't appreciated being batted around—no woman would. Maybe she'd decided to take matters in her own hands. She was wealthy. For less than someone might think, she could have hired a hit man to end her problem. There were so many grease bags in Montreal that if she put out the word, they would have been lined up at her door. Maybe she'd taken care of Willis Steele, too, for another reason. Maybe she'd done the same to her first husband. Maybe she'd hired Eddie to throw suspicion off of her. Maybe that was why she hadn't wanted the police involved.

There were a lot of maybes. Too many. He tucked them away for now. He'd perhaps pick at them later, one at a time.

He pulled up to police headquarters downtown and went inside to see Jack Macalister. He walked down a long hallway, stopped at a door, knuckled it twice, and then stuck his head inside.

"Glad to see you're still alive, old buddy," Macalister said, looking up from his desk.

"Glad to be alive." Eddie entered the office and took a seat beside Macalister's desk.

"You been ducking any more bullets lately?"

"Not since Monday night. Listen, are you busy right now?"

"I'm always busy. What do you need?"

"I'm working on a particular case. The name Thornton Hill came up. A missing person's report apparently had been filed by his mother. Could you pull his jacket?"

"It wasn't my case, but I'll see what I can do. You got some time?"

He looked at his watch. "It says here that I've got all the time in the world."

Macalister got up and left his office. Eddie entertained himself by looking at his shoes. They needed polishing. Macalister was back in fifteen minutes. He sat down at his desk and opened the folder.

"Let's see now," he said. After skimming a few pages, he said, "Mr. Hill looks like an interesting character. He's got a number of assault and battery charges against him, filed by different women over the years. He spent a few nights in the clink but didn't do any hard time for them. The victims never followed through, so we had to release him. We still have his prints on file. The last entry here is the missing person's report filed by his mother, one Mrs. Florence Hill. It looks like there was a preliminary search, and then the case went dry. Says here that the mother thinks he might have moved to the States. My guess is that's when they stopped looking. He definitely was a bad boy, but I've seen a lot worse. How does he tie into your case?"

Eddie told him everything about the Steele case and that Hill had been engaged to Chanel Steele before he went missing.

"Let me get this straight. Her husband was murdered about five years ago—I remember that one. Guy Dupont. A hotshot banker. Shot in the back of the head. No arrests were made, and we had absolutely no leads. If I remember correctly, we chocked it up as a random shooting. Then her current husband goes missing, and last year, the man she was supposed to marry went missing. Is that right?"

"On the button."

"She's a busy lady," he said, grinning and leaning back in his chair. "You ever hear of the case back in the early forties in Three Rivers?"

The case involved a woman, a Madame Couture, who had killed four of the five husbands she'd been married to, overdosed them with prescription medications and tranquilizers. When husband number three had refused to die, she borrowed her neighbor's car and ran over him a half dozen times.

"Who hasn't?"

"Maybe we've got budding Claudette Couture on our hands.

"Yeah, maybe."

"Sounds like you want me to do something about it."

"Sounds like it. Can you?"

"Sure. No problem. Just get me some evidence. I can't arrest her on the grounds that we think she was a naughty lady. That's a sure lawsuit. I'd be pounding the beat again. If she murdered Guy Dupont, prove it. If she had anything to do with the missing fiancé and her current husband, prove it. I'll get a warrant for her arrest and have her behind bars before you can say Jack Robinson."

Eddie nodded but remained silent for a short moment.

"I'll see what I can do."

———«◎»———

What were these hands that clutched and grasped? What were these arms that grew out of this unyielding mass of fifth and grime? What was this tortured brain that could not sleep? He did not know. He could not guess. He saw only the splintered images, saw only the dead remnants of rotting sewage that was his soul. There was no shelter; there was no relief. Only a dried bed of mud-cracked earth where once a river flowed. Only the skeletons of dead trees that stood naked and imponent under the sun. He was neither alive nor dead.

There was a shadow before him that sat immoveable, tractable, restrained. Head reposed, leaning, the room as silent as death.

His mind was a broken cup that lay shattered upon the floor. Rational thought had departed. That much he knew. That much he was aware of: troubled; confused; prolonged; undone. Yet the flames deep within him urged him on, spread out with savage indifference, and glowed brilliantly with no sign of diminishing.

After the words had been spoken; after the numb silence and then the shaming reply; after the derision and mocking; after the wild laughter and the contemptuous stares, there was no shelter—there was no relief.

Only these and other withered fragments of a young life retold a thousand times, and a thousand times the anguish stirring the blood, arousing the soul, evoking hatred again and again. He got up, walked forward, and leaned into the shadow. He listened intently to the steady breathing, peaceful and inviolate. His head suddenly jerked to the side. What was that noise? He strained to hear. Nothing. Nothing. Nothing. Only the steady breathing of the man in front of him, the erratic beating of his own heart, and a cold draft of air at his back.

Not tonight, he thought. He'd let the man sleep.

The laughter in his head, the insufferable disdain year after year coursing through him, the unrelentingly shame burrowing itself deeper and deeper left him but an empty vessel afloat in a sea of fear and reprisal. There was no one to rescue him; no one to throw him a life raft; no one to comfort and shelter him from the coming storm.

London Bridge is falling down, falling down, falling down.

London Bridge is falling down.

My fair lady.

Chapter 13
I'LL DRINK TO THAT!

THE MOON SANK BELOW THE HORIZON AT 4:05 on Saturday morning. Dawn appeared seventy-two minutes before sunrise at 5:49. Eddie opened his eyes two minutes after that. He had two woolen, military, olive-drab blankets over him that he'd purchased at the Army Surplus store down on Dollard just off of Notre-Dame years before, but he could feel it was cold beyond them. The tip of his nose told him so.

It was one of those mornings that he didn't want to get out of bed. He was warm and cozy under the blankets, but he wished he had someone to share it with—like Angel. Sometimes they'd sleep in her bed at her apartment in town; or more likely, it was this bed here at his office. He remembered how they'd linger in the warmth on frigid mornings, never wanting to escape it. The heat emanating from each other's bodies—safe in each other's arms. The world was at peace. The universe made sense. As long as they were under the blankets, no harm would come to them. But once they got up, all bets were off.

Underneath those thoughts, though, was Chanel Steele, and like flowing lava, she carried along the potential of destruction in her wake. Could she be another Claudette

Couture, the killer from Three Rivers who Jack had mentioned yesterday? She'd killed four of her five husbands before getting caught. Chanel might have killed three, counting her husband-to-be. What was her potential?

He threw back the blankets and got out of bed. He had a lot to do today.

He pulled his thick socks on, slipped into his robe, and went into his office to put the coffee pot on. While it was percolating, he shaved and showered and then dressed in his dark blue suit. He returned to the office and poured some coffee. Then he sat down on the couch, trying to wake up; he did so in stages.

If Chanel had something to do with the murder of Guy Dupont and the disappearances of her fiancé and present husband, then she was using Eddie to deflect her guilt. But that was a big *if.* The thought annoyed him; he didn't like to be manipulated, especially by a beautiful broad. No wonder she'd wanted nothing to do with the police. However, as long as she was paying him, as long as the money kept coming in, he'd continue with the case—but on his terms.

Antoinette and Henri appeared at his feet and started to do a little dance in front of him. He watched them for a moment, entertained by their style and feline grace. When they started to headbutt his ankles, he got up and filled their bowls and then went to his desk and sat down behind it. He picked up one of his pipes from the rack, put it back and picked another one, filled it, and then lit up, sending a cloud of smoke above him.

Rays of sunlight cut through the Venetian blinds and shot through the smoke, making the office seem like a hazy netherworld where souls were forever doomed to wander aimlessly in an underworld of uncertainty. He would interview Chanel's parents later today; maybe he could gain more insight into the complexities of their daughter, if they cooperated. They sounded like reasonable people on the phone. Knowing that interviews could go haywire with just a wrong word spoken or an incorrect facial expression, he hoped they'd remain reasonable throughout the interview. He got up, refilled his cup, putting a little Canadian Club in it this time, went to the door, opened it, picked up the morning paper, and sat down again to have a read.

Spiked coffee, a pipe, a paper, and contented felines—life was good on the home front.

An hour later, he reached over to his phone and dialed Sylvie Boucher's number. When she picked up and said "Hello," he hung up. She was home. That was all he wanted to know. He threw on his overcoat and hat, folded the paper under his arm, grabbed his camera, and went to his car.

He drove to rue Blondin in Rosemont and parked across the street from her house but down a few houses from it. Two cars were in the driveway. One was hers, but who did the other one belong to? He'd planned on staying there a good chunk of the day, or at least until there was some movement or action. He opened the paper to the sports section, spread it out over the steering wheel, and lit his pipe.

Puff-puff.

The Canadians were still on a winning streak, even without their star player. They had a good chance playing in the Stanley Cup finals next month. He guessed they'd play the Red Wings. Should be a good series.

Puff-puff.

He glanced to his left. No movement at the Boucher house yet.

He continued to read the paper and smoke his pipe. Then, less than a half hour later, a man in a brown overcoat exited the house. He was carrying his hat in his hand. Before the man got into the second car, Eddie grabbed his Kodak Bakelite 35mm rangefinder from the passenger side and took a series of pictures. Click-click-click. The man got into his car and drove away.

That could be important. Was he her lover? Was the widow-woman back in the game so soon after her husband's untimely departure? Was there some sort of a conspiracy going on? Maybe the guy was nothing more than her brother who had come to console her. But something didn't smell right; he had to find out what.

He sat there for a few more hours. Nothing else happened, so he decided to drive over to the Gazette to get the film developed.

And maybe have a Birdbath.

Or two.

———«◉»———

From the Gazette, he drove up Sainte-Catherine to the Ellis Detective Agency, two doors down from the Forum, where the Canadians played. The area had been trashed and the shops looted in the riot nine days earlier over the suspension of their top scorer. In the days that followed, the street had been cleaned up, but there were still remnants of debris of broken glass and rubbish, as well as discarded hopes and dreams. The city of Montreal would recover but not anytime soon. The resentment ran deep.

The office was small, with two wooden desks pushed side to side in the middle and filing cabinets along the walls. The space looked as if it could have been a neighborhood candy store or bookie's hideaway in the past. There was a large window in the front facing Sainte-Catherine, with the agency's name in big letters printed in a semicircle on it: gold on a black background. In theory, the window could have let in sunshine, when there was any to let in and if it had been any cleaner. In short, the office was basic by anyone's estimation, but its occupants were some of the best investigators around the city, especially when it came to doing in-depth research. They were better than the PhD candidates at McGill.

The agency consisted of a husband-wife team of Sully and Angie Ellis. Sully's father, Herbert, had opened it up in the 1930s, and Sully went to work with him after the war at the same time Eddie got into the game. In the late 1940s, while working a divorce case, Herbert had been shot in the head by the irate husband of his client. It happened right there in the office. He had lingered in a coma at the Old Vic for three days before he died. Sully had taken over the reins. Angie, his new wife, became licensed up, and they'd been partners ever since, both in the business and in life. Eddie and the Ellises helped each other out on cases periodically, exchanging services—and bottles of whiskey occasionally—instead of money for their fees.

"You're as ugly as ever, Wade," Sully said as Eddie entered the office.

"You haven't improved on that front yourself. Why Angie stays with you is beyond me."

"It's a mystery I've never been able to solve."

Sully was a big man, standing six four, a few inches taller than Eddie. He had long brown hair that was usually tousled and a thick mustache hiding his upper lip. In his late thirties, his face showed signs that he'd been around the block several dozen times. It was chiseled out of granite with strong jawlines. His eyes were dark and deeply set. They looked as if they could bore a hole in steel. When he stared at you in a certain way, you immediate felt the need to pee. He had a light brown leather shoulder holster strapped on over his white shirt with a .45 semiautomatic inside, the same kind of gun Eddie carried. He got up, and they both shook hands.

"Good to see you, Eddie. Sit down. Get off your feet. I'd offer you a cup of coffee, but I drank the whole pot, and Angie is gone at the moment. How 'bout a little cognac?"

"Business must be good if you're offering cognac, but no, I'm fine."

"Refusing a drink? Jesus, that must mean you're on a stinker of a case. I guess we can forego the idle chitchat. What's up?"

Eddie gave him the lowdown on the Steele case, everything he had so far.

"I'd like to have a background done on the Dupont family, see if there's anything dark in their past. I want to either establish a connection between Guy Dupont's murder and Hill's and Steele's disappearance or eliminate one. Dupont seemed to have been a straight shooter, but you know how that goes."

"This sounds like fun." He flashed a big, wide smile. "How far back do you want me to go?"

Eddie knew that Sully would be eager to put on his work boots. It was right up his alley. He enjoyed researching the moneyed families in the city to see how many boulders he'd have to heave out of the way to get to the dirt underneath. His clients paid him good money for the juicy stuff.

"I'll leave that for you to decide. I need the information as soon as you can get it. Don't spend too much time on it though. I know you and Angie must be busy. I'd do it myself, but the Steele case is getting complicated, and I need to pick up more leads. I'm also doing some work for London Life."

"Christ almighty, let me guess. Reginald Nithercott is having you run around in circles."

"Something like that."

"You're a glutton for punishment, Eddie. The last time I worked for Reggie, I told him my fees were doubling. Cost of living, you know. He hasn't called me since. Just the way I like it."

"I might have to try that. By the way, how's Angie doing?"

"Aw, she's doing fine. She's at the pistol range right now. Goes whenever there's down time. She's become a better shot than me, not that she'll ever need it. She made me a bet the other day, so we went out to the range. Beat me fair and square. I have to take her out to a fancy restaurant for the next three weekends. But I still do the legwork. She's here working the phones and getting new clients. She's still bugging me to let her loose in the field. 'What good is my license,' says she, 'if I can't use it?'"

"Why don't you let her do some footwork?"

"Because I don't want to have to worry about her." He ran his big paw over his hair and sighed. "It's a goddamn jungle out there. You know all about that. Anyway, we have a new client as of today that she doesn't know about. I'm going to let her run with it alone. See what happens."

"If things go south, she can always just shoot him, since she's so good with a pistol."

"Hah, that's what I figure," Sully said with a smile. He tugged at his shoulder holster a little in the front and then found a more comfortable position to sit. "So, Eddie, you doing a line with anyone yet?"

"Nary a one, Sully. Happily unattached and planning to stay that way."

"You should hook up with someone. Get married. Then you could team up with her. Make her your partner. It'll be good for the marriage. Best thing Angie and I ever did. We can keep an eye on each other that way."

"Two private eyes keeping an eye on each other."

"That's what we always say." He reached into the bottom drawer of his desk and pulled out a bottle of cognac and two glasses. "Let's have a quick one in celebration, now that the business is finished," he said, pouring two fingers in each glass and giving one to Eddie.

"What are we celebrating?"

"Angie's first official gig as a bona fide snoop and all the dirt I'm going to dig up on the goddamn Duponts."

"I'll drink to that!"

And he did.

They talked for another hour, catching up on things since they last saw each other. When their conversation began to peter out a bit, Eddie looked at his watch. He had an interview with Chanel's parents. He hoped to get another lead out of it.

Chapter 14
IT'S COMPLICATED

NINE DAYS INTO THE STEELE CASE, AND HE WAS no closer to finding Willis than when he started. Eddie wasn't surprised. It was damn well nearly impossible to find a schmuck who skipped out on his wife and didn't want to be found. He could be anywhere. There was a lot of territory to cover in Canada. The same with the States. A lot of hiding places. A lot of stones to uncover. He'd told that to Chanel when she first hired him—in so many words—and it was panning out to be true. What he hadn't told her was the possibility that her husband could be dead and buried in some remote forested area. The likelihood wasn't great, but he knew it could happen. He'd seen it before. A guy runs out on his wife after stealing from her. He lives it up, flashes the cash around, which catches the eyes of some unscrupulous person who decides to relieve him of the money. He kills the husband and then drives up north to bury the body. All sorts of possibilities. There were plenty of dark places in the world that the average person knew nothing about.

On the other hand, maybe Chanel knew about those dark places all too well.

From the Ellis Detective Agency, he drove a short way

to Côte-des-Neiges to interview Serge and Brigitte Fournier, Chanel's parents. They owned and operated a small neighborhood bakery in Monkland Village on Grand, just off of avenue Monkland. While Sully and Angie were looking into the Duponts, he wanted to look into Chanel's own past on the off chance he could learn something significant that might help him with the case. Even an offhanded remark or a facial tick in a response to a question could be noteworthy. Chanel had been open about her past but only to a degree. She proved to be unreliable, failing to mention something as important as the disappearance of Thornton Hill. Eddie knew she was being closemouthed about other things as well; he just didn't know what. Maybe he could find out from her parents.

The Fourniers took him in the back of the shop so they could talk in private while their other daughter, Josette, held down the fort in the front. It was a family operation. They sat down at a small table that was probably used to eat lunch. Huge bags of flour and other baking ingredients sat on shelves that lined the walls. They weren't that surprised that Willis had run out on Chanel. It was the first they had heard about it.

"We always had mixed feelings about Willis," Brigitte said. She was a small, elegantly attractive woman in her early to middle sixties. Eddie could tell that she had been a beautiful woman in her youth. Chanel obviously got her looks from her. She had gray hair, which looked as if she had it done by a coiffeur, and wore a fashionable, brightly colored dress. She probably worked the front counter, serving the public. "They grew up together, you know. Our families lived in the same neighborhood. Would you like a doughnut? Maybe a brioche or a croissant? Freshly made this morning."

"Appreciate it but no thanks. Why mixed feelings?"

"When Willis was a young boy, he was very nice. We had him over for supper many times. We liked him. But as he got into his teens, he seemed to change. I know a lot of boys do, but he became sort of wild. Got into trouble a lot, and we worried that he might have a bad influence on Chanel. We hadn't forbidden Chanel from seeing him because we knew she'd go behind our backs, but we did discourage her when we could. He wasn't a bad boy, just wild. We thought his parents hadn't been teaching him the correct values."

"Yeah, we were glad she dumped him for good, when she met Guy," Serge chimed in. He was solidly built with thick hands and arms. Bald and wearing a long white apron, he looked like a baker should look. "We couldn't have been happier. She had a good life until her husband was murdered. But she's set for life."

"Any ideas who might have murdered your son-in-law?"

"None whatsoever," Serge continued. "He was a decent, hardworking man who had been deeply in love with Chanel. The police never came up with a suspect, but I suppose you looked into that. Like I said, she's set for life. That's the kind of guy he was. He looked after his wife. Sure I can't get you a brioche or something? Made them myself. They're as fresh as you can get!"

"I appreciate it, but I just had lunch, and I'm stuffed up to here," he said, raising his hand to his chin. He lied, but that was the only thing he could say that would circumvent another round or two of offers. After a moment, he said, "I hope I'm not being out of line, but do you see your daughter very often these days?"

There was an uncomfortable period of silence. Serge looked down at his hands on the top of the table. Brigitte shifted her eyes to the right but otherwise didn't move her head.

"Since Guy was killed," Brigitte said, finally breaking the silence, "it's been rather difficult."

"How so, if I can ask?"

"It's Percy. Have you met him?"

"I have. He seems like a good kid."

"Oh, he is. A very good young man. But Serge and I believe he has an unhealthy attachment to Chanel. We had many discussions with Chanel about it."

"Discussions?" Serge said, scoffing at the word. "They were more like battles without all the artillery."

"We thought that Percy was being overly protective of Chanel since his father's death. He's at the age where he should be on his own—you know, be with friends. He should be out there dating and making a life of his own. He's making no attempt to get a profession. We're not certain he has any skills that could make him independent. Instead, all he does is stay home with his mother. If you know Chanel just a little, you know she doesn't need to be protected. Yet Percy believes it's his job to protect her."

"Protect her from what?" Eddie asked.

"That's a damn good question," Serge said.

"From harm?" Eddie asked. "In light of what happened to his father?"

"That's the obvious answer," Brigitte said. "But in all likelihood, Guy's death was just random. He was probably in the wrong place at the wrong time. That's what the police thought. And Chanel has never had any threats against her. You know she's a wealthy woman."

"Anyway," Serge said, "we tried to talk Chanel into encouraging the boy to get on with his life, but we always ended up in an argument. She doesn't seem to think anything is wrong. We're not the kind of parents that meddle in their kids' lives, but we couldn't sit back and say nothing. The situation just isn't right. It isn't normal."

"Do you think there's anything wrong besides the unhealthy attachment?"

Again, they went silent. They looked at each other. Serge nodded at his wife, as if to say, "You might as well tell him."

"The boy just doesn't act normal to us," Brigitte said. "It's hard to pinpoint, but he broods a lot and spends a great deal of time by himself. Too much time. He doesn't have friends; never had a girlfriend. It's just not right, and Chanel does nothing to discourage him. And the way he talks to us and his mother. He's overly polite to the point that we'd like to take him and shake him up. There's a distance between us that's hard to explain. We see it with his mother as well. I know that seems to be a contradiction, but it's not. There's no intimacy like there should be in families. It's gotten to the point that we rarely see them anymore."

"We'd actually be thrilled to pieces to learn he went out and got plastered with booze and crawled home on his hands and knees, cursing the world," Serge said. "At least he'd show a little spunk—a little emotion."

"Serge doesn't really mean that," Brigitte threw in, "but you get the point."

Eddie got the point.

They talked for a few more minutes until there was nothing more to say. He shook their hands, thanked them for their time, and walked through the shop to leave.

As he had his hand on the doorknob, Josette, Chanel's younger sister, hurried over to him and gave him a folded piece of paper, then went behind the counter again. He opened it; it was a note: *Please meet me in fifteen minutes at the café three doors down the street.*

———— «•» ————

Josette Fournier did not have her sister's beauty. She was one of those rare women whose features were plain but exuded a certain elegance, poise, and self-assurance that made her attractive to the opposite sex. Eddie sensed it immediately.

They sat at a table in the back of the café over coffee.

"I couldn't help but overhear your conversation with my parents."

"Oh, were we talking too loudly?" He feigned a surprised look, maybe overdoing it a bit. Actually, it was bordering on flirtation. "I hope we didn't disturb you too much."

"OK, so I was deliberately listening. Guilty as charged." She stuck her wrists out. "Arrest me and take me away."

She was being playful. Eddie liked that.

"I left my cuffs at the office, but I'll take a rain check on that," he said, winking at her. "Is that why you want to see me?"

"It is, but I don't know anything about Willis. I knew him when we were kids, but that was about it. I haven't seen him in a few decades." She stopped and looked around the café. There were a few people scattered about, minding their own business. Unless they had electronic eavesdropping devices, they were too far away to hear them. "But you should know that Guy Dupont was having an affair at the time he was murdered."

Her voice was soft and smooth like silk, with a slight French accent. She didn't waste any time getting to the point. Eddie's ears perked up.

"Go on," Eddie said, sipping his coffee.

"Maybe that had something to do with his murder. Maybe Guy was involved in some shady dealings. I don't know."

"Do you have any proof of that?"

"He was seeing a dancehall stripper and prostitute who worked at the Gayety. It had gone on for quite some time."

"Do you know her name—the prostitute?"

"She goes by Samantha L'Amour, but her real name is Samantha Dubois. Apparently, she was Lili St. Cyr's protégé before the morality police closed the Gayety."

Sam. Eddie knew her well.

"I always believed that Guy was murdered for a reason.

You know, I had a feeling deep down. I never bought the idea that his death was random."

"Who was selling it?"

She squinched her face. Eddie thought she looked cute.

"The police. My parents even."

"Have any theories?"

"If you're asking me if I know the reason, I don't. But it doesn't take much to know that that side of life can be … dangerous. Where there's prostitution, there are usually other things, illegal things that spell trouble. You should know that as a private detective."

"How did you know about Samantha?"

"I had suspicions about Guy and followed him to the Gayety one night. Then I hired a private detective to do the rest."

"Did you tell your sister?" A quick thought flashed through his head. *She'd make a good investigator.*

"Yes, but she got angry with me. Told me to stay out of her business, and I did. Our relationship isn't the greatest now. We hardly talk or see each other anymore."

"I assume that your parents don't know."

She nodded.

Eddie hesitated to ask the next question, but he thought she could handle it.

"Do you think Chanel was capable of taking matters into her own hands?"

"I love my sister dearly, but I know she's capable of doing a lot of things that most people would never even think of doing. Besides, she was having her own little flings on the side. Being married never stopped her. But to answer your question … I just don't know."

Something didn't feel right to Eddie, so he retraced his steps.

"What made you initially suspicious of Guy?"

She looked down at her coffee cup. She had her hands wrapped around it as if keeping them warm. She seemed to have gone into a sudden trance.

"Josette?"

She looked up. "Yes?"

"I asked why you were suspicious of Guy in the first place."

"Because I did a stupid thing."

Eddie kept quiet, waiting for her to continue.

"It's complicated."

He kept his trap shut; he was going to wait her out.

"I had an affair with him." The words came out, one by one. "I'm not proud of that. I knew that my sister had been seeing other men, so when Guy showed me some attention, I just let it happen. I had become smitten by him, just like a teenage girl. He was handsome and manly, and I just fell into his spell. I was terribly ashamed of myself afterwards. Still am. It goes against everything I believe in."

Eddie sensed that she thought he was being judgmental. He needed to say something to smooth it over. He didn't want her to pull back.

"Sometimes decent people make bad mistakes. That's the way life is. I've made my share of them."

She stared at him for a moment. There was a trace of a smile.

"How long did the affair last?"

"A few months, maybe a little longer. Then one day, he broke it off, just like that." She snapped her fingers. "I thought that he had found someone else, so one night I followed him to the Gayety. That confirmed my suspicions. But I was curious, so I hired a private detective. Over the next few weeks, he was able to substantiate it. But by that time, I had come to my senses. I went to Chanel with the information, but I didn't tell her about my own affair with Guy. She blew her lid. She told me to stay out of her business. It got pretty ugly. Things haven't been the same with us ever since. Please don't tell my parents. I don't think they could take it."

Eddie had no intention of talking to her parents about it, but he did want to have a little chat with Samantha L'Amour.

—————≈«❂»≈—————

The walls of the Lion's Den were a shrine to professional prize fighting. Framed photographs of some of the most important fights in the last twenty years across North America hung like sacred relics, taken by Bruno himself. One wall in particular was dedicated to a local hero of Montreal's fight scene.

Eddie stood in front of one specific photo and stared at it. It was his last fight before enlisting in the American Army. It showed him throwing a left hook at his opponent, Jack "The Bomber" Zielinski. Bruno had clicked his camera just as the punch landed on the Bomber's right jaw. He had gone down like a sack of cement and never made the ten count; Eddie won by a knockout in the third round. He hadn't known it at the time, but that would be the last punch he would ever throw in the ring. He continued staring at it, wondering where life would have taken him had it not been for the war. In all likelihood, he would have stayed in the ring and won a few world championships in different weight classes and never become a private investigator. He might still be fighting today, at the tail end of his career. He might be rich, driving a fancy car and living the high life, or he might be penniless and punch-drunk, living in some flophouse in skid row. He would never know.

"Hey, Eddie," Bruno shouted from the bar. "You drinking or what?"

Eddie turned away and walked toward the bar.

"A Molson, Bruno."

He sat down at the bar and looked around.

"Where's Benedict? Where's everyone? It's Saturday night."

Bruno set the beer in front of Eddie and slid a cardboard mat underneath.

"That's two separate questions and very distinct but not unrelated. The answer to your first question is this. Me and Benedict were standing around here scratching our asses when the phone rang. It was for Benedict. Someone's toilet was overflowing, and the apartment smelled like horse shit. Which brings us to your second question. As we didn't have any drinkers here, I gave Benedict, who is a highly trained plumber as we know, the night off so he could fix the toilet and give its owner some peace of mind."

"The place is usually packed. Where's everyone?"

"There's a dance in the rec room of the church. The wives of all our regulars got together and demanded their husbands take them to it. Let me tell you, Eddie, when those ladies get together, they are a force to be reckoned with. Hence, it is only me and you and an empty Den."

"I've never seen it this quiet during opening hours. It's eerie, a little spooky."

"To say nothing about what it's doing to my wallet. I saw you looking at the Zielinski picture. That was some knockout. He had wobbly legs for the next ten minutes."

"I bought him dinner the following week. I felt sorry for him."

"That was the last fight of your career."

"My last punch too."

"Memorialized by yours truly. I was lucky with that shot. I just kept clicking away."

Eddie gulped down some beer and filled his pipe.

"Met a young lady today," he said, puffing out some smoke.

"So, when are you going to get married?"

"I think I'm in love," he said with a grin.

"It's about time you do something. Let me tell you, buddy boy—one of these days, you're going to wake up and look in the mirror. And when you do, you're going to see an old man, just like me. But by that time, the game's over."

"Will I be bald like you?"

"That's a distinct possibility. Think about that for a moment. You look in the mirror and see me. That alone should shock you into doing something. Is she a beauty queen?"

"Not in the sense that you mean, but there's definitely something about her that I'm attracted to. Can't figure it out. Only met her earlier today."

"She's not married, is she?" Bruno gave him a look that said she better not be.

"I don't think so, but I guess I don't know for sure. She wasn't wearing a ring, and she was flirting with me."

"That's a good sign. Where did you meet her?"

"She's the sister of my client. I interview her and her parents today."

"Jesus, Mary, and Joseph! How many times have I told you—"

"I know, I know. Don't go after anyone involved in an investigation. That's one of my own rules. But I'm not going after her. I just mentioned that I was attracted to her; that's all."

"Anyway, what I said still stands. Find yourself some gal and have children with her. You can thank me later, even when you're changing shitty diapers. Don't be like me—an old man with no one to hand down his possessions to. You'll regret it."

"I'll give it some consideration."

"You do that."

Just then, the door swung open, and a group of men came in—five of the regulars. They said their hellos to Bruno. Eddie turned around in his stool and waved at them. He knew three of the five.

"They're all bachelors," Bruno whispered, leaning into Eddie. "They'll be here until closing."

Bruno excused himself to take their orders. Eddie tamped his pipe and relit it.

Josette Fournier was still on his mind. Setting aside the marriage and children thing that Bruno had been talking about, Eddie was ready for some steady female companionship. It did seem like the older he got, the more he craved it. Living in the back of his office with two cats was getting old. The fact of the matter was he was lonely. He had had a long, serious relationship that abruptly ended a few years back. And now he was ready for another one. Dating women as he had was fine in its own right, but it wasn't the same. He wanted something more. He really hadn't thought much about marriage and children. At that point in his life, he just wanted someone to share his life with.

In spite of Bruno's warning and his own rules, he decided that he'd have to see Josette again. If she was married, it would end there. If she wasn't, then he'd take it from there and see what happened. He'd call her tomorrow on the pretext of wanting a second interview. If she agreed, then there would be all sorts of possibilities.

Chapter 15
THE ROSE COTTAGE

SUNDAY MORNING IN LATE MARCH.

The month had the reputation of going out like a lamb or a ravenous tiger on a rampage. Quebecers would take sides; they always did. It gave them something to talk about over morning coffee. They'd even place bets. So far, the odds-on favorite was the lamb. But there was a nasty chill in the air made worse by spiteful winds, which necessitated a winter coat for anyone loony enough to be out in it. Notwithstanding, by the middle of the day, the sun would be out, the winds diminishing to a slight breeze—a time to switch to a spring jacket. No blizzards were forecasted for now. However, Quebecers would still keep their winter duds handy.

Eddie Wade knew with a degree of certainty that he would find Cecil Becket on any Sunday of the year at the Rose Cottage. Not that he wasn't there all the other days of the week. He was. Rumors had circulated a few years before that he would take the occasional Saturday off, but it was never substantiated.

Eddie took boulevard Saint-Laurent into town and parked his car in the usual spot, whenever he'd make the trip, near the Notre-Dame Basilica. He walked a block and stopped at a decrepit stone building sandwiched between two newer ones: the Montreal Morgue. No sign outside; nothing to hint that the edifice housed dead bodies. Becket liked to call the structure Rose Cottage. He thought it sounded cheerier than city morgue. Eddie opened the door and went down a flight of stairs to the basement. He walked down a long, narrow, claustrophobic tunnel with gray cinder blocks as walls. The closer he got to the morgue, the chillier it became. Industrial-strength disinfectant and other smells hung in the air and bit at his nose. The door was unlocked, so he walked in.

Becket was lounging behind his desk as if he were on a sunny beach somewhere in the South of France, reading a book and smoking his pipe. Peace and quiet among dead bodies. His legs were up, with his ankles resting on the edge of the back of a chair. He looked up over his glasses when Eddie came in.

"Bonifacio!" he said. "I was just thinking about you the other day."

Becket was one of only a handful of people who consistently used Eddie's actual first name. Eddie's late mother had at times in his youth, but only when she wanted to straighten the kid out. Usually, it was followed by a good ear twist. Becket hadn't resorted to that yet.

"Good thoughts, I hope."

"Always. Whenever I have bad thoughts about you, I do headstands until they go away."

"What're you reading?"

"What does any upstanding coroner read? A book with dead people in it! In this case, *The Black Mountain* by Rex Stout. You've got to listen to this," he said, paging to the front of the book. "Here it is. I underlined it. It's beautiful prose! Listen to this." He cleared his throat. "'I pay him the tribute of speaking of him and feeling about him precisely as I did when he lived; the insult would be to smear his corpse with the honey excreted by my fear of death.' Now, isn't that just beautiful, I ask you?"

Cecil Becket was the city of Montreal's chief coroner. With long, curly white hair and deep creases in his face, he looked much older than he actually was. He'd been born in Manchester, England, but hadn't lived there in decades. Notwithstanding, he still retained his class accent.

"You just can't get away from corpses, can you?"

"Try as I may."

Eddie took off his overcoat, draped it over the back of a chair at the side of Becket's desk, and then sat down. He kept his hat on but tilted back. He grabbed a tobacco humidor off the desk, opened it, stuck his nose inside, and then looked up at Becket.

"The usual Blatter blend," Becket said. "Virginia and Latakia. A little Perique. Help yourself."

Eddie filled his Dunhill with the blend and lit up.

"Not bad," he said.

"Not bad, says the novice. Not bad? I'll have you know I smoke only the best!" He twitched his nose, narrowed his eyes, and, positioning himself figuratively in the center of the ring, declared, "Non ducor, duco. I am not led. I lead!"

Becket was playfully showing off his English public school education again, at the same time challenging Eddie to a pugilistic battle of words. Eddie had had his fair share of Latin in school and could go toe to toe with him.

He shot back with "Vincit qui se vincit. Before you lead, get yourself under control; master first your urges and temptations."

Becket put his legs down and slapped the desktop with his palm in mock anger.

"Flectere si nequeo superos, Acheronta movebo. If I cannot bend the will of heaven, I shall move hell!"

Eddie came back strong.

"Acta deos numquam mortalia fallunt. Mortal actions never deceive the gods."

"Well, you got me on that one. Carpe vinum! Let's seize some wine and partake."

Not to be left without the final word, Eddie said, "Alea iacta est. The die is cast. I want a drink!"

Becket laughed and reached for an opened bottle of Cabernet Sauvignon in the small refrigerator he kept behind his desk. He uncorked it and poured the wine in two crystal glasses. He liked his red wine cool like his white, a habit from working in a morgue.

"Here's to the wind and the rain," he said, raising his glass. "May we forever be blessed with nature."

They clicked glasses and drank.

"What's in the hopper?" Becket asked, running a finger over his lips and then relighting his pipe. That was his usual opening to Eddie whenever he thought Eddie came here on business.

"A corpse. Why else would I be here?"

"Ah, yes, a cadaver. Anyone in particular in mind, or just cadavers in general?"

It was clever and subtle, but he managed to squeeze the word *cadaver* in twice. As he was the last one to use a Latin word or phrase, he won the contest—for now.

They both puffed on their pipes, sending a blast of smoke between them.

"Martin Boucher."

"Martin Boucher. Sad, very sad. What do you want to know about him? Are you working the case?"

"For London Life." Puff, puff. "I want to know whether there's any way to identify the body without using the ID found in his wallet."

"Well, for one thing, the body was fairly well preserved

because the river was cold and icy. On the other hand, his face was beyond recognition. There could be a number of reasons for that."

"Yeah, like someone didn't want him identified."

"Of course, there's that. I do have my best print man coming in. If there's a way to get any prints from the corpse, Maxime's the man."

"Did you get a probable cause of death?"

Becket ran his hand through his hair. He looked down at his pipe, tamped the ash down with a nail, and then relit it.

"Or am I not supposed to ask?"

"If it were anyone but you, Bonifacio, I'd be closemouthed about it. But I know you can be closemouthed too, when the situation calls for it, and it does call for it. The cause of Mr. Boucher's death was a gunshot wound to the chest. There was no water in the lungs which means—"

"He was shot dead and then dumped into the St. Lawrence."

"Precisely. It's a homicide case. The chief constable withheld that from the public, pending further investigation, but not from the insurance company. Needless to say, you have to keep it under wraps. But, Jesus, you already know this if you're on the case."

"Mum's the word. Just wanted an official confirmation."

"The bullet ricocheted inside and tore his organs all to hell and then somehow managed to lodge near a bone. He was a bloody mess inside. But on the bright side of things, miraculously, it looked pretty clean for matching, if there happens to be a weapon around to match it to."

"At the moment, there's not, but I'm working on it."

They both stopped and put their glasses to their lips.

"He's reposing quietly over yonder. Want to have a peek?"

"Not on an empty stomach." He relit his pipe and then stood up and put his overcoat on. "Requiescat in pace. Let him rest in peace." Eddie didn't like losing. "Gotta go. I'll let you get back to your book. Thanks for the wine. I'll check back later on the ID." He walked to the door and had his hand on the knob, about to open it, when Becket called out to him. He turned around.

"Si vis pacem, para bellum. If you, yourself, want peace, prepare for war, my friend. I fear that one is coming your way."

"That's my intent, Cecil. Incepto ne desistam. May I not shrink from my purpose."

Eddie saw Becket's lips part, about to reply, but the words died in his mouth. He gave him a wink instead and nodded his head.

———————«◉»———————

Percy sat in his bedroom alone, fingering a photo album.

He liked the solitude. It was his refuge from the harsh and sometimes indifferent world that seemed at times to envelop him. He spent many hours there each day thinking about the past. In fact, his bedroom was an echo chamber where he encountered only past events that reverberated and then mingled with his existing beliefs, reinforcing them, giving them strength and him courage to navigate the present and ignore the future.

His bookshelf contained mostly classical literature written by men who were now lying in their caskets, as dead as anyone could be. Why read someone who was still alive? The author would still have the power to change; hence, he'd be confronted with the possibility that his previous works would all be negated. Then Percy would have to throw those books in the garbage where they belonged. That wouldn't do at all. Percy wanted things to remain as they were, steadfast and unalterable.

He had photo albums of all the past trips his mother had taken him on when he was younger—one album reserved for each trip. It was just he and his mother—never his father. In retrospect and with a certain amount of distance between then and now, he thought that had been a good thing. And then there was his tennis racket. He hadn't used that in years. It, too, like most things in his life, was relegated to the past. About the only significant thing he owned that embodied the present, the here and now, was the gun he kept in his closet, in the secret compartment behind the wall. But even that had a past.

He wasn't complaining; he like it that way, preferred it even—his room. The past was manageable for him; it always made sense when he thought about it long enough. There was a certain order to it, a certitude that things couldn't change. He drew comfort from that. As a youngster, he remembered his mother sending him to his room several times as a punishment for some infraction of the rules. He had long ago forgotten what he'd done wrong—probably something idiotic—but he always remembered the warm and heartening feeling of being there. It was as if the walls had grown arms and caressed him. She had stopped sending him to his room when she realized it really hadn't been a punishment at all.

As much as he was reassured by the past and troubled by the present, the future was abhorrent to him, so much so that he did his best never to think about it. At infrequent times, he wondered whether it really existed. He wasn't sure. He remembered reading in one of his philosophy books in high school that some people believed the past and future didn't exist, that only the present did. He was certain that that was incorrect, because for him, the past was vividly alive. If he could understand the past, then he could control the present. Things happened in the present, and in a microsecond, they became the past; when they did, they could not be undone. But if you could control the present, if you could manipulate it to conform to your beliefs, then you could intervene and change it the way you wanted before it slid into the past.

To Percy, the past was all that mattered. That was where his soul was sheltered; that was where his unencumbered mind roamed free.

He opened the photo album; it was their first trip to the Adirondack Mountains when he was ten years old. It was one of the most memorial trips his mother had taken him on, because on that trip he had gained much insight—even at that tender age—into his mother that had lasted even to this day. He looked at one of the photos and then ran his hand over it. His mother was sitting on a lounge chair, leaning back, holding up a drink. She was young and beautiful. He remembered it well because he had taken the picture. In fact, he had taken every photo in every album he had. And because of that, he had never been in one.

Just before the trip, his father had bought him a Brownie camera. It was an F model that used 120 film and had a viewfinder and handle. His father had been a stickler for details and insisted on sharing every little thing about it with his son. It was an aluminum box camera rather than the cheaper cardboard model, invented by Eastman Kodak and named after Palmer Cox's cartoon characters, the "brownies," who were household spirits that came out at night while the owners of the house were asleep and performed household chores and farming tasks. Percy had been greatly impressed by his father's obsession with details.

He flipped through the album, stopping randomly somewhere in the middle. His eyes were drawn to the middle of the page. This one had been taken at the activity center at the main lodge of the resort they stayed at. His mother was smiling, happy with a little help of several drinks. She was standing with her arms around a man, a stranger she had just met shortly before. The next photo was the cabin where she and the stranger had spent the night.

Percy had spent his night in their own cabin alone. It had

been his first night in the forest, and he hadn't been used to all the night sounds. It was quieter than the city, certainly, but he was unnerved by all the unfamiliar sounds—the hoots, thuds, and screeches. He was sure they were made by animals; no humans could make them, at least not by any he had ever known.

He stood at the screened window and saw unsettling shadows cast by the moon and the trees. Occasionally, he would hear footsteps crunching over twigs, adding to his sense of fear and isolation. Because he was unaccustomed to the chilling sounds, they startled his imagination to dread the worse. Later, he would realize that those sounds were nothing more than giant toads, amorous foxes, rutting deer, screeching owls, and even hungry hedgehogs—a cacophony of spooky nighttime sounds. On subsequent trips there, he had gotten used to them and even looked forward to hearing them, but on that first trip, he would have felt much better with his mother's arms around him instead of a stranger.

He flipped through some more pages, more photos of his mother with strangers, more laughter, and more nights alone in his cabin. He wasn't resentful, as one might think. Instead, he looked at it as being afforded an opportunity to know his mother better; it had been a valuable lesson. The past was important if you knew how to control the present. He was doing a good job at that. And it all started in the middle of the Adirondacks among the trees and noisy animals.

He closed the album.

His mother needed his protection, whether she knew it or not, or she would one day find herself walking off a steep cliff and into a never-ending abyss.

Chapter 16
THE TWO FACES OF JANUS

"MR. WADE," PERCY DUPONT SAID. "THIS IS A surprise. I assume you've come to see my mother. Unfortunately, she's not here at the moment."

"That's a shame. Mind if I come in and ask you a few questions?" Eddie flashed him a smile; he was just a harmless, friendly guy. He used the same smile on clients, prospective clients, con men, Mafia dons, and anyone pointing a gun at him. It got him what he wanted most of the time. "Could help your mother's case," he added.

Percy paused a few seconds too long before answering. Either he wasn't thrilled with the idea, or Eddie caught him at a bad time—or maybe Percy just didn't like him.

"Yes, of course," Percy finally said. "I should like to be of help anyway I can."

They went into the small sitting room where Eddie initially had interviewed Chanel.

"Would you like a refreshment?" Percy asked. "I could have our maid prepare something for you."

"Naw, that won't be necessary, Percy. I'm just coming from lunch, but thanks anyway."

"Yes, of course, Mr. Wade. Should you change your mind

later, please let me know, and I'll tell the maid. We keep a large selection of beverages, so you'd have many to choose from."

The kid didn't do anything for a living, but Eddie thought he'd make a great head butler. All he needed was a waistcoat, gray striped trousers, a white shirt with a Windsor cut, and a black tie. He had the lingo down pat.

They sat down on the davenport facing the fireplace.

"I hope I'm not taking you away from something important," Eddie said. "It's Sunday, and well, people usually do special things like go to church or socialize with friends."

"Oh, Mother stopped going to church when Father died. She said she could never tolerate all the smells. I still go on holy days of obligation myself. However, it might just be out of habit at this point in my life. I don't know where Mother is at the moment. She was gone when I got up. She usually leaves me a note"—he paused for a few beats—"but she didn't this time."

"Anyway, I appreciate that you're willing to take the time to talk with me. I'm just trying to see the larger picture here, Percy. Your father had been murdered. Then your mother's fiancé, Thornton Hill, disappeared last year, and now your stepfather, Willis, disappears with your mother's money and jewels. Don't you find all that strange?"

Percy sat with his fingers interlaced on his lap, staring at the cold fireplace. There were fresh logs in it with newspapers that had been twisted into rolls on top of them, with kindling on top of that. The maid had probably prepared it for this evening. One could imagine a single match sending the whole thing into a fiercely burning blaze. He ran his fingers through his hair, which had gotten into his eyes, and turned his head toward Eddie.

"Strange? Can you be more specific, Mr. Wade?"

"Well, that's a lot to have happened to one woman, don't you think? Most women don't experience any of that in a lifetime."

Percy considered that for a time and then said, "That seems to be a reasonable conclusion. How long have you known my mother, Mr. Wade?"

"You can call me Eddie. I just met her last week when she came into my office."

"I've known her all my life. Can I ask you how, exactly, you see my mother?"

"I see her as a strong woman who's capable of taking charge of things."

"That ... perception is quite right, Mr. Wade. She is that. But because I've known her all my life ..." He paused in thought, then continued. "I know a different side of her, a side that needs protecting."

Percy was talking, which was good, but he was weighing his words carefully. Was it to protect his mother? Himself?

"You wanna tell me about that side?"

"I don't mind, Mr. Wade, but please don't share this with her. There are some things I tell my mother, and there are some things I don't. I prefer that what I say now isn't shared with her."

"Of course. We're speaking in confidence."

Percy turned his attention to the fireplace again.

"Chanel is strong, and she does like to take charge of things, as you said. But there are times when—and I'm very accurate in this, Mr. Wade—there are times when her judgment isn't very good."

Chanel? He switched to her first name. It wasn't common for sons and daughters to call their parents by their given names, but it wasn't unheard of.

"Like when it comes to men? You mean Willis?"

"I mean Willis, and Mr. Hill, and even my own father."

Eddie noticed him tensing up, fisting his hands on his lap. He still wasn't making eye contact.

"So, you disapprove of her choices?"

"It's not up to me to approve or disapprove, Mr. Wade. The most I can do is observe, and what I observe leads me to conclude that her judgment isn't what it should be."

"Can you give me an example?"

"Certainly, Mr. Wade. I was prepared to do that, or I wouldn't have mentioned it. Willis and Chanel were always arguing. They had been married for only two months, one week, and five days at the time he left, but it started before that. As you can imagine, living in the same house with that going on was very uncomfortable for me. It wasn't just the occasional disagreement. I won't say that it was every day, but it was frequent. I could hear them shouting at each other from other parts of the house."

"Would the arguments ever become physical?"

"That I can't say, but if you're asking me for my best guess, I'd say no, they weren't."

Eddie nodded, more out of acknowledgment than anything else.

"Anything else?"

"When Mr. Hill was coming around, they would argue as well, but I often heard him slapping her. He might have done more than that, but I was never in the same room to see it. I only heard them. But I had seen marks he left on her—her face, her arms. She tried to hide them from me with makeup, but it didn't work. On those occasions, I think he had been drinking."

Eddie watched him fisting his hands again. His body was tense as he talked. He seemed to be working himself up into a frenzy, experiencing all that again. Had Eddie probed him too far? Should he pull back? He decided to let him continue.

"And then there was Mr. Legrand and even my own father. There was so much chea—so much disloyalty. I tried my best to protect her, but there always seemed to be another one to take his place."

He suddenly stopped talking. Eddie waited him out. It was a long moment of silence. Percy seemed to be reining himself in, regaining control again.

"Mr. Wade, I'm becoming a little uncomfortable now," he continued. "I think we should end this conversation and you should leave." He wasn't impolite, just matter of fact. He got up and offered Eddie his hand. He seemed calm again. "You could go back to your office, or if you have something else to do, you could do that. You have two options as I see it. Maybe you have more that I'm not aware of. If you're about to ask me for my opinion, I would say that it's up to you to choose. I regret not being able to help you with that."

Outside, Eddie sat in his car with his notebook and pen.

Percy seemed to have a pretty good grasp of his mother's behavior and relationships with men, and he obviously didn't approve, going so far as to question her judgment. He mentioned that she needed protecting. Of course, an adult son would want to protect his mother from any harm, but how could he have possibly done that?

Surprisingly, Percy had added another name to the list of men who'd been in Chanel's life: Mr. Legrand. That name had been front-page news last Friday. Eddie remembered reading about it. A Luc Legrand had been shot to death outside his home on Thursday night. The name stuck because he was a bank executive at the Royal Bank of Canada, the same bank that Chanel's first husband, Guy, had worked for. Percy implied that his mother had had a relationship with him. And then he mentioned his own father. Did Percy somehow know he'd been cheating on her with a prostitute? And was any of this relevant to his case of the missing Willis Steele?

All good questions with no answers.

Eddie had been considering the possibility that Chanel had been killing off the men in her life. The motives were there.

Now he discovered that Luc Legrand had been yet another person in her life who was either killed or disappeared. This was all circumstantial, of course, but it looked promising. If he decided to pursue that angle, he'd have to hire someone else to work with him. He couldn't do it by himself. There was just too much to look into. Maybe Sully and Angie Ellis would jump at the chance.

Then, for just a split second, a thought rushed into his head like a tidal wave. Was Percy capable of violence? There was something strange about the kid. Chanel's parents, Serge and Brigitte Fournier, had been spot-on about Percy. He was a loner, living his life through his mother. It seemed as though his mission in life was to protect her. Percy was obviously intelligent and articulate, but his demeanor most of the time was polite to the point of being obsequious. That wasn't normal. Eddie guessed he spent most of his time wanting to please others, most of all his mother. But was he capable of violence? How far had he gone to protect his mother?

Was Percy Dupont a killer?

―――――――◈――――――――

That evening, Eddie sat behind his desk, typing up his notes from the last few days. He had his pipe going and a glass of whiskey near the typewriter. Antoinette was sprawled out on some folders on his desk, and Henri was ignoring both of them from the couch. He had the radio on, listening to Lucille Dumont, la grande dame de la chanson, singing "The Sky and the Sea." Whenever he heard that song, he was always reminded of Angélique Charbonneau. It was her favorite.

After Eddie's visit with Cecil Becket at the Rose Cottage that morning, they had decided to have lunch together at Bens Delicatessen and catch up on each other's lives. Eddie had his usual, a smoked meat sandwich; Cecil had a huge bowl of matzo ball soup. Regrettably, Cecil had brought up Eddie's former longtime girlfriend, Angélique Charbonneau—Angel, for short. Eddie and Angel had been a hot item for years. She was an artist (Eddie still had a few of her paintings on his office walls). They had loved each other, they had been comfortable with each other, and they had gotten used to each other, so much so that their relationship had gone into neutral with the engine left idling.

One night, during the course of a murder investigation (the murder had taken place on a tram in the early morning—a tram that Eddie himself had been on) Eddie and Angel had been returning to his Mile End office when someone decided to put a few bullets into him for good measure. The shooter had missed Eddie completely but ended up putting a round in Angel's shoulder instead. That had put her in the hospital for a time. While she lay on her bed, surrounded by flowers, with tubes running on all directions, Eddie was just about to ask her for her hand in marriage. However, she spoke first. Anticipating what he was about to ask her, she'd told him that she couldn't see a future for herself married to a private dick. She hadn't used those exact words, but her point was clear. Maybe the next bullet would hit something other than a shoulder.

And that was that. Eddie hadn't seen her since that night at the hospital. Fortunately, he had years of wonderful memories; unfortunately, none of them would keep him warm at night in his bed.

He tamped his pipe again and set his fingertips on the keys. Antoinette got up, stretched, and then joined Henri on the couch. She seemed indifferent to the vicissitudes of humanity. Henri opened his eyes to see what was going on but otherwise didn't move. He closed his eyes again, shutting out the world around him. Eddie felt like doing the same thing.

The door to his office suddenly flung open, ending his

train of thought. The wooden coatrack went toppling over. He'd have to remember to move it to a safer place. A man in a black fedora wearing a long gray overcoat came in. He had two days' growth on his face. He slipped his hands into his pockets.

"You Wade?" he asked. His voice was gravelly, and he had a pug nose, as if it had been flattened several dozen times in the ring.

Eddie stared at him but remained in his chair. The guy wasn't particularly pleasant to look at, at least not for anything beyond a few seconds. He spelled trouble. Eddie's gun was in the safe behind his desk, but maybe he wouldn't need it. Still, he wasn't in any mood to play games with this lunkhead.

"You're impolite. You knocked down my coatrack."

"You Wade?" he asked again. He did something strange with his shoulders, moved them around a bit, and dug his hands deeper in his pockets.

"That's what the sign outside says."

Eddie had seen this pug somewhere before, recently, but he couldn't place him. He rarely forgot a face, especially an ugly one.

"Then let me give you a piece of advice." Again, he did the shoulders' routine. "Stay away from Sylvie Boucher. She's a widow woman. She's mourning a loss. She don't need some ding-dong like you coming around making trouble for her, if you catch my drift."

He caught his drift, but he didn't like it. Who the hell was this guy? Did Sylvie send him? He was becoming concerned by this dimwit's hands in his pockets. He didn't like surprises.

"I caught your drift," he said. Puff, puff. "And you might be ...?"

"Never mind who I am. Din't your mother ever tell you to stay away from grieving widows?"

"She told me to stay away from a lot of things but never

grief-stricken widows. Maybe I would have listened to her if she'd told me. Maybe not."

"Well, let me be the first then, smartass. If I find out you've been snooping around again, I'll come back, and I won't be so pleasant."

"Pleasant? Yeah, you've been a load of laughs. Don't let the door hit you in the ass on your way out."

"Just remember what I said, hotshot." He backed up to the door, which was still open. "For your own health," he said and then slipped out.

Sylvie Boucher, he thought. *London Life. Where have I seen that guy before?*

He set his pipe down and took a sip of whiskey, then got up, went to the door, and closed and locked it. He picked up the coatrack, moved it away from the door, and returned to his desk. *Sylvie Boucher,* he thought again as he sipped some more whiskey. Edith Piaf was now singing away on the radio. *Where have I seen that chump?*

He reached over his desk, where Antoinette had been lying, and picked up a manila folder. He opened it and took the photos out that he had had developed yesterday. He looked at the first one. There he was with the same hat and overcoat. He was coming out of Sylvie's house yesterday. A clean shot—unmistakable. Now he knew that the woman's claim was fraudulent. How was this guy involved? And how was he going to prove it?

That was it for the night.

He decided to turn in early. He knocked back the whiskey, cleaned his pipe out, and thought, *What an idiotic thing to have done,* referring to his late-night visitor. Coming in here, threatening the investigator on the case, and then expecting everything was going to be hunky-dory. Well, one thing was certain: he was dealing with a bunch of morons.

But then he remembered the night someone shot at him

through the window. Initially, he thought Branch York had done it, because he'd had a run-in with him that morning, and York threatened him. But on the same day, he'd also interviewed Sylvie.

Besides being stupid, were these people also dangerous?

Chapter 17
FOOL ME ONCE

EDDIE SAT AT THE COUNTER OF THE LOCAL greasy spoon, finishing up his toast and coffee. *La Presse* was spread out in front of him. He'd read the first paragraph of an article and had no idea what it meant. The prose was clear and concise like a newspaper article should be, so he read it again. And then he read it a third time. Finally, he gave up. It wasn't the writer; it was him. He was preoccupied with Percy Dupont and the idiot who threatened him last night in his office. The Boucher case could wait another day or two; the Steele case was becoming hot, and the snags were worrisome. It was spreading its wings in several directions, and he couldn't cover all of them. He thought again about calling Sully and Angie this morning and getting them on the case. He decided to hold off for another day and see what came up. He didn't want to offer some of the legwork to the Ellises and then not be able to follow through. He knew they'd be eager to run with it.

He folded the paper, put it under his arm, walked over to the pay phone in the back of the restaurant, and dropped a dime into the slot. He called his answering service and was told that Jack Macalister wanted him to get his ass downtown to police headquarters pronto, if he knew what was good for him. The operator hadn't actually used those words, but the meaning was clear enough. He got into his car and shot down Saint-Laurent, driving over the speed limit most of the way.

———«◉»———

Macalister was sitting at his desk going through some files when Eddie walked into his office.

"OK, I'm here," he said. "What's up?"

Macalister swung around in his chair, leaned back, and laced his fingers behind his head. A great big smile spread across his face.

"And good morning to you, too, Mr. Wade. How're you doing, old pal o' mine? How was the weekend? Out chasing women? Good for you! My weekend was a doozy, if you'd care to know."

"You left a message and said you wanted to see me. I think you used the word *pronto*. I made it pronto."

Macalister swung around again to his desk. Eddie stood over him like a tall pine tree.

"I've got the ballistics report back."

"That was fast; must have set an all-time record. Could make the 'Guinness Book of Records.'"

"I asked Alain to run it through as quickly as he could. I even said please and thank you. A bottle of Johnny Walker probably helped a little as well. Red Label it was."

"I owe you."

"You certainly do, and don't think I'm not keeping track. You were in arrears last time I checked." Rising slightly from his chair, he reached to the far end of his desk and picked up the report. "OK," he said, sliding back in his chair again and opening the folder. "The three bullets that were meant for you but ended up lodged in your office wall instead of your body and the shell casings that we found outside on the sidewalk all matched one that we had stored in the evidence room on a past murder case."

"Shit! Who was the victim?"

"You need to sit down for this one."

Eddie dragged a chair from the wall to Macalister's desk and sat down.

"I think you may have heard the name before: Guy Dupont."

Eddie stared at Macalister. Then, slowly drawing out the words, he said, "Christ Almighty."

"There's more."

"Should I lie down for this one?"

"You told me you were working on a case for London Life. A constable had fished Martin Boucher's body out of the Saint Lawrence."

"That's right. I just saw Cecil Becket yesterday about making a positive identification on him. He was having your best print man come in."

"That would be Maxime. He started his vacation today, so he went to the morgue late yesterday afternoon to do the job. We wanted a positive ID on the body before he left. He wasn't too happy about it. He was packing up the car when I called him in. He's probably in New Jersey now, heading for Miami for a few weeks. His wife was very upset about it. She gave me a piece of her mind. You should have heard what she said to me."

"And?"

"And he made a positive ID. It wasn't Martin Boucher."

"Who was he then?"

"You know the guy you asked me about last time we talked? Chanel Steele's former fiancé who disappeared? His mother thought he might have skipped off to the States?"

"Thornton Hill."

"Thornton Hill—that's the guy. We had his prints on file

from a previous arrest on assault and battery charges. They matched."

"Christ Almighty."

"You already said that. You want to hear the kicker?"

"I don't know whether my heart can take it, but go ahead."

"The bullet that killed Hill matched the bullet that killed Dupont, and both of them matched the bullets we pulled out of your wall."

Eddie was either in shock, or he was still processing the information, because he sat there as still as an infantryman on an ambush and as white as a chunk of crystalline metamorphic rock. For the next minute, Macalister's office was as cold and silent as Cecil Becket's Rose Cottage.

"You know what I think?" Macalister asked.

"What?"

"You should hire three bodyguards and put them on eight-hour shifts."

"I'll give it some consideration." He just managed to get that out.

"In the meantime, find the gun, and you'll be a step closer to finding the killer."

"Are you guys going to do anything?"

"Of course, we will, but do you know how many homicide cases we're working? Anyway, keep this to yourself. We don't want to give the killer a heads-up."

"Of course."

Eddie stared at the wall behind Macalister. *It's all tied together: Dupont, Hill, and now me. Find the gun, and you'll be a step closer ... Was Chanel capable of murder? Was Percy?*

"Can I ask another favor of you?"

"It'll cost you another bottle of Johnny Walker. You already owe me five."

"Really? That many?"

"Like I said, I keep track."

"Remember that banker who was murdered outside his home last Wednesday night? His name was Luc Legrand. Any leads on that?"

"It's my case, and no, I don't have a single lead yet. His killer disappeared, and no one in the neighborhood saw or heard anything, as usual. You think it has anything to do with these cases?"

"I don't know, but Legrand worked at the same bank as Dupont and at the same time."

"I know. I'm working on any connections between them, but the murders were five years apart. That's a stretch."

"But maybe not too much. I interviewed Chanel's son, Percy, recently. He didn't come right out and say it, but he certainly hinted at an affair between Legrand and his mother."

"Jesus!"

"Could you let me know if you find anything interesting?"

"Sure, but don't give me the Red Label. I only use that when I want a favor from someone. When someone wants a favor from me, I require Johnny Walker Black Label only."

"Black Label. I'll have to write that down."

"You do that. That's six bottles now."

"So why was your weekend a doozy?"

———— «•» ————

Eddie had an appointment to meet Josette Fournier in Côte-des-Neiges, but it was too early. He needed to kill some time, so he drove over to the Flamingo, which was nearby. It wouldn't be open, but Pierre would be there with a pot of coffee on.

He pounded on the door until he got Pierre's attention.

"Eddie, it's early," he said, opening the door. "Come in anyway. You're always welcome here." He stepped aside, and when Eddie passed him, he locked the door.

"Thanks, Pierre. Mind if I just sit an hour?"

"Sit all day if you want. You want your usual? I've got coffee on too."

"Coffee's good," he said, sitting down at the bar. "Don't let me bother you. I know you have work to do before you open."

"Actually, I was doing yesterday's receipts in the back," he said, setting Eddie's coffee in front of him. "If you don't mind, I'd like to finish them before we open."

"No, no, go ahead. I'm just killing a little time. Pretend I'm not here."

"Help yourself to more coffee. Let me know when you want to leave, and I'll unlock the door." With that, he disappeared in the back office.

Eddie took his coat and hat off and set them on the stool beside him. He filled his pipe and then took a sip of his coffee. It was hot.

He thought about what Jack had told him just an hour before. A picture was starting to come into focus, but it was still blurred at the moment. It was staring him in the face, but it was distorted. The murders were linked by the evidence, and whoever the killer might be was coming after him. Whoever it was had to be connected to the Dupont-Steele family somehow. He thought of Chanel and Percy again. Was either one capable of multiple murders? If not them, then someone close to the family that he wasn't aware of?

Several years ago, he had had a lesson that things were never as they appeared to be. An old man had been murdered. Eddie had known him from a restaurant where he sometimes had his morning coffee. The guy was always there. His name was Al. That was all he knew about him, except that he was in his sixties and always well dressed. Over the course of a year, they had talked many times, mostly about the weather, and the Canadians in the winter, and the Royals in the spring and summer months. He'd been a terrific guy, always laughing and telling jokes. Eddie had enjoyed their conversations and even looked forward to the next morning, especially if there had been a game the previous day. They'd spend an hour drinking coffee and analyzing it, breaking it down and reconstructing it, explaining how the game should have been played.

The police had looked at the case as a random shooting and hadn't given it much manpower. Of course, Eddie had been devasted when he heard the news. There was no identification on the man, and the newspapers referred to him simply as Al. The police had no information on him and had his picture all over Montreal, hoping that someone knew him. No such luck. People were killed all the time, mostly bums on the street though, and were never identified. But not being able to identify someone like Al was unusual. So, Eddie decided to investigate the case on his own when he had the time. After a few months, Eddie didn't have any leads.

While he was having a drink with a longtime investigator friend of his, Tommy Callahan, he'd told the story to him. Tommy was in his late fifties and looking forward to retirement soon. His wife and son had been brutally murdered twenty years before, and he never remarried. He volunteered to help Eddie with the case, so they worked it together, but after a few weeks, they hadn't uncovered anything useful. Eddie knew Tommy hadn't done much legwork, but he hadn't minded it, because after all, he had volunteered, and he was about to retire anyway. It had been more of a goodwill gesture than anything. But when they got together, he was always curious to know what Eddie found out, which, as it turned out, hadn't been much.

Then one day, Eddie had tracked down a man from a vague lead who had known Al well. At first, the guy wasn't willing to talk much. He was down-and-out and lived in a single room at one of the skid row hotels. The guy maintained he'd known Al for years when they were younger, so Eddie had helped his memory along by giving him fifty bucks. The story he told had been worth more than that.

Decades ago, Al—his full name had been Alphonse "the Ghost" Marchand—had been a loan shark, extortionist, and murderer who kept a very low profile, using others to do his dirty work. He lived under the radar, so he didn't have a police record because he had never been arrested; hence the nickname "The Ghost." Few people knew who he was and what he did. This news shocked Eddie. He couldn't believe what he was hearing. Could this guy be the same one he'd had coffee with most mornings for a year? He thought the guy was lying to him just to get the money. Maybe he just had a vivid imagination. Then the guy told him something else, and everything suddenly made sense. The guy went on to tell him about a double murder Al had one of his men do. He had had the wife and son of some private dick killed because the guy was on to his operation. The murders had been grizzly and brutal—done with a knife. As far as the old guy could remember, that had happened nearly twenty years before.

Several days later when Tommy and he met up, Eddie confronted him about it. Tommy had not denied it. It turned out that he had been collecting evidence against Al to give to the police. When Al found out about it, he threatened to kill his wife and son if he didn't stop. Tommy hadn't relented. Instead, he had made arrangements for his wife and son to stay in Quebec City until Al was behind bars. The night before they were supposed to have left, they were murdered. At the same time, his office had been broken into and the evidence stolen. For the last twenty years, Tommy had been trying to get the evidence that Al ordered the hit on his wife and son. He finally threw his hands up and gave up. There would be no justice for his wife and son, so he took matters into his own hands. Tommy had used Eddie to find out if he was on to him. Alphonse "the Ghost" Marchand had been dying of heart disease anyway; Tommy just helped him along.

Eddie had been fooled by both Tommy and Al. In the end, it hadn't mattered. Tommy had had his long-overdue justice; Al was in a grave that should have been dug decades before. Eddie couldn't see his friend behind bars, so he kept his mouth shut. He might have done the same thing as Tommy, given the circumstances. He learned a valuable lesson about humanity: things were never as they appeared to be. There were always other stories to be told, other songs to be sung, other people to die.

Chanel? Percy?

Their imagines were still distorted but slowly coming into focus.

Fool me once, shame on you, he thought. *Fool me twice, shame on me.*

"Pierre!" Eddie shouted over his shoulder. "I'm ready to leave now."

Chapter 18
AN AURA

EDDIE DROVE OVER TO MONKLAND VILLAGE IN Côte-des-Neiges again to meet with Josette Fournier, Chanel's sister, at the same café on boulevard Grand where he first interviewed her. He wanted to pump her for more information. He also wanted to have a second look at her. He was definitely attracted to her, but he didn't know why. It wasn't that she was gorgeous; she wasn't. And her features were unremarkable. She did seem to have a little of her sister's spunk though, which he found sexy. In fact, everything being equal, he wouldn't have given Josette the time of day. But there was a certain aura about her that he found appealing. She had something that exuded an undefined scent that wasted no time at all going to work on him; he was certain it hadn't been all the doughnuts and chocolate croissants she spent her days selling.

"Thanks for seeing me, Josette."

"We're busiest early in the morning, then it slacks off until noon. So right now's a good time for me to take a little break."

It was there again—that aura. He hadn't been imagining it the first time he saw her. He couldn't put it into words; it was just a sensation that enveloped him in her presence. The only thing he knew for certain was that it excited him.

"You like working in the family business?"

"I do. My parents made me a partner. At some point, I'll own the shop. They're thinking about retiring in the next five years."

"It looks like the shop's doing well."

"Even when the economy is doing poorly, people still want their doughnuts and coffee. I can't see that changing anytime soon. We're actually talking about expanding."

"Open a shop in Mile End, and I'll be a steady customer."

"I'll see what I can do," she said, picking up her cup and sipping some coffee. "I'll hold you to that. If it turns out that you're the only customer, it'll cost you a lot to keep the doors open."

Eddie could only see her eyes looking at him over the cup. Her mouth was hidden. Was she smiling at him?

"You mentioned that Chanel was having flings on the side. I assume you meant while she was married to Guy."

"Chanel always had flings on the side since high school. She always had someone steady—mostly Willis—but that never stopped her. Even when she married. So, yes, while she was married to Guy."

"Did you know any of these men? Any names stand out?"

"Like I said, we haven't seen much of each other since I told her about Guy. But she had garnered quite a reputation for herself over the years, so I usually found out from other people that we both knew. It was mostly gossip, but it fit Chanel to the T. Certain things are difficult to hide—not that she tried very hard."

"Do you think that Guy knew she was having affairs?"

"Listen, after our argument, I didn't care how they chose to lead their lives. If they wanted to sleep with half of Montreal, that was their business. But Percy is my nephew, and I was worried about him. That could have a lasting effect on him. I think it already has."

"How so?"

"I love him dearly, but he's sort of weird in his own way. He's too attached to Chanel, and it's unhealthy. I hate to say this, but he's really a mommy's boy. It's as if it's his job to protect her. I think he wants to be her knight in shining armor. At his age, he should be out on his own, living his own life. Instead, he lives in that big house of hers, hardly goes out, and doesn't have friends of his own. It's just not normal, and Chanel has done nothing to discourage him."

"You said that his mother's behavior has had a lasting effect on Percy. How so?"

"Just like I said. I never talked to Percy directly about it, but from the conversations we had over time, I think he's obsessed with wanting to protect Chanel from men. Otherwise, why would he choose to live like he does? You have to admit that it's quite strange."

It was. Eddie wanted to ask her whether she felt that Percy was capable of violence but decided not to. He couldn't predict how Josette might take that question, and he didn't want to put a roadblock up between them.

"It is strange, yes," he said. "More coffee?"

"Just a quick one. I've got to get back soon."

Eddie motioned with his hand to the waitress standing behind the counter. She came over with a pot and refilled their cups.

"How do you like being an investigator? It must be interesting."

"It keeps food on my table and in Antoinette's and Henri's bowls."

She looked at him quizzically.

"I have two cats."

"Oh, I just love cats!" she said.

And they were off and running for the next ten minutes, laughing and joking about the weird behaviors of felines and how independent and yet cuddly and lovable they were.

When they squeezed as much as they could out of that, and after a slight lull in the conversation, Eddie said, "Do you mind if I ask you a question?"

"That's all you've done for the two times I've seen you. What's one more question? Ask away."

For just a split second, he thought he was talking to Chanel. He knew that what he was about to ask her broke the first rule of his professional ethics, but he didn't care.

"What would you say if I asked you to have dinner with me some night soon?"

"Let me see," she said, squinching up her face as if she were in deep thought. "I don't know. I guess I'd have to think about it." She took a long sip from her coffee. "Why don't you get back to me in a few months, and we'll discuss that possibility."

Eddie smiled.

"Actually, I'd been thinking about how I was going to ask you the same question, without being unladylike. Thanks for eliminating my dilemma. What did you have in mind, bud?"

Eddie stared at her, the aura clearly about her. He liked the shape of her nose and how her lips moved when she talked. It was captivating.

That's what he was.

Captivated.

———— «◉» ————

That night, he drove to the red-light district. The Gypsy Flower Cabaret was at the end of rue Sainte-Catherine. During Eddie's first interview with Josette, she'd mentioned that Guy Dupont had been seeing a dancer named Samantha L'Amour. That was her stage name. Eddie had known her when she was simply Samantha Dubois. He always called her Sam. She'd been a prostitute who saw higher stars in the sky for herself to hang onto. Several years after Minneapolis-born Lili St. Cyr arrived in Montreal, she'd taken Sam under her wings. She'd taught her how to really *dance* and all the tricks of the trade, which included the "Flying G." At the end of a performance when the stage lights were dimming, she'd attach a hook to her G-string. The hook was on the end of a fishing line that was in the hands of a stagehand in the balcony. The moment just before the lights were turned off to end the routine, the stagehand would yank the line, and the G-string went flying up to the balcony. The rest was left to the imagination of the audience. They couldn't get enough of it!

Sam had been St. Cyr's protégé, who at the time was the most famous woman in Montreal. That was well before the Gayety Theater closed down, which had created quite a sensation. Quebec's Catholic clergy thought St. Cyr was the devil incarnate and had ignored her corrupting the souls of men for long enough. They had gone after her with a righteous vengeance. They declared to the press that whenever Lili danced, "the theater is made to stink with the foul odor of sexual frenzy." The ears of the Public Morality Committee perked up. St. Cyr was arrested and charged with "immoral, obscene, and indecent behavior." One wonders whether they had even seen the Flying G? She had been acquitted on the charges, but the city's moralists nevertheless closed the doors of the Gayety. St. Cyr loved Montreal, but she went back to Hollywood to resume her career, and Sam was out of a job, at least until she was picked up by the Gypsy Flower, where she still performed what St. Cyr had taught her, including the G-string routine. But she never completely got out of prostitution. There was too much money to be made.

If you didn't scrutinize her too hard, Sam was a double for Marilyn Monroe, the "Blonde Bombshell." More accurately, she resembled Lili St. Cyr herself, who Marilyn had patterned herself after. Notwithstanding, Sam was a knockout in her own right.

"The last time I saw you, Eddie, you had to duck out of the way of my G-string. You were in the first row, off to stage left."

"That was at the Gayety."

"So it had to be at least a few years ago."

"Just before Lili was arrested and the doors were padlocked. It was her night off. You were substituting for her. I think it was your last show there."

"You've got quite a memory. I must have made an impression on you."

"You've got quite a routine."

"It was Lili's routine first, but thanks anyway."

They were sitting in Sam's private dressing room. Since the closing of the Gayety, things in Montreal had settled down a little, but the Gypsy Flower might very well be the next to go. Everyone in the city believed that it was just a matter of time—which was why Samantha L'Amour was playing to a packed house every night. Even the mayor himself took in a couple of shows a week. When it's gone—it's gone.

Eddie told her why he was there, specifically mentioning Guy Dupont's name.

"Gee, Eddie, that was a long time ago." She paused a moment in thought. "He was a handsome devil, though, for an old guy. Shame what had happened to him."

"Were you having an affair with him?"

Eddie and Sam could always talk freely. There had never been any embarrassing subjects between them. They just picked up where they'd left off.

"An affair? God no! I do a lot of things, but affairs aren't one of them. It was strictly a business arrangement; that's all. He was a steady customer who paid well; he was a safe bet."

"Safe in what way?"

"He wanted normal sex, nothing kicky. Know what I mean?

No chains or handcuffs. Nothing like that. Hell, sometimes we wouldn't have sex at all. Sometimes, he just wanted to talk, so I got to know him pretty well, just like his son."

"What?"

"His son, Percy. Do you know him?"

"Percy is seeing you?" He couldn't believe his ears.

"Yeah, he's seeing me, but it's never for sex. Some guys are just like that. They're lonely and have no one to talk to. I have a few customers like that, but they're all older men. Percy's the youngest by far. Oops. Maybe I shouldn't have said anything."

Eddie wanted to ask her for a detailed transcript of their conversations, but he didn't want to put Sam in the awkward position of having to say no; instead, he asked her whether any of their little chats were about Percy's father.

"Only that he knew his father had been seeing me."

"Don't you find that strange? I mean, this father-son thing?"

"It wasn't as if we were having a ménage à trois. He started seeing me long after his father died, so no, I don't find it strange. And we don't even have sex. And just for the record, lover boy—if you're keeping score—I have customers who bring their sons to me when they become a certain age, because they trust that I'll give them a decent first experience. I'd use the word *righteous* if I were talking to a priest. You haven't become a priest since we last saw each other, have you?" She gave him a coy wink.

"Do me a big favor, will you, Sam? Don't see him again until I get back to you."

"Why? What am I supposed to do if he calls for an appointment?"

"Just stall him. Say you're booked up. Say you're going on vacation. Just don't see him."

"Now you're scaring me, Eddie. Do you know something you should be telling me?"

"You don't have to be scared, but just don't see him until you hear from me."

"OK, Eddie, I won't see him until I hear from you. Are you going to tell me why, or are you going to let me have sleepless nights wondering how I'm going to have to protect myself?"

"Don't worry about that. Just don't see him."

"If you say so."

Once outside, he reached into his overcoat and pulled out his pipe. There was still tobacco in the bowl. He struck a match and lit it. A light breeze blew the smoke over his shoulder.

Maybe he had Chanel all wrong. Maybe she had nothing to do with the murders. More and more, Percy was beginning to come into focus, and what he saw, he didn't like. Everyone he'd talked to, including Percy himself, suggested Percy was obsessed with protecting his mother. He had even told Eddie that his mother lacked judgment when it came to men. Could Percy be protecting Chanel by killing them, including his own father? It was a bizarre thought, but bizarre things happened all the time. Was this one of them? The same person who had killed both Guy Dupont and Thornton Hill had a go at Eddie at his office. The ballistics report proved that. Was Percy after him because he was on the case? Had he killed Willis Steele as well? Luc Legrand? He had to do something about this soon before he became the next victim, but he had absolutely no idea what.

He tamped his pipe and walked to his car, turning over possibility after possibility.

Chapter 19
THE PLAN

TUESDAY MORNING.

Eddie sat in his car across the street and down away from the Boucher residence. Beside him on the passenger side was a thermos jug with hot black coffee. Beside that was a mason jar with a wide opening he used to pee in. A hermetically sealed jar was absolutely necessary; doing surveillance work alone was hard on the bladder.

As the Boucher case was gaining speed, he planned on staying there all day and night if necessary. The body at the morgue had been proven not to be Martin Boucher. As Sylvie had identified the body as her husband and filed a claim for the $20,000 life insurance payout, the case was now considered to be a matter of fraud. Eddie's job was to get conclusive evidence that would stand up in court for any wiseass judge who might want to sympathize with the grieving widow and give her the benefit of the doubt. Court cases like this were always a roll of the dice without solid proof. The one big question that needed to be answered was, "Where was Martin Boucher?"

Eddie glanced over at the house. No movement. It was as still as a corpse on a concrete foundation. He reached for the thermos, unscrewed the top that doubled as a cup, and poured some coffee into it. After he took a long sip, he checked his Kodak rangefinder, making sure it was ready to go on duty. He forgot to bring a newspaper, so he loaded up his Dunhill and lit up. Then he hunkered down and waited.

Percy, he thought.

What was he going to do about him? If he was correct about the kid, Percy might have another go at him. Maybe this time he wouldn't miss. Percy had been at the center of all the men in his mother's life. There seemed to be a never-ending stream of them. It all made sense to Eddie now. But Chanel herself wasn't out of the woods yet. She had a better motive for killing them than Percy. Her sister, Josette, even implied that Chanel was capable of murder. Could mother and son have planned and carried out these murders together, assuming Willis was also dead? One question eluded Eddie at the moment: if either Chanel or Percy had killed Thornton Hill—and the probability was great that one or the other had—how did Martin Boucher's wallet get in his pocket? Could Sylvie somehow have been involved in this too?

An hour went by. Still no movement in the house.

More coffee.

He turned the radio on. "Mr. Sandman" came on. He lowered the volume.

He tamped his pipe and then relit it. A quick glance at the house.

Puff-puff.

He tamped the ash down.

Puff-puff.

Another sip of coffee. It tasted good.

He adjusted the volume. A little higher this time. He liked the song.

His eye caught movement to his left. He shifted his gaze. Sylvie came out of the house. He picked up his Kodak rangefinder from the seat. Click-click. That done, he'd have to follow her, see what she was up to. Oops. Wait for her to get into the car. One more picture of her behind the wheel. Click.

Then—

The door opened again, and a man wearing an overcoat and hat came out of the house. Then another one. Click-click. They opened the doors of the car in the driveway. Click-click-click. The three of them inside—two in the front seat, one in the back. Click-click.

Eddie was too far from them to recognize the men. One of them, however, looked like his late-night visitor. The car pulled out into the street, turned left, and sped away. To follow or not to follow? No, he wanted to get the film developed right away.

He wanted to know who the other guy was.

———•«◉»•———

Eddie put his ear to the door. He could hear a voice. He knuckled the door twice and let himself in. Reginald Nithercott, claims adjuster for London Life Insurance Company, sat behind his desk alone.

"Talking to yourself again, Reggie?" Eddie asked.

"Thinking aloud would be a more accurate term, Mr. Wade. And it's Reginald, as you know."

"OK, Reginald, I've got some interesting information on the Boucher case," he said, sitting down in front of the desk. "And you're going to like it."

"*Interesting*, of course, is a nebulous word. Abstract even. I would prefer you use a more refined one."

"How about the word *fraud*? Is that refined enough for you?"

"You have my full and undivided attention." He adjusted his tie, scratched his mustache several times with his right index finger, and then folded his hands in front of him, fingers interlaced. He stared a hole through Eddie as if to demonstrate that his attention was truly undivided.

"First of all," Eddie said, "what was supposedly Martin Boucher's body was positively identified yesterday. It's not him."

Nithercott's eyebrows jumped a notch.

"And the cause of death, as we guessed, was the gunshot wound to the chest. For the moment, we have to keep this information to ourselves. The police haven't released this information to the press yet."

"Of course."

"Because Martin Boucher's wallet was found on the body, we could use that as evidence of fraud, because the only way it could have gotten there is if it was planted." He paused briefly after seeing Nithercott's expression. "OK, there could have been other ways, but I'm giving odds that it was planted. Any way you look at it, we need more evidence in case Sylvie Boucher hires some cute defense attorney or the judge sympathizes with her."

"I knew you were the right man for the job!"

Eddie took out the large manila envelope he'd brought with him, reached inside for the newly developed photos, and placed them in front of Nithercott, side by side.

"I took these pictures this morning and had them developed and enlarged. You can plainly see in this one," he said, pointing, "that Martin Boucher is alive and well. The other guy appeared at my office a few nights ago and threatened that if I continued to investigate Sylvie's claim, he'd return and take care of me. He implied he had a gun in his pocket. I believed him. I have a sneaking suspicion that that's against the law in the province of Quebec."

Nithercott munched on that for a moment and then said, "So, it appears that the three of them were in on this together."

"Bingo!"

"I don't understand something."

"What's that?" Eddie knew what was coming.

"How did Boucher's wallet get into the dead man's pocket?"

"Planted, like I said. Beyond that, I can only speculate."

"Speculate away for God's sake."

Eddie didn't want to tell him that the body was identified as Thornton Hill, only because he didn't feel like taking the time to go over the Steele case. It was too complicated. He would have to reveal too much information for the case to make sense to Nithercott. Although he trusted him, the fewer people who knew about the case, the better.

"The only way the wallet could have gotten on the body, at least the only way that makes sense to me, is if one of the three put it there. Whether the person was alive or dead at the time is another matter of speculation. The only thing at this point that matters to us is—"

"We have a case of fraud."

"Bingo again! We'll let the police figure out the rest."

"We have to proceed cautiously, Mr. Wade."

"Eddie, just Eddie."

"You win. We have to proceed cautiously, Eddie. If we rush it—you know, get the police involved right away—the wife will surely hire a cleaver defense attorney. He'll look carefully for any missteps we might make, any technicality that could get her off the hook. So, we have to have a plan."

Eddie thought about that for a moment. He wanted to look out the window, but there was none in the office.

Nithercott leaned back in his chair and looked up at the ceiling.

After a long minute, Eddie said, "How about you make out a check to Sylvie Boucher, and I personally take it to her? That would cinch it, wouldn't it? I'd be a witness that she took the check."

Nithercott leaned forward in his chair.

"You never know what the courts would do, but yes, that should put the nail in her coffin. But we'd have to have the police involved at that point to arrest her and her two accomplices."

"That sounds good then. Let me know when everything is set up. Can I use your phone?"

Nithercott pushed it toward him.

He dialed his answering service. Sully at the Ellis Detective Agency had left a message. He and Angie had completed the background on the Duponts, as he had requested.

When he hung up, Nithercott said, "I think I'll be able to get you a bonus for this. You saved us a lot of money."

"That's what I live for, Reggie," he said as he opened the door.

"I'll call soon, Mr. Wade."

Eddie knew it wouldn't last long.

As he was going through the front door of the building, he was looking straight ahead. Directly in front of him, sitting on a public bench across the street, was that bum again. Eddie stopped dead in his tracks. Once again, he was in a rush—this time to find out what Sully and Angie had dug up on the Dupont family. He was convinced the bum had been following him around town. Coincidences couldn't account for all the times he'd seen him.

Who was this guy? More importantly, what did he want?

Chapter 20
BLOODLINE

SULLY ELLIS SAT BEHIND HIS DESK, LEANING back with his hands behind his head and his shoes on his desk. Angie, his wife, was at her desk, finishing the report on the family background investigation of the Duponts for Eddie. Eddie was sitting in front of their two desks, smoking his pipe. Each had a glass of cognac in front of them.

"We would have had the report done sooner," Sully said, "but Angie and I drove down to Boston on Sunday to see the Canadians get their clocks cleaned in the semifinals."

"I saw the score in the paper: four to two," Eddie said. "They're still going to win the Cup."

Without looking up or stopping her typing, Angie said, "Fifty bucks says Detroit wins this year."

"You're on," Eddie said, puffing the words out with the smoke. "Did you guys stay the night?"

"Naw, we headed back right after the game. Took turns driving. Made it in six hours without breaking the speed limit."

"Mostly," Angie put in.

"Had to get your report done," Sully said.

"Why don't you give me the highlights, and I'll read the full report later?"

The Ellises were terrific researchers, so Eddie expected the report to be detailed.

"Sounds good to me," Sully said and downed the rest of his cognac. "Well, Guy Dupont was a direct descendent from the American branch of the family," Sully said. "You go back far enough, and you'll end up in France. At some point in the late eighteenth century, his part of the family crossed the border into Quebec—or to be more precise, Lower Canada—and put down roots."

"Anything directly related to the Steele case?"

Angie stopped typing and pulled the paper out of the machine. *ZZZip!* She put the paper under some other sheets and stapled them together.

"We don't know how directly related this is, but it sure is interesting," Angie said. "One of Guy Dupont's distant relatives here in Quebec was charged with murder in the middle of the 1800s. Pretty brutal." She winced. "It involved an ax. The official records and the local newspaper accounts weren't clear in the details, and we couldn't find anything that suggested he did any time. It was on a farm, and it involved a neighbor. Apparently, there had been a longstanding feud about land rights. The Duponts did have money, even back then, so he might have bought his way out of a prison sentence. But maybe not. It just wasn't clear."

Angie had long black hair that fell down her shoulders. Her olive skin, smooth and clean of any blemishes, and her facial features suggested Mediterranean, maybe southern Italian. She was petite and stood all of five three to Sully's six four. Eddie always felt that he could have fallen head over heels for her if circumstances had been different.

"Given the time period," Sully added, "it wouldn't have been uncommon, even for murder. Money can get you a lot of things. We couldn't find anything about the guy's mental state or how long exactly the feud went on for, except that it went on for a long time. The guy might have just blown his cork one day, and the ax was the handiest thing. Or he could have given considerable thought to it. And it didn't say anything about self-defense. We just don't know."

"The only other thing we found," Angie said, "that I know will brighten your universe was that Guy's great-grandfather was in and out of an insane asylum several times. No record of criminal activity, but that could have been hidden if there was any. Money again. The details are in the report. Also, Guy had a great-uncle who was in an insane asylum as well. We found only one newspaper article that gave an account of the man going after a family with a butcher knife. Plenty of blood spilled but no deaths."

"Murder and insanity in the Dupont family," Eddie said. "Well, that's something."

"Every family has its little secrets," Angie said, handing the report to Eddie.

"Thanks so much, guys. I owe you."

"Yes, you do," Sully said.

"And me, when the Red Wings win," Angie added.

Eddie left his car outside the agency and crossed Sainte-Catherine to Cabot Square. Although the street and shops had been cleaned up by the city's maintenance crews and business owners since the St. Patrick's Day riot over the treatment of Maurice Richard at the hands of the NHL, the square still looked awful, with broken glass and beer bottles strewn about. Eddie found a bench beside John Cabot's statue, sat down, and smoked his pipe. He wanted a few moments of undistracted thought. The Steele case was coming to a head, and he needed a plan. As of the moment, he had none.

Murder and insanity.

By no means was Eddie an expert on the subject, but he had taken an interest in how certain traits and characteristic were passed down from one generation to the next in families. He often wondered how bad blood from previous generations long ago could be passed on to the present. Was it like dripping contaminated water into an ocean? There would be little or no pollution. Or was it like dripping contaminated water into a thimble?

He'd read articles written by academics rather than the scientists themselves because of his lack of scientific knowledge. He was fascinated by the subject. He often wondered just how much of his father had been passed down to him. How much of his bad blood did he have in him? He supposed that was the underlying reason for the interest in the subject to begin with.

Some of the so-called science he knew to be utter nonsense. He'd never bought into the idea of eugenics in spite of the fact that some pretty prominent people had supported it. He knew he was right when the Nazis used the theory to purge people they thought were inferior. Now the movement was fully discredited. Still, he wondered whether the genetic makeup of a murderer or someone who was insane could be passed down to a family member. If so, was it passed down to each successive generation, or did it skip certain generations and then reappear decades later?

Murder and insanity.

Eddie had been a private investigator ever since the end of the war. He'd investigated many murders in the past, but never in his career had he seen so many murders and missing people associated with one person—except, of course, for the Mafia—as he had in the Steele case. Guy Dupont; Thornton Hill; Willis Steele; Luc Legrand. The common denominators: Chanel Steele and Percy Dupont.

Was Percy Dupont a murderer? Was he insane? Was he the one who had been infected with the bad Dupont blood? It made more sense than Chanel doing the killings, although both had motives. Was she covering them up to protect him, as he had been protecting her from these men? Were they in on this together?

If Percy was a killer, then he was dangerous.

Eddie didn't have any evidence that would stand up in court—it was all circumstantial at this point—but he had to do something before someone else was killed. Like him. But what? Maybe he could push Percy to the breaking point—Chanel as well—so that either one would do something incriminating.

He was treading on thin ice, but he had to do something now. Tonight.

Chapter 21
HIDDEN SECRETS

LATER THAT EVENING, EDDIE SAT IN HIS CAR ON avenue Mount-Pleasant in Westmount outside Chanel Steele's house. It wasn't actually a house—not really—and it didn't look very pleasant to him; it was a mansion by anyone's yardstick. *Mansions have names,* he thought. Did Chanel call hers "The Dupont"? Did she change the name after she married Willis? Maybe it was called "The Steele Manor" now. If so, there would be some irony in that. Nevertheless, the Victorian structure was concealed behind eight-foot-high privacy hedges—unseen, invisible from the world. *Hidden secrets,* he thought, *tucked away, out of sight.*

It was cold, so he left the car idling with the heat on. He turned the knob on the radio; Oscar Peterson was playing "Come Rain or Come Shine" on an all-night jazz station. He lowered the volume. Snowflakes were slowly falling, disappearing before his very eyes—melting as they hit the cement, leaving the street glistening under the streetlights, glittering in the urban landscape of the wealthy in Westmount as in a watercolor painting—dazzling and splendid, misty and mysterious—the colors running into one another, forming new shades, some with a hint of spirited, uplifting complexity, some with a hint of dark obscurity that ran as deep as the soul. Falling snowflakes, slowly falling, melting away, disappearing, transmuting, resplendent under the night skies—marvelous, vivid, intense, and deadly hypnotic.

Secrets.

Everyone had them. Some wouldn't tell their secrets to another person, except maybe to their closest friends. Others wouldn't even dare tell them to their friends, keeping them safely to themselves. And yet there were still others who were deathly afraid even to acknowledge their secrets to themselves—a burden far too great, so they stored them away forever, out of sight. Eddie had his fair share of those. So did Chanel, he guessed. So did Percy.

As a general rule, Eddie avoided confrontations like the plague. Not that he didn't have enough confidence in himself to handle most situation. He had, and he did. It was just that confrontations were, to a great extent, unpredictable. In point of fact, he found the behavior of people rather predictable, but under certain circumstances, when life went sideways, when the flames rose from a fire high enough to burn the flesh off an otherwise rational person, the ensuing response was always problematic. Thus, Eddie could either make a wild dash like an Olympic runner or stand his ground with lethal intensity. He certainly had done both. But given the choice, he preferred to deal with problems that had predictably peaceful outcomes, so that both parties could walk away in one piece, with the issue resolved to the mutual satisfaction of both.

But sometimes that wasn't always possible.

Like now.

Instead of avoiding a confrontation, Eddie was going to use it as a means of pushing Chanel (and Percy if he was there) into doing or saying something reckless so that she'd show her hand. It was risky business, but Eddie wasn't reckless. The evidence, albeit circumstantial, pointed to Percy. His accusations against Percy were going to be so serious and spoken with such fervor that any response to them would be unpredictable. That was why he had brought his .45 semiautomatic with him. After all, three people were dead, one was missing and presumed dead, and he had been shot at. Under the circumstances, it was a reasonable thing to do.

For the next fifteen minutes, as the snow kept falling, occasionally being blown sideways by gusts of wind, and glistening under the streetlights, he sat there rehearsing what he was going to say. Then imagining any number of possible responses, he addressed each one. It would lessen his chances of saying something foolish and unproductive but wouldn't fully eliminate the risk. Would she have a gun at her fingertips? Would Percy? The murder weapon was probably somewhere in the house. The situation cut through him with a serrated blade; there was an element of unpredictability that he just couldn't avoid.

He turned off the engine and sighed heavily. This wasn't the first time he'd been hired by a client to investigate a crime that Eddie later found out had been committed by the client or someone very close to them. He was getting tired of it. He got out of his car and walked up the cement path. He rang the doorbell and waited. Instead of the maid answering the door, Chanel did. She was wearing dark slacks with a woolen jumper, her hair flowing over her shoulders. Eddie took a few seconds to admire her beauty, like a spider admiring his mate just before she devoured the poor soul after copulating with him.

"Eddie!" she said, surprised. "I wasn't expecting you."

"Sorry for the intrusion, but I need to go over something with you, and it can't wait."

He followed her to the sitting room to the left of the vestibule. He glanced to his right to see whether the armless Venus de Milo was still there. It was—armless, helpless. Once inside, Chanel closed the door. He was inside her web.

"Take off your coat and hat and have a seat, Eddie. Would you like a drink? I was just going to pour one for myself."

"I'm fine on both accounts."

"You sound so serious, Eddie," she said, pouring a whiskey. She walked to the love seat, sat down, and then crossed one leg over the other. She patted the cushion. "Come sit beside me."

She had stopped calling him ducky. He didn't know whether that was a good thing or bad.

"I'm fine," he said again. "I can't stay long."

"I could take offense with that." She lowered her head coquettishly and pouted.

Without moving his head, he scanned the room as much as possible, especially around Chanel. He was concerned about a gun. There weren't many places right around her where one could be hidden. He hoped there wasn't one under the cushion she was sitting on.

He caught her eyes. "It's Percy."

"What about Percy?" She flicked the tip of her tongue out slightly, and then her lips curled up at the sides.

Outside in the car at the last minute, he'd decided to talk to her as if she were innocent of knowing anything about what he believed Percy had done. He wanted to see her reaction. If she knew or had conspired with Percy, she would be defensive about the accusations. She'd perceive that Eddie was attacking her personally instead of defending Percy.

"I have reason to believe that Percy killed his father because he was cheating on you."

The room suddenly became as silent and cold as Kaffeklubben Island.

"You're kidding, right?" she asked, the smile frozen in place.

"He also killed Thornton Hill because he was beating you."

"You're not kidding, are you?" The smile became a pucker, and the skin between her eyebrows creased into rivulets of uncertainty. She tried to say something more but wasn't successful.

"What had Willis been doing to you that warranted his murder?"

She was shocked into silence.

"Percy had the combination of the safe. In all probability, he took the money and jewels as a ruse to set up Willis. They're probably somewhere in the house. When you hired me to find Willis, Percy got nervous, so he went after me with the same gun he used to kill the others. The police have the evidence; all they need is the gun. That, too, is probably somewhere in the house."

The door suddenly opened. Eddie and Chanel turned their heads at the same time. It was Percy.

"Come on in," Eddie said, "and join the party. It's a small one, but I think you'll like it. And while you're here, why don't you explain to your mother why you've been seeing your father's personal prostitute, Samantha L'Amour." He turned to Chanel. "Her clients call her Sam for short." He turned back to Percy. "Isn't that right, Percy?" After a moment, he said, "Speak up, Percy. We can't hear you. Tell your mother all about it. You should probably leave all the juicy details out though. It wouldn't be right. What's wrong, Percy? Cat got your tongue?"

Percy looked like a trapped animal with nowhere to run. He looked at Eddie and then at his mother.

"I just came in to see whether you wanted some tea." The words came out slowly and softly.

Eddie pushed even harder.

"Were you planning on killing Sam as well, Percy? While you're at it, why don't you give us the lowdown on Luc Legrand? You can explain how you stalked him outside his house and shot him." He turned to Chanel and said, "He knew about your affair with him. He's quite the little killer, you know."

Chanel suddenly stood up. She began screaming at Eddie.

"That's enough! You're absolutely insane!"

Insane? Eddie thought a moment about bringing up the insanity found in the Dupont lineage but decided against it, even though it was on the tip of his tongue.

"Where's the gun, Percy? The cops are going to find it eventually."

"Get out of my house right now!" Chanel shouted. "You're fired. I never want to see you again! Leave!"

"That's fine with me, sis," Eddie said, not taking his eyes off of Percy but talking to Chanel. "I'll send you my bill, but the case isn't over yet. The police will stop by with a mop and bucket in a day or two, after I have a nice, long talk with them."

"Get out now!"

Eddie got out.

He sat in his car again and turned on the engine.

Well, that was interesting, he thought.

Eddie believed Chanel had acted with genuine disbelief. It was difficult but not impossible to feign that. Anything was possible, but he no longer believed that Chanel knew anything about what Percy had been up to. She wasn't out of the woods entirely, but it did give Eddie something to focus on: Percy.

He was sure Percy had been listening at the door before he came into the room. The kid said nothing in his own defense. He had that same look on his face—the vacant stare, the mouth slightly parted—as Eddie had seen on the faces of criminals when they were confronted with their crimes and had never thought ahead of time to come up with excuses because they never thought they'd be caught. He had his killer.

But how was he going to prove it?

He needed the murder weapon, and he needed to find the body of Willis Steele. Finding the body was going to be nearly impossible without a confession from Percy.

By all accounts, Chanel had pampered Percy and protected him from the cruel, hard realities of the world. To show his gratitude, Percy protected her from her lack of judgment concerning men by killing them. He could kill again, if so provoked. Maybe Eddie was next in line. The Dupont insanity hadn't skipped Percy. Eddie had to do something and soon. But what? In spite of what he'd told Chanel, he couldn't go to the police. The evidence wouldn't hold up in court. He'd have to do something himself, but Chanel had just fired him again.

He never let little details get in the way. He put the car into gear and drove away.

Inside the mansion, Chanel and Percy were recovering from the slings and arrows of Eddie Wade's outrageous accusations.

"I could still get you some tea, Mother, if you want some," Percy said. "It's Irene's night off."

"Oh, forget the tea, Percy," Chanel snapped. "Can't you see I poured a drink for myself?"

"I'm sorry if I offended you, Mother. That was not my intent."

They were sitting on the love seat, looking into the fireplace. It was blazing.

"Didn't you hear what that moron said about you? You were listening at the door, weren't you?"

"Mr. Wade's voice was quite loud. It caught my attention when I was walking by."

"Then you know the terrible things he said about you. I wish I had never hired him in the first place."

"Do you think what he said was true? Do you think I murdered all those men, even my father?"

"Percy, how could you ask me that?" she said, wounded by Percy's question.

"If one doesn't ask, how would one know? I'm sorry that I—"

"Stop apologizing, Percy. You have nothing to apologize for. It's that awful man who should be apologizing to you. He said some dreadful things about you. We shouldn't let him get away with that."

"Is there something I could do, Mother?"

"I just don't know, Percy. I should have said something more to him to defend you. It's just that he took me completely by surprise. He said he was going to the police to tell them. This could ruin my reputation—our reputation. I just don't know what to do." She shook her head and then took a sip of her drink. "I just don't know."

For a moment, she thought about asking her son about Samantha. Of course, she knew Guy had been seeing her; knew it from the very beginning. She knew all the gory details, but that was a long time ago. Water under the bridge. But Wade had said that Percy was seeing her too. Was this true? Percy seeing a prostitute? Of course not. After Wade found out about Guy and Sam, he must have decided to make up a story about Percy to torture her. Not that she was tortured about Guy. She had Luc Legrand after all. And how did he find out about him? Did Percy really know about him as well?

"Yes, I heard him say he was going to the police. Do you think he will? Maybe he was just threatening us."

"Maybe, but if he could accuse you of something so absurd as murder, he might be capable of anything. If he does go to the police, we might have a big fight on our hands. This little nest of ours might be disrupted, maybe beyond repair."

"That wouldn't be good at all. Right, Mother?"

"No, it wouldn't be good at all, Percy."

Chanel turned to her son and thought she saw the wheels spinning in his brain. Maybe it was just the reflection of the fire she saw in his eyes.

Later that night, a few hours after Percy had spun his wheels sufficiently in Westmount, Eddie and Josette were having dinner.

The Café de L'Est, as one might guess, lay east of downtown on Notre Dame, down by the river just off the Jacques-Cartier Bridge. It was as close as restaurants in Montreal came to being Parisian. Eddie hadn't wasted any time in inviting Josette out for the night. If this was going to be his only chance with her, he wanted something special, something memorable to leave her with. If it turned out to be the beginning of something serious, then this was just the right spot—a cabaret with the best French food in town, along with a magic show and song and dance. Besides, he needed a night out with a date; he couldn't remember the last time he'd been on one.

The café was packed for a Tuesday night. They had a table at the edge of the large stage. A magician wearing black tails was performing his act, while Eddie and Josette were halfway through dinner. After a few glasses of wine, they had started with a Lyonnaise salad made of frisée lettuce, tossed in a warm vinaigrette and topped with crispy bacon and a poached egg. After that, the waiter had brought Eddie boeuf bourguignon, a beef stew made with red wine, pearl onions, mushrooms, and bacon. Josette had ordered coq au vin, a red wine chicken stew also from Burgundy. Eddie was impressed by her appetite; it equaled his, even though she was petite.

After a piece of beef melted in his mouth and he swallowed it, he asked Josette how she liked her chow.

She gave him a coy smile.

"If you mean *'Comment est cette magnifique cuisine française?'* I would have to say that it's gorgeous. How's your chow?"

Embarrassed somewhat, he said, "Mine's gorgeous too!"

They both giggled at that.

They were mostly quiet while they ate, even somewhat shy. Eddie was known to be a lot of things, but shy wasn't one of them. He didn't know whether it was because the food was so good and they were enjoying it so much, or they were both slightly uncomfortable with each other in this particular setting. That certainly hadn't been the case the two times they had met before. Maybe he should have taken her to a smaller, more intimate restaurant with fewer distractions.

Their attention was drawn to the stage at the same time. The magician was showing his top hat to the audience. He reached inside it—nothing! He spun the hat around a few times and then reached his hand inside again, and this time, he pulled out a white rabbit. Everyone set their forks and knives down and chapped. It was a standard trick, but it always elicited the *oohs* and *aahs* on cue. Josette leaned over the table a little and whispered to Eddie, asking him how the magician did that. Eddie leaned in and whispered back that he didn't know, but he was thinking about hiring him. Maybe he could pull Willis out of the hat too.

The magician took a bow and left the stage. Spirited music started playing, and five seconds later, a line of girls dressed in colorful costumes with long feathers sticking out every which way danced in a row onto the stage, not unlike what one would see at the Moulin Rouge.

At the same time, a waiter came to their table and collected the plates and silverware, while another placed espresso and crème brûlée in front of them. It was difficult to have a conversation, so they enjoyed the show and ate their dessert. When they finished, Eddie suggested they go to one of the cozier bars inside the restaurant.

It was far less crowded. They found a table in the back and ordered drinks.

Eddie wanted to avoid talking about work. It was a night out for him, and he didn't want to spoil it by bringing up the

Steeles. He wanted to tell Josette that her sister just fired him today because he accused Percy of being a murderer, but this was the wrong time and the wrong place.

"So, have you ever been married?" he asked instead. Josette must have been around his age, give or take, so he thought it was a reasonable question to ask.

"Nothing like jumping in without testing the water first," she said, laughing. "The answer is no; I've never been married before. Twice, I was going with guys who wanted to get married, but they were fairly traditional. They wanted a wife who would have children and sit in their cute little house, waiting for them to come home from, work with their slippers, a newspaper, and a pipe, and, of course, with a four-course meal on the table waiting for them. There's nothing wrong with that—there really isn't—but I wasn't the right one for them. Not by a longshot. How about you?"

"Almost once. She couldn't see being married to a private investigator."

"Really? I would think it would be exciting! Such a shame."

"It's not very exciting most of the time. A lot of hard work and frustration."

"Just the same, it must be very interesting. I like what I'm doing, and there's definitely a future in it, but I'm stuck in the shop every day of the week, and the work can be tedious, even boring at times. But there is security in the job, so that's something." She paused a moment to sip her drink. "Being an investigator—one day has got to be so different than the next day."

"It is, but sometimes I wish it wasn't. Sometimes I could do with a little boredom."

"Is it dangerous?"

"Mostly not, but it can be. You just never know."

"Have you ever known a female investigator?"

"They're around, but I know only one personally, and she's

very good at what she does. She works with her husband. They make a great team."

"A team! Wow! Husband and wife gumshoes. Now that's something!" She stared off into space for a moment. Then she brought her face back to Eddie, looking directly into his eyes. "What do you say we finish our drinks here and then go to my place for a little nightcap? We can kick off our shoes, relax, listen to a little soft music, and continue our conversation. It'll be fun!"

Nothing like taking charge of the situation. Eddie wasn't antipathetic to that idea, not by a longshot.

"What say we do!"

Chapter 22
A SURPRISE AND THEN ANOTHER

THE NEXT DAY, WEDNESDAY, AT 9:00 A.M. SHARP, Eddie phoned Mrs. Sylvie Boucher to say he'd be at her house at noon with the check from London Life. As the sole beneficiary of her husband's life insurance policy, she was entitled to the $20,000. She sounded a little more chipper on the phone than the last time he'd seen her at her house. Once she had the check in her hand, she could be arrested on the spot. However, he also needed her not-so-dead husband, Martin, as well as the other male accomplice, the one who had appeared at Eddie's office and threatened him. To do that, Mrs. Boucher had to have surveillance on her after he delivered the check so that she'd lead Eddie to them, if they hadn't already shown up at her house.

At a little before noon, Eddie pulled up to the pale yellow clapboard house on rue Blondin in Rosemont and parked. Her car was in the driveway. He walked up the path and knocked on the door. It opened immediately. She must have been on the lookout for him.

"Mr. Wade," she said, "how nice to see you."

She was definitely more cheerful. She was wearing a colorful, flowered dress—quite the contrast to the black dress she'd been wearing when he first met her. This time, she had makeup on. Eddie had to admit she looked quite attractive—sexy even—someone he might have been interested in if circumstances had been different.

"Hi," Eddie said. "Can I come in? I need you to sign a few papers."

He followed her to the living room, and they sat down on the couch. He placed the folder he was carrying on the coffee table in front of them.

"Would you like something to drink? Coffee, tea—maybe something stronger?"

She had a great smile. She seemed like a different woman. But why wouldn't she? Twenty grand, even split three ways, is still a lot of money. Eddie made a wild guess that her mourning days had ended.

"No thanks, Mrs. Boucher. I've been drinking coffee all morning. I'm coffeed out, and it's a little too early for a drink."

He opened the folder and reached into his pocket for a pen.

"I just need your signature on a few places here," he said, angling the papers toward her. "London Life's a stickler on paperwork, you know." He pointed to the places on the three documents where she had to sign her name. "You should read each one before you sign."

"Oh, that won't be necessary," she said as she signed her name to each one. "Most of the time, lawyers write these legal documents, and you have to have a translator to understand them."

That was fine with Eddie. In large print on the third sheet, just above her signature, was the following statement: "Fraud committed against London Life Insurance Company is a criminal offense." It was both in English and French. It wouldn't need to be translated.

He gathered up the documents and reached into his inner pocket of his coat and took out the envelope with the check.

"And this belongs to you," he said.

She took it from him and set it on the coffee table.

"I want to say again how very sorry we are for the loss of your husband. I know these are trying times for you."

She took the linen handkerchief she'd been holding and dabbed her eyes, which were as dry as two shrivelled-up raisins.

"Not having Martin here has been terribly difficult, Mr. Wade. His clothes, his stamp collection, his toothbrush in the bathroom—I keep thinking he's going to walk in any minute and ask me what we're having for supper. Yes, it's been difficult."

Sniff-sniff; dab-dab.

She would probably be having supper with her dearly departed, miraculously resurrected husband tonight. Eddie wondered what they were going to have to eat. At their house or a restaurant?

"I hope you have friends or family to help you through this."

"Oh, yes. They've been wonderful. But at the end of the day, it's just me and this empty house."

Eddie didn't know what to say to that, so he said nothing. She was playing her part well. He stood up with the folder containing the papers with her signatures.

"I'll be leaving now. If you have any questions or concerns, please be sure to contact London Life."

He walked to his car, got in and started it, and drove two blocks south. He spotted a black, four-door Ford Fairlane sedan with two men inside wearing fedoras, parked at the side of the road. Eddie pulled up behind them. He got out of the car, walked up to the Ford, opened the back door, and got inside.

"Bingo," he said, holding up the folders.

"You got her signature?" the guy in the passenger seat asked. "Got to see it for myself before we go any further."

Eddie handed the folder up to the guy. He opened it and looked at all three sheets.

"That cinches it," he said. "Let's move."

The driver started the car and pulled out from the curb.

After it had become apparent to London Life that they were dealing with a fraud case, claims adjuster Reginald Nithercott arranged with the police department to have two plainclothes detectives accompany Eddie so that they could do the surveillance and make the arrests. Johnny Longchamp sat behind the wheel; Myron Banaszynski sat shotgun. Both men were close to retirement. Easy assignment. No legwork required.

"That's the house, the yellow one," Eddie said, pointing between the detectives.

Johnny pulled to the curb across the street and four houses down from the Bouchers. They had a good view; Sylvie's car was still in the driveway.

"Hey," Myron said, looking over his shoulder at Eddie, "we ID'd that photo Reggie gave us. You know, the one you took of that guy leaving the house?"

"Who is he?" Eddie asked.

"He's a two-bit hood by the name of Cosmo Degaré."

"He's got a rap sheet as long as my dick," Johnny chimed in. "I had the privilege of putting him in Bordeaux for two years back in '48. A real asshole. I hope we end up getting that son of a bitch today."

"What about Martin Boucher?" Eddie asked. "Any record?"

"Clean as a whistle," Myron said. "That is until we nab him."

They were quiet for the next hour. No activity at the Boucher house.

"What the hell is she doing in there?" Johnny asked. "I

would think she'd be off to the bank to cash her check by now. Or meet up with her husband."

"I hope we're not going to be here all damn day," Myron said. "My better half and I have tickets to see Carmen Basilio whip Tony DeMarco at the Forum tonight. My wife will kill me if we miss that. By the way, anyone want to bet against Basilio? Any takers? Ten bucks says Carmen knocks him out in five."

Silence.

"Cowards. You could have beaten either one, Eddie. That left hook of yours was wicked, man. I once saw you lift Jack Banyan off the canvas at least four inches. He was stone-cold for five minutes. You should have stayed in the game."

"My knee, remember? The war."

"Yeah, that was a crying shame. You could have been the middleweight champion of the world—another Marcel Cerdan. With your size, you probably would have gone up to light heavyweight or even heavyweight. I always said that—"

The front door of the Boucher house opened and then closed again. That caught the attention of all three of them.

"OK," Johnny said, "a little action! Come on, sweet lady. Come on out and take us to daddy."

The door swung open again, and this time Sylvie came out—alone. She locked up the house and got into her car. She backed out of the driveway and drove up the street. Johnny started the Ford and let her get up away before pulling out. They followed her at a distance to Assumption going south, eventually ending up on Notre-Dame.

"She's meeting them in town somewhere," Eddie said.

They followed her to St. Laurent going north. When she hit Dorchester, she made a right, drove another six or seven blocks, made another right turn onto Mountain, and parked. Johnny passed her as she was getting out of the car. He quickly pulled over, and they all got out.

"She turned left," Myron said, pointing. "Let's go!"

They were all on Dorchester in time for them to see Sylvie go into Slitkin's and Slotkin's, a popular downtown restaurant; the food was fast and good.

"I'll go in and see if all three are there," Myron said. "None of them know me."

Five minutes later, he came out.

"They're sitting in the back," Myron said. "All three of them. I walked by them. They were having drinks and laughing like thieves. Sylvie was waving the check around and kissing it. It's pretty crowded in there. Johnny, what say we let them celebrate and then take them when they come out? Safer that way, in case they put up a fuss."

"Sounds good to me," Johnny said. He turned to Eddie. "You staying for the show? It could be awhile."

"I don't think you boys need my help. As long as I'm downtown, I think I'll go see Reggie and give him the lowdown. Make his day. Maybe he'll even pay me."

"Your car's sitting in Rosemont," Myron said.

"I'll get a ride from Reggie. That's the least he could do. I bid you adieu, gentlemen. Bonne chance." He turned and walked a few steps and then turned around again. "Myron, I never told you this, but I once sparred with Basilio in Canastota."

"Jesus, no."

"I knocked him down with that left hook you were talking about. I was a little embarrassed to tell you before now. He was sixteen at the time, long before he turned pro. I didn't mean to hit him so hard, you know. He was only a kid. That was a few years before I went in the army, at the end of my career. I was in Canastota for a fight, and he was one of the amateurs I sparred with to prepare for the fight."

"Jesus, Eddie. You knocked down Carmen? What happened then?"

"He got up and knocked me down. I saw stars for the next half hour. I wouldn't have beaten him on a good day."

"Jesus."

———«◉»———

Late that night, Eddie sat at the bar of the Flamingo with Reginald Nithercott, claims adjuster extraordinaire of London Life Insurance Company. Eddie had gone to his office to tell him the good news after leaving the two detectives outside of Slitkin's and Slotkin's. Nithercott had been so relieved that he offered to buy Eddie a drink for the occasion. The drink had turned into many, and as the clock was approaching ten, they were still sitting there. Eddie had decided to take the tram home and pick up his car tomorrow.

"You know, Eddie," Nithercott said, "I'm glad we decided to go out tonight. We've known each other for eons now, and yet I somehow feel I know you better now on a personal level."

Nithercott had dispensed with "Mr. Wade." It was all *Eddie* now.

Eddie stared at him and smiled, holding up his drink as if in a toast.

"Well, thank you, Reggie. The feeling's mutual."

Nithercott flattened out his mustache with the tips of his thumb and forefinger.

"It's quite all right. No need to verbalize your grat ... grat ... gratitude." He was beginning to show signs that he had reached his limit. "It is I, however," he continued, with a nod of his head and the palm of his hand flat against his chest, "who need to show you my grat ... grat ... gratitude for assuaging the legitimate concerns of the executives upstairs on the fifth floor. They can be bastards, you know. You saved the company a whopping sum of money by exposing the Bouchers' insidious sub ... sub ... subversive scheme."

Nithercott was a fastidious, single-minded bore. He looked at the world in terms of black and white with nary a hint of gray. His habits and mannerisms were such that they could send a grown adult reeling into a corner of a room, weeping from anguish and frustration. Yet he was an exceptional claims adjuster, a solid citizen who did his civic duties, and a pretty good all-around guy. Eddie liked him.

They said their goodbyes at the bar, and Eddie stepped outside into the chilly night. He stretched, breathing in the fresh air, and then proceeded down the street toward Dorchester to catch a tram to Mile End. As he got to a narrow alleyway between two buildings where garbage cans were kept, a man appeared from around a car and called his name. Eddie stopped, turning his head in that direction.

"Mr. Wade," the person said again.

"Percy," Eddie said, astonished. "What are you doing?"

Percy held his right arm out straight, pointing a gun at Eddie. He walked forward a few steps, backing Eddie into the shadows of the alley. Eddie held his arms up at the elbows. His .45 was strapped under his arm, but there was no possible way to get at it without being shot first. The kid was standing about three feet in front of him.

"You said some very bad things about me last night; you used some very harsh words. You made my mother upset. I'd have to say your behavior was shameful."

All of that had happened so fast and unexpectedly that Eddie was at a loss for words, yet he had to say something, anything.

"I'm sorry she was upset, Percy. We can talk this out, but first you should put the gun down."

The war suddenly flashed in his mind—Germany. After all he'd gone through, after all the heartache and bloodshed, after all the pain and agony of liberating Germans from maniacs, here he was, about to be murdered in a dark alley by some insane kid who was trying to protect his mother from—what—harsh words?

"You weren't very nice to me, Mr. Wade. My mother was very distraught after you left."

"I know, Percy, and I'm sorry, but that gun isn't going to solve anything. Let's talk about it."

"You should have stayed fired the first time. That way, things would be fine now."

Eddie's eyes caught movement in front of him. The silhouette of a large man appeared behind Percy. He reached for Percy's wrist and directed the gun upward, and then he clubbed Percy on the back of his neck just below his head with the side of his opened hand. It was a terrific blow. The gun fell to the cement, and Percy collapsed after it.

Eddie moved forward, knelt down, and picked up the gun. He looked up; Branch York was staring down at him. Two surprises in one night.

"Branch!" he said, standing up. "Where did you come from?"

"I was downtown at the bank, across the street from Slitkin's and Slotkin's, when I saw you standing on the corner. I followed you to that insurance company, and then I followed you and that other guy to the Flamingo. I waited for you to come out. I was going to rough you up a bit, teach you a lesson about blaming the theft on Willis. Then I saw this kid hiding between two cars when you came out of the bar. I knew something was off. Then I saw him pull his piece on you. That's when I came to my senses. I don't like you, but I don't want to see you dead."

"I'm grateful; thank you. You saved my life."

"I'm still pissed that you think Willis stole the jewels and money."

Eddie asked York to call the police from the Flamingo. When he came back, they talked while waiting for a prowl car to arrive. Eddie couldn't tell him much about the Steele case, but he did say that Willis was no longer a suspect. York seemed relieved. Without giving too much detail, Eddie went on to tell him that his friend was probably dead. He didn't want York to learn about it from the newspapers. He took it hard. He left as you might expect one would leave after hearing that his best friend had been murdered: completely dejected.

Percy had been knocked unconscious by the blow. He was lying where he fell. Soon after York left, he started to come to.

"Just lie still, Percy. Help is on the way."

He moaned and tried to get up.

"Stay still. Don't move. You might have a concussion."

Eddie tried to make him as comfortable as possible. He took his hat off and wedged it under Percy's head. He didn't harbor any ill will toward the kid. He felt sorry for him—the Dupont insanity. In a way, the murders weren't Percy's fault. He had contaminated blood, passed down from generation to generation. Unfortunately, it hadn't skipped him. He wasn't responsible for that, so how could he be responsible for the murders?

Eddie felt guilty about involving the police. More than anything, the kid needed help, not punishment. He needed a psychiatrist, not a prison cell. Of course, he had to be kept away from society, but Eddie couldn't see how being locked up at Bordeaux would help him. He was certain that the province wouldn't execute him. He just hoped that they'd take mercy on him and put him in a hospital rather than behind bars.

Eddie finally had the evidence against Percy in his hand: the gun. The police would run a ballistic test on it, matching it to the bullets that killed Guy Dupont, Thornton Hill, Luc Legrand, and to the ones found in his office wall. Percy probably used the same gun to kill Willis Steele.

Wherever he was.

Chapter 23
IT WON'T MATTER

EDDIE GRABBED A TAXI TO ROSEMONT TO PICK up his car, then drove to the house on avenue Mount-Pleasant. It was as black as a psychopath's soul.

He turned off the ignition and sat still outside Chanel's house. Either the police had gotten there already to break the news and take her down to headquarters, so she wasn't at home, or she was at home and asleep. Perhaps she was merely sitting alone in her bedroom, enveloped by the darkness, protected and nourished by the four walls like a womb, with her knees pulled up to her chin, her arms around her legs, her eyes closed, her hair gently hanging down at the sides.

Whatever the reason for the stony stillness of the mansion, he felt despondent. Notwithstanding the fact that Percy was a murderer, he deserved a certain amount of compassion. A killer pointing a gun at his victim would elicit little sympathy from most people, but Percy hadn't been able to control his animal impulses; there was little he could do when bad blood coursed through his veins. Civilized society had little patience for people like him—and maybe rightly so. But to merely punish without compassion was a horrifying thought to Eddie.

And then there was Chanel. Was she not deserving of

compassion as well? It would be ravaging for any mother to find out that her son was mentally ill and a murderer. Over the course of the last two weeks, Eddie had grown to dislike Chanel intensely. But now, he couldn't help but feel sorry for her. He hoped that the police hadn't been there yet; better that she learn the news about Percy from him than a stranger.

Eddie got out of the car and walked up the long path, feeling as if he were walking a road that led to purgatory, where the souls of sinners were expiating their sins. He knocked on the door and waited. He kept knocking for the next five minutes. Finally, the overhead light went on, and the door opened. Chanel was in a bathrobe. He could smell liquor on her breath at a distance that he shouldn't have been able to.

"Before you slam the door on my face, I need to talk to you. It's about Percy."

"Percy's upstairs sleeping. What's this about?" Half-drunk and half-asleep, the words stumbled out of her mouth, tumbling head over heels before plummeting to the floor.

"He's not upstairs. Can I come in?"

Once again, he followed her into the sitting room. She immediately poured some whiskey for herself. She didn't offer one to Eddie. She turned around, facing him.

"So talk," she said. "I need my beauty sleep."

"I'm afraid that's going to have to wait. The police have Percy, and he's in a lot of trouble."

She flinched and then set her drink down. She darted out of the room. Eddie could hear her calling Percy's name as she ran up the staircase. She was back downstairs after a few minutes.

She picked up her drink and gulped half of it down.

"Tell me what happened, goddammit. It's probably your fault with your incessant nosing around."

Eddie's compassion had its limits. She was a nasty witch, standing in front of him. The strands of her hair were twisted and went every which way. Her woolen bathrobe made her look twenty pounds heavier. Her breath reeked. Without her makeup, she was just another person. Maybe this was as disgusting as she ever got. Served her right. But her eyes glowed hatred, unsettling him. He tried hard not to let her affect him. What he was about to say might cause another firestorm. He wanted to be compassionate, but she was making it difficult for him.

"I already told you what he did last night, but you threw me out of the house. Tonight, he pulled a gun on me. He was going to kill me. I'd be dead right now if someone hadn't been there to help."

She plopped into an armchair. Was she surrendering, or was this another one of her little games?

"He had a gun? Oh my God." She started crying; her tears seemed genuine.

"He's probably being interrogated right now. He's in a lot of trouble. You'll need to get him a good lawyer, maybe a team of them, experienced in homicide."

She looked up at Eddie. She wiped her face with the palm of her hand, suddenly appearing more sober than drunk.

"Why would he want to harm you?"

Eddie was getting impatient.

"Chanel, we went over this last night. He killed his father and Thornton Hill. He probably killed Luc Legrand. He tried to kill me nine days ago, a few days after you hired me to find Willis. The police have the gun; they'll match it to the bullets. He tried to kill me again tonight. He knew I was onto him. In all likelihood, he killed Willis and stole your jewels and money to make it seem like Willis took off with them. He did all of this to protect you. At least that was how he rationalized it. Your son is seriously disturbed."

"I refuse to believe he did all those things. He's a little different, but he's no murderer."

Eddie didn't want to bring this up, but he had no choice now.

"You're not seeing this the way you should. You're too

close to him. I had some investigators look into the history of the Dupont family. They discovered something alarming. I don't know whether you're aware of this, but there was insanity in the family. Two family members, maybe more. It skipped generations but not his."

She stood up.

"That isn't true. You're wrong."

"I wish I were. You said yourself that Percy is a little different. I'm afraid he's more than just a little different."

"Yes, I said that, but I never said he was capable of murder."

"I'm really sorry about this, Chanel."

"You should be." She paced the room for a minute. In spite of the heat from the words exchanged, the room was artic cold and silent. Suddenly, she turned to face him. "I never told a soul about this, so don't you dare either. I'll have you crucified if you do, if it's the last thing I ever do. Percy is not a Dupont, at least not by blood. I was pregnant with him for a month before I married Guy. I kept it a secret all these years. Even Guy hadn't known."

They stared at each other for a long moment. Eddie couldn't believe what he'd just heard.

"So, who *is* Percy's father, if you don't mind me asking?"

She stared daggers at him.

"OK, that's fine; it's none of my business. I shouldn't have asked."

That didn't change anything. As far as the courts would be concerned, the motive was the same. In Percy's twisted mind, he murdered those men in the belief that he was protecting his mother from harm. Maybe he wasn't insane after all; maybe he was just a killer with a mission in life, plain and simple. That was for the Crown attorney and the courts to decide.

Eddie walked to the door to let himself out. Before reaching for the doorknob, he turned around.

"If the bullets match up to his gun—and they will—it won't matter who Percy's father is."

—————————«•»—————————

From there, he drove to Josette's apartment. He knew she had to get up at four o'clock and would be sleeping, but he had to tell her what happened, and it had to come from him. The apartment was a few blocks south of the Fournier Pâtisserie. With little traffic, he made it in fifteen minutes.

After he pounded on the door for a few minutes, Josette finally opened it.

"Eddie," she said sleepily. "It's late."

"Sorry, Josette, but we've got to talk. Can I come in?"

"Of course," she said, stepping to the side to let him in. "Talk about what?"

Eddie took off his hat and coat and threw them on a chair. They sat on the couch in the living room. The apartment was small but nicely furnished. Eddie told her about what had happened yesterday, about his accusations against Percy and about her sister firing him. She listened wide-eyed, not interrupting him. And then he told her what had happened that night.

"Oh, my God!" she said when he finished. She was fully awake now. "He had a gun? Percy? He's a strange kid, but do you really think he's capable of murder? Capable of killing his own father?"

"He was pointing a loaded gun at me, Josette. I'm only alive right now because someone stopped him. But it really doesn't matter what I think he's capable of doing. It's the evidence that counts. And the evidence points directly to him. When the police run the gun through ballistics, it's all over for him. And there's something else."

"God, I don't think I'm ready for anything else," she said, pulling her legs up onto the couch and wrapping her arms around them. "What is it?"

"I was with Chanel tonight, just before I came here. She told me that Guy Dupont wasn't Percy's real father. She'd been pregnant with him by a month when she married Guy. She said she hadn't told Guy."

"Does Percy know?"

"She didn't say, but she did say that she hadn't told a soul."

They both stopped talking. Eddie could see that she was thinking.

"Then it must be Willis. She was going with him up until she got married to Guy. That's got to be it."

"That's what I figured. Maybe Percy figured it out too. So, he wasn't killing his biological father, Guy."

"What are you going to do?"

"There's nothing left to do. I can only believe that Percy killed Willis as well. He probably stole Chanel's money and jewels to make it seem as if Willis had done it and then skipped out. We don't know for sure whether or not he knew Willis was his real father. It's up to the police now to sort things out."

"Poor Chanel. I should be with her now, only I don't think she'd want me around. My parents will have to know. They would go to her."

"Maybe you should tell them yourself. It wouldn't be good for them to find out in the papers. It'll be plastered in the headlines in the morning editions."

She threw her head back.

"God, what a mess."

"I should be going."

"Why don't you stay? I could use a little comfort after all this."

"You sure?"

She shifted her position on the couch, resting her head on his shoulder and slipping her arm around his waist.

"I'm sure."

Chapter 24
WHO IN THE HELL ARE YOU?

ON HIS WAY TO LONDON LIFE TO PICK UP HIS check the next day, Eddie thought about Chanel and Percy. Percy'd been so protective of his mother that he resorted to murder. Not even wealth could prevent the destruction of a family. It was just one of those heartbreakingly sad things that happen all too frequently in life.

Although history was full of examples of patricide, killing one's father was not very common in the modern era. The fact that Guy Dupont wasn't Percy's biological father didn't matter; Percy believed he was. When Percy pulled the trigger and shot Guy in the back of the head, he was killing his father. And what had been Guy's crime that required the death penalty? It was infidelity. Infidelity could certainly be used as grounds for divorce, but it wasn't a crime, except in Percy's mind.

On the other hand, if Willis was Percy's real father, and if Percy knew it ...

Percy may not have had the Dupont blood, but Eddie believed that a case could be made for insanity. If it was just one murder, then maybe not. But with four cases and his attempted murder of Eddie, the possibility that Percy was insane and would likely be institutionalized for the rest of his

223

life was great. The kid just wasn't wired right; society had to be protected from people like him. He was an adult who didn't know right from wrong; he was a ticking time bomb that had gone off and would have continued to go off if he hadn't been caught. But he belonged in a hospital for the criminally insane, not in a prison or under the hangman's noose.

Eddie was curious about who exactly Percy's father was. Chanel, by her own admission, liked men, so there was no lack of candidates for that position. High on that list, Eddie guessed, was Willis himself. He remembered Chanel telling him that she had been seeing him for a very long time, right up to her marriage with Guy Dupont. If Willis turned out to be Percy's father, then Percy had inadvertently committed patricide. But from Chanel's reaction to Eddie's question last night, she would probably take that secret to her grave. That would be best for everyone concerned.

Tragedy—we read about it in the newspapers every day. It is inflicted on people all the time. High-profile cases get in the papers and on radio and TV. People seem to not get enough of it. But what happens even more is the tragedy that people inflict on themselves and those closest to them behind closed doors. Unlike the Steele case, they will never make the news. They are hidden from society and guarded by domestic maniacs. Thornton Hill would have been one of them had he lived and married Chanel. But there are thousands of Thornton Hills still out there, terrorizing their wives and children, unnoticed, unrecorded—concealed from all except their victims.

He pulled up to London Life and parked out front on Sherbrooke. He shut off the engine and took the key out of the ignition. *Poor Percy,* he thought. Whatever could go wrong in his life did. Chanel would have to shoulder some of the blame.

Eddie entered the building, walked down the corridor, and opened Nithercott's door without knocking.

"That's right, Mr. Wade. Just come right in while ignoring the usual civilized custom of announcing oneself first vis-à-vis the receptionist. Even a slight knock on the door would have sufficed."

"We're back to Mr. Wade now, are we? What happened to Eddie?"

"As you might expect, if you've been paying attention to the world around you, things change with amazing speed."

Eddie sat down on the chair in front of Nithercott's desk and stretched out his legs, resting his shoes on the edge of the desk.

"Make yourself at home," Nithercott said, looking over his glasses.

"What do you mean, as I might expect?"

"It simply means that while I greatly enjoyed your company last night, and getting to know you better was an educational experience, our socializing was an anomaly. My game was off; I let my guard down and became ..."

"Plastered?"

"That wasn't the word I was looking for, but for the moment, it'll do."

"Reggie, you've got to loosen up once in a while."

"I was quite loose enough last night, thank you very much. Considering what you did for the company, I'll ignore the Reggie part. Speaking of the company, I have this envelope for you." He reached across the desk with it. Eddie placed his feet on the floor, leaned forward, and took it. "You deserve much more, but I did manage to squeeze out a modest bonus for you. I trust you'll find we covered everything, including your fee and expenses."

Eddie slipped the check halfway out of the envelope to peek at the amount and raised his eyebrows.

"I thought you'd like that. I prepared you with the word *modest,* knowing that when you saw the actual amount, your eyebrows would jump. And they did—right on cue."

"Be sure you give the executives upstairs on the fifth floor my regards."

"I most certainly will do that."

"What happened to the Bouchers?" he asked, sliding the envelope in his coat pocket.

"They, along with their cohort, confessed to fraud. They played their hand and lost. The evidence against them was sitting right there—the husband, Martin. The third charlatan was Cosmo Degaré, a small-time swindler with a long arrest record. Apparently, he was the mastermind of the *escroquerie*."

"Good for them. They earned it."

"They said that they found the body in an alley by the river and threw it in after taking out the deceased's wallet and putting in Martin's. They had talked about it for months, but when they came across the body, they decided that then was the time. Spur-of-the-moment, you know. Degaré confessed he mangled the face so it couldn't be identified. The police are bringing added charges against him for that. Disfiguring a corpse; something like that. Apparently, there's a law against it."

Eddie thanked Nithercott for the bonus and left. A nice little payday. With his two cases completed, he felt unsettled—antsy. Working eighteen-hour days for the last two weeks and then suddenly having nothing to do, he felt ousted from humanity. He stood on Sherbrooke with his hands in his overcoat pockets. What was he going to do? He didn't have any cases on the horizon, but that could change anytime. In the meantime, he felt like a fish out of water. He could relax for a few days, perhaps take a vacation in the Adirondacks. Do a little fishing in the streams, a little boating on Lake George. Dammit—the fishing season wouldn't start for another few weeks for trout. Maybe he'd just go back to his office and clean up his files, something that was long overdue. Keep busy. That was the key.

As he walked around his car to get inside, someone or something across the street caught his attention. He squinted for a better look and noticed a guy sitting on the sidewalk, leaning against a building. It was that bum again. Eddie had seen him three or four times before—he couldn't remember the exact number—in different parts of the city, even in his own neighborhood in Mile End. That wasn't coincidence. The guy must have been following him. But why? Now was the time to find out. After all, Eddie had all the time in the world now.

He crossed the street, dodging traffic. He walked up to the guy and stood over him. The bum held a steady gaze straight ahead, not acknowledging Eddie.

"OK," Eddie said, "here I am. What do you want with me?"

The bum said nothing.

"Do you remember me? I bought you lunch at Bens a few weeks ago. You've been following me around since then. Why?"

Still nothing.

"You hungry? You want lunch again? OK, let's go."

Nothing.

"OK then, let me say a few things. If you don't want anything from me, fine. But stop following me. I don't know how you did it, but you need to stop. If I see that you are—" He stopped. What? What was he going to do? That was stupid. "Just don't." He turned around and walked to the curb, looking left and right at the traffic.

"Mister," the bum said.

Eddie turned around.

"So you do have something to say."

"I know you," he said, lifting his arm and pointing a finger at Eddie. He let his arm drop to his lap. "You're Bonifacio Wade. Your middle name is Eddie—I mean Edmondo. You were named after your grandfather on your mother's side of the family. You were born in Brooklyn."

Stunned, Eddie walked over to the man and looked down. The man looked up at him, shielding his eyes with his hand from the brightness of the sky.

"Who in the hell are you?" Eddie asked. The words came out gentle and soft.

"I'm your pa."

Chapter 25
THE LONG, SAD STORY

"YOU DID ALL RIGHT FOR YOURSELF, KID."

Eddie sat on his swivel chair in front of the couch, staring at his father. He wanted to reach over and strangle the bastard. He held him directly responsible for his mother's death. He had had to work through a lot of *ifs* in his life, not least of which was that if his father had never abandoned the family in Brooklyn, Eddie and his mother would have never gone to Montreal, and his mother would never have been hit by a car; she'd still be alive today. And there was always this: if his father had been responsible and had a steady job and normal life like other fathers, Eddie would have had a better life, never having grown up in the harsh realities and meager existence of Mile End, with his mother working day and night to make ends meet. One man was responsible for all of that, and he was sitting in front of him right then after all those years: Lincoln Wade.

"With no help from you," Eddie said matter-of-factly.

After his father had exploded the bombshell on rue Sherbrooke, Eddie brought him to his office. The man stank like a sewer, so much so that Eddie insisted he have a shower. As they were both the same size, he gave him some of his clothes: underwear, socks, shoes, shirt, and pants. He threw his clothes in the trash outside in the back. He wasn't going to bother having them washed.

"OK, you got me," Lincoln said. "You're right, Bonifacio. I never helped you. You have a right to be pissed."

What could Eddie say to that?

"I've been going by Eddie since I was nine. Just call me that."

"Before that. I started calling you Eddie first. Your mother never liked it."

Eddie stared at the man with contempt. What could he say to him? Were they going to have a nice little chat, catching up on the last twenty-six years as if a grievous wrong had never been committed? He took out his wallet and pulled out the picture. He handed it to Lincoln. Nine-year-old Eddie stood between his mother and father. They were all smiles.

"We had just returned from a Chinese restaurant to our apartment in Brooklyn. I had egg foo young. That's the last time we saw you. You said you were going for a pack of cigs, that you'd be right back. Mom and I waited for you. You just disappeared with the man who had taken the picture."

"Geez, you've got a good memory."

"I've lived every day of my life with that image in my head. Where did you go?"

That was the question he'd asked himself since he was nine. Now he was asking the one person who could answer it.

"That's a long story, Bonifacio—I mean Eddie."

"Don't I deserve an answer?"

"That you do," he said, shaking his head. "That you do."

Lincoln Wade had never been an ideal father or husband—not even close. He'd been a compulsive gambler and alcoholic most of his adult life and hung around the wrong crowd. But he was bound and determined to change that. He wanted a better life for his family, and he wanted to be a good husband and father. All that he told to Eddie.

"I tried my best to cut my ties with these people, but you see, I owed them a lot of money from gambling. You gotta understand, these were really bad people."

In fact, they had been associated with the mob. They told him that if he didn't pay up, they'd kill his family. But he didn't have any money and had no way of getting it.

"I thought about skipping out with your mother and you and going out west, maybe to California, some place, any place, but I knew we couldn't hide from them forever. They have long arms, these people; they'd find us eventually, and that would be the end for all of us."

But then they gave him a way out: they offered him a job, and it wasn't as if he could refuse it. That was the only way to save himself and his family, his only way out. But he couldn't very well tell his wife that he was going to work for gangsters. After Lincoln and his family returned to their apartment that day from eating out at the Chinese joint, one of the gang members was there to collect him. That was when Lincoln thought about the camera. He wanted his wife and son to have a picture of them all together in case he never returned.

"So, the guy who took this picture was a gangster," Eddie said.

Lincoln nodded. "He wasn't such a bad guy as gangsters go, but he had a job to do. It was the others who were rotten to the core. No respectable young lady would ever want to bring one of them home to meet her parents."

"What did you do then? Where'd you go?"

"I figured that your mother would take you to Montreal to live, which is what she did. What did I do? I became a bodyguard for a time to one of the underbosses."

As he became more familiar to the others, it came out that he had been an expert marksman in the Great War. He knew his guns and could use them. When Lepke Buckalter started to organize his "hit squad" (a carryover from Bugsy Siegal and Meyer Lansky), the underboss Lincoln had been working for volunteered him. The squad was really an enforcement arm for the Italian and Jewish gangsters in New York and the surrounding area. Eventually, they took murder contracts from mob bosses around the country. Lincoln Wade had been a well-traveled hit man. Toward the end of the squad's reign of terror, the newspapers had dubbed them "Murder Incorporated."

Of course, Eddie had heard about them.

"I thought they were just Jews and Italians. Why were you let in?"

"Well, Eddie, that's another story."

He went on to explain Eddie's lineage. Lincoln was a first-generation American. His parents had come from Poland. After being processed through Ellis Island, Lincoln's father had decided to do two things immediately: he first changed his name to avoid being discriminated against. He shortened it to Wade from Wadowski. Then he converted to Christianity. Like magic, he was no longer a Polish Jew.

"So, I'm Jewish," Eddie said, astonished by what he was hearing.

"Only half of you; the other half is Italian, thanks to your mother.

"Did she know?"

"I never told her."

In the late forties and early fifties, when the New York authorities had begun their push to round up members of Murder Incorporated, many of the hit men fled the state—the ones who hadn't been killed or arrested—and so did Lincoln Wade. He had gone first to St. Louis. When it got too hot for him there, he went to Detroit, which turned out to be no better. He finally ended up in St. Paul, Minnesota, which for the last few decades had been a nesting spot for criminals on the lamb—a neutral zone.

"What did you do there?"

"Not much. There weren't a lot of opportunities for a hit man. It was a quiet city, and the police wanted to keep it that way. I washed dishes in a dive for a few years and shined shoes until I hit rock bottom. I've been living on the streets ever since, with a bottle."

Eddie wondered whether he had heard about his mother. She'd been hit by a car crossing the street after the driver held up a liquor store. Only it wasn't the robber who'd hit her; it was a police car that was chasing it. Eddie had investigated the case years later and found out the truth. Agostina De Luca Wade died at the scene. Eddie had been in Europe at the time, fighting in the war. She had died alone—Eddie in Germany, Lincoln in God knows where.

"Did you hear about my mother?" Eddie asked.

Lincoln nodded sadly, his lips curving downward.

"I wanted to go to Montreal, but there was no way I could get across the border at the time. My name was out there. I'm sorry, kid."

"Why come now?"

"The doctors in St. Paul gave me six months, maybe a year. Hell, maybe two weeks. They couldn't tell me for certain. The bottle, you know. My liver's shot to hell. I just wanted to see you one last time before I croaked. I wanted to set the record straight. I didn't want you thinking that I didn't care about you and your mother. It's just that I was pulled in another direction, and I didn't have the wherewithal or the courage to unpull myself. I wanted to say I'm sorry to you, face-to-face, like a man."

Eddie stared at him. He was everything Eddie despised in a man. He'd been a loathsome excuse of a father. He'd been worse as a husband. He was a pathetic human being—and a murderer to boot. Yet he'd traveled in his condition fifteen hundred miles to seek out his son. No doubt it was his own fault that he had gotten involved with the gangsters. You don't owe the mob money and then just walk away from them without consequences. They threatened to kill his wife and son, so he joined the mob to protect them. Lincoln would be sixty-eight now, and he was dying from cirrhosis. Was there anything more to say to him? Was there anything else that needed to be done?

Just then, his telephone rang. Before answering it, he asked his father a question, because that was all he could think of saying.

"You hungry? We could go out for a bite to eat. Let me get the phone first."

He got up and reached to his desk for the receiver.

"Wade Detective Agency," he said.

"Eddie! This is Jack. Get your ass down here. You're not going to believe what we discovered!"

Chapter 26
CUI BONO?

THE BITE TO EAT WOULD HAVE TO WAIT. Detective Jack Macalister had been closemouthed on the phone, which made Eddie go through all the possibilities as to why he wanted to see Eddie at police headquarters. The only reason he could think of was Percy.

"Sit down, Eddie," Macalister said, "because if you don't, what I'm about to tell you is going to knock you off your feet."

Shit, Eddie thought. *A goddamn monkey wrench.*

Eddie sat down, crossed one leg over the other, slumped down a little, tilted his hat back on his head, put his elbows on the armrests, interlaced his fingers, and propped them under his chin, waiting for Macalister's news. *Goddammit.*

"It's the Dupont kid."

A thought flashed through Eddie's mind. *He hanged himself in his cell.*

"What about him?"

"Our ballistics man couldn't match his gun. We've got the wrong guy and the wrong gun."

"Shit."

"During our interview with him, he confessed that the gun had belonged to his father, Guy Dupont. He knew where his father had kept it. After he was murdered, Percy retrieved it and put it in his room behind a false wall. I found the wall myself. There was a box of rounds in there. I think the kid is telling the truth."

"But he tried to kill me with it."

"He said that he was only trying to scare you with it so you'd leave his mother alone. He seemed sincere, very open. He said he doesn't even know how to use it. He knows the basics, but he's never fired a gun in his life." Macalister picked up a pencil from the desk and began twirling it in his fingers. "I've interrogated a lot of people over the years. There's something odd about this kid—weird. I think he's got a couple of his noodles loose up here," he said, pointing the pencil to his head and twirling it. "Actually, more than just a couple."

"He could be faking it."

"He could be, but I doubt it. I don't think he's capable of lying, at least not to that degree." He flipped the pencil back on his desk. "We've got the wrong man, Eddie. None of the evidence you gathered would hold up in court. Even an incompetent defense attorney would destroy it without the gun."

"Dammit."

Eddie was absolutely certain that Percy had committed those crimes. The evidence *did* point to him in spite of what Macalister had just said. But without the murder weapon, there was no case.

"You're going to free him?"

"I've got no choice. We could charge him with pointing a loaded gun at you, but what good would that do? I really don't think he meant to harm you."

Maybe Eddie had obsessed over Percy so much that he hadn't really considered someone else might have committed the murders. Cui bono? Who'd benefit? The only other person he had considered was Chanel, but he was now convinced she had nothing to do with them.

Who else then? Who else benefitted? Who had ties to Chanel that he had overlooked?

And where was Willis Steele?

———«•»———

Before he left the police station, he used Macalister's phone and called Josette at the bakery. Could she meet him in twenty minutes at the café where he first interviewed her? She was going to be taking a break at that time anyway, so, yes, no problem. He left the station, got into his car, and sped off, all the time thinking about Willis Steele. When he arrived at the café, Josette was sitting at the same table with two cups of coffee on it. Eddie sat down opposite her.

"I don't know whether I want to hear any more bad news," she said.

"Then I won't tell you any bad news. Percy's gun didn't match the bullets."

She was stunned for a moment.

"You mean he didn't kill all those people?"

"That's what I mean. If he did, he used another gun."

"What about you? Didn't he try to kill you?"

"He told the police that he only wanted to scare me, because I upset his mother. He thought I was out to ruin their reputation. He wanted me to back off."

"The police believed him?"

"They're releasing him soon, if they haven't already. He doesn't know anything about Willis's disappearance."

"Do you believe him?"

There was a long moment before Eddie answered her.

"I think he might be telling the truth." He sipped his coffee and then set the cup down. "You asked me the other day what it was like to be an investigator. I said that it was sometimes frustrating. This is one of those times. All the evidence pointed at Percy. I think it would have stood up in court if it was supported by the ballistics report. It wasn't, so I'm back to square one."

"What will you do?"

"I need to apologize to Percy and Chanel first. Then I have to find out whether Chanel still wants me on the case. After all, Willis is still missing. Chanel paid me to find him."

"Do you think she will?"

"I don't know. You know her better than I do."

"I think she'll rehire you—after she throws something heavy at you."

"I know how to bob and weave, so that won't be a problem."

"You really don't know her, do you?" she said, laughing.

"Listen—do you know anyone who is or was close to Chanel that might be capable of multiple murders? Think hard."

"I actually thought about that for the last few days, and I just couldn't come up with a name, other than Willis. But that's unfair of me, because I really don't know him all that well, and I don't know what he's capable of."

"OK, don't worry about it."

He didn't want to talk about it anymore, so he changed the subject.

"I really enjoyed Tuesday night. I hope you did as well."

"I had a great time, Eddie. Enjoyed every minute of it. But ... I think I enjoyed last night even more. Lucky for you, I had an extra toothbrush handy, eh?"

"Lucky me!"

"I've got to get back to work. My mother's up front while I'm on break, and she needs to get back to baking. She's working on a special order of birthday cakes."

They got up, and Eddie walked her to the front door of the shop. They stood facing each other.

"So, will I see you again before the end of the year?"

Eddie grinned.

"I think that might be a distinct possibility. The weekend's coming up. You never know what could happen."

"Call me," she said, and then she reached up and kissed him long and hard on the mouth.

Eddie left Josette and went to the Flamingo. He spent the next four hours thinking about the case and downing shots of whiskey. It was a pleasant evening for the end of March, so he decided to walk around town; the shops were open late on Thursday, and he needed a diversion. Also, he wasn't in the mood to see his father yet. He'd left him at his office and told him he might be back late. He had given him ten bucks, told him where he could eat, and said if he felt the need to drink, the Lion's Den was right next door. He was already dying from booze; a few more weren't going hurt him if he felt comfort in them. Eddie was prepared to let him sleep on the couch for the next few days, but after that, he'd have to find a place for him to stay.

Eddie walked aimlessly for a while and soon found himself on rue Sainte-Catherine. It was crowded with shoppers and those looking for a night out on the town. Montreal was a city with many moods. You found them all on Sainte-Catherine. A police car roared by him, followed by a hook and ladder. Someone's business or flat was on fire. He passed a hurdy-gurdy man grinding out his music. He caught a whiff of smoked meat from Dunn's Deli. He walked on and saw a man sitting on the sidewalk with his back to a building, his legs crossed in a way that wasn't physically possible for a regular Joe, holding out a cigar box to passersby, his crutches next to him on the cement. Eddie stopped to throw some coins in the box and then moved along with the crowd.

Ahead of him, he saw that Loew's theater was showing *Dial M for Murder*, and a few doors down from that, the Capitol Theater had *Rear Window*. Both Hitchcock movies. He wasn't in the mood for either one. He passed a loan shop and next to that Chez Maurice's Danceland, featuring Sonny Dunham and his Orchestra in big letters for all to see. He'd catch him the next time Sonny was in town.

The green, blue, red, and yellow flashing neon lights were trying their best to get everyone's attention, reminding Eddie of Times Square. A neon outline of a waitress waving a hand overhead beckoned him to come in for a meal. The smell was wonderful as he passed the restaurant. He wasn't hungry. Another police car roared by with its sirens blasting. Another emergence; another murder? A newsagent smoking a cigar was hawking the late edition of *La Presse*. "Paper, paper. Get your paper here." Next to him, a lost soul was asking a constable for directions to Union Square. *Three blocks down and five to your left, bud*. Lovers hand in hand pushed by him in a hurry. In a hurry for what? Did they even know? He stopped outside the Tip Top Tailors to fill and light his pipe.

The city was full of life, even for a March evening. But somewhere in the city limits, not far away, inside the paneled rooms of exclusive clubs, the captains of industry, the bank presidents, board directors, and corporation lawyers were discussing the ebb and flow of the nation's commerce. And in other kinds of clubs, Frank Sinatra, Edith Piaf, and others were entertaining Montrealers. In a few hours, the nocturnal army of workers would be deployed to clean up the mess left by all the shoppers, the captains of industry, and the famous entertainers.

The diversion hadn't worked. Eddie was still thinking about Willis Steele.

Maybe, just maybe, Willis was behind all this. Cui bono? How would he benefit from killing Guy Dupont, Thornton Hill, and Luc Legrand? He would have free rein to marry Chanel, as he had done, and secure her fortune. But then why had he taken off with her jewels and cash when he could have had so much more? It didn't make sense. By all accounts, Willis felt uncomfortable living in Chanel's world. Chanel even admitted that they'd argued about that. Notwithstanding, the motive was there, and that counted for something, if nothing else did.

At the end, he may have to reconsider Chanel.

Just then, a man passed by him, then stopped and turned around.

"Eddie? Eddie Wade?" he said.

"Fred?" He squinted for a second and then recognized the man. "Fred!"

"Yes, how are you doing? God, it must be a year since we've seen each other."

"You look great."

"I'm retired now and catching up on life. Listen, I'm late for a show down the street, but let me call you in a few days. I'll buy you dinner. We'll have a lot to talk about."

"I'd like that, Fred."

Indeed, Eddie hadn't seen Fredrick Churchill in over a year. He'd been a professor at McGill whose name had come up during a case. They had become very good friends but just lost contact with each other. The last time Eddie had seen Churchill was when he intervened and saved Eddie's life when a gun had been pointed at him.

Fred had saved his life last year, and now Branch York had saved his life this year, even though Percy had told the police that he was only trying to scare Eddie. True or not, Percy had pointed a loaded gun at him. It could have gone off. York had prevented that. That had to count for something too.

How many more times was that going to happen?

How many more times was he going to be in the wrong place at the wrong time? Everyone's clock was ticking away.

Sooner or later, they would stop. Most would be in old age when they did. So why was Eddie trying to move his along? Maybe he should find something else to do before his luck ran out.

Surely there had to be a better way to make a living than peddling his services.

Chapter 27
APRIL FOOL'S DAY

IT WAS FRIDAY, APRIL 1.

Eddie had slept in. There was no particular rush to get up. The Boucher case was closed, and Eddie had been fired from the Steele case. He had climbed out of bed at nine thirty. His father—he couldn't get used to the word, so he called him by his first name—was already up and dressed. They went to Beauty's for breakfast. The most that could be said about their conversation was that it was polite. What could Eddie say to the man who had taken a twenty-six-year hiatus from Eddie's life and then suddenly reappeared out of nowhere? The weather was always a safe bet.

When they returned to the office, Eddie sat behind his desk, trying to figure out what to do. It had been two weeks and one day since he had taken on the Steele case. Willis was still missing, and Eddie was still fired. He didn't like that. If asked, Eddie would readily admit that he was a flawed human being. He had personal imperfections and professional foibles, not the least of which was that he was prone to getting too close to some of the people on the cases he was working on. At times, this caused problems that inexorably spilled over to his personal life. In short, he had a difficult time separating his two lives.

He couldn't tell you whether his relationship with Josette prompted him to make a decision, but it was no small wonder that he found himself driving over to Westmount to find out whether Chanel wanted him to continue looking for her missing husband. He hadn't deluded himself into believing that Chanel would embrace him with open arms. He had prepared himself for an onslaught of verbal abuse. More likely, she would call the Mounties to have him removed from her property. Willis Steele had sucked him into a virtual vortex that left him spinning in a thousand different directions. He had to have one more go at finding him, if Chanel would allow him to. The very least he would do was apologize for cruelly and wrongly accusing her son of murder. So, he'd gotten into his car, pointed it east, and hoped for the best.

Chanel opened the door after Eddie knocked several times. That was a positive start. But she said nothing; instead, she simply stared at him with her arms crossed in front of her.

"Hi, Chanel," he said. After waiting an uncomfortable minute and she hadn't reciprocated, he said, "I was wondering how Percy was."

He watched her eyes narrow at him like some she-cat ready for the kill. A mother of any species protecting her young was always a dangerous proposition.

"He's upstairs sleeping peacefully, no thanks to you."

"I'm sorry about that. I truly am." He made no excuses. "There's some unfinished business. You paid me a lot of money to find Willis. I haven't earned all of it. I'd still like to try."

She narrowed her eyes even more at him, as if she was going on the attack to scratch his eyes out. Then she suddenly sighed and dropped her arms to her sides.

"Do you think it's worth the effort?"

"If you want to know where he is and you want your money and jewels back, I do."

She went silent again, but this time she seemed to be thinking it over rather than planning some offensive move to destroy him right there on the front porch.

"Come in then. We'll go in the kitchen. I just made some coffee."

The kitchen was tiny. It was one of those houses where the meals were prepared there and then brought into the dining room by the servants for the family to eat. The table was small and pushed against the back window. Chanel poured some coffee, and then they sat at either end, warming their hands on the cups.

"The last time you were here," Chanel said, "making your accusations against Percy, you mentioned Samantha L'Amour. What does she have to do with Percy?"

There was resentment in her voice that burned through Eddie like a firestorm.

"Somehow Percy found out that Guy was seeing her. He was curious about his father's behavior and followed him one night. Sometime long after Guy was murdered, Percy started seeing Samantha, wanting to know why he'd been cheating on you. It was just curiosity. They talked. That was all. Nothing happened between them. Percy confessed this to the police. I talked to Samantha myself; she verified Percy's story."

"Guy and I had a mutual arrangement; he could cheat if I could. We both did. I didn't know that Percy knew about it." She sighed and looked down at her coffee.

Eddie reached in his coat pocket and took out a piece of folded paper.

"I'd like to believe that Willis is an isolated incident, that he took your money and jewels and just skipped town. But I believe his disappearance is linked to the murders." He didn't mention that he thought Willis might be the killer. When all else failed, he'd have to say something.

"Why the murders?"

"Hill's body was pulled out of the St. Lawrence. He'd been shot in the chest and dumped there. His body was just ID'd recently. He didn't just take off on you. He was murdered."

"Oh, my God." Her reaction seemed genuine.

"The bullet that killed him matched the bullet that killed Guy. They were fired by the same gun but not by the gun Percy had. It was the same with Luc Legrand. I believe that Willis's disappearance is somehow connected to the three murders and that whoever did the killings wasn't a stranger." He unfolded the paper he was holding and set it in front of her. It was the list of names she had prepared for Eddie of family members and friends of Willis. His coffee had cooled down enough, so he gulped down half of it.

She stared at the list. Eddie had scratched through the names of people be believed couldn't have possibly committed the murders.

"Think hard, Chanel. Is there anyone on this list who you think is capable of murder or had a motive, whether I scratched through their name or not? These murders aren't random. They were personal—very personal. Someone hated an awful lot, and I don't think that hatred was directed at Guy, or Thornton, or Luc, or Willis. I think that hatred was directed toward you. I think this person wanted to punish you for something you might have done in the past. Think hard. Who on that list hated you so much that he would kill the people you were involved with? Think hard; this might be our only chance, Chanel."

She set the paper facedown on the table.

"I have something to tell you," she said.

She was as distraught as he had ever seen her. Her hands were shaking. She curled them into fists to stop them.

"Go on," Eddie said and then sipped his coffee.

"Willis and I had been together ever since I can remember, like I told you. He had been my first love from the time we played show and tell. At that time, I had never been interested in anyone else. Oh, there had been others but nothing serious. But when we were in our teens, sixteen or seventeen, another boy appeared on the scene and showed some interest in me. He was persistent, sometimes following me home from school and around the neighborhood. He had asked me out on dates numerous times. I wasn't at all interested in him. I should have told him so straight off, but I was foolish, so I led him on, making him think he had a chance. It was idiotic of me; I know. This went on for months. I was just having some fun with him. That was all.

"At one point, I got bored by it all. Instead of being entertained by his doggedness, I became annoyed by it. One day outside of school and in front of a bunch of kids, he declared his love for me. Everyone around us had heard him. They were giggling; some were laughing outright. I was thoroughly embarrassed by it. I handled the situation like a foolish and ruthless teenager who had been humiliated. I wanted to get back at him, so I did. In front of everyone there, I asked him why he thought I would like a moron. I told him I'd go out on a date with a bug before I'd go with him. And those were the nice things I said to him. I went on like that for the next two minutes, although it seemed like an eternity. I don't think I would have been so brutal with him if we'd been alone. But with the other kids there, I thought I had to save face, so I laid it on really thick."

She stopped to sip her coffee and then continued.

"I never talked to him again, although we saw each other in the hallways in between classes. It was apparent he was avoiding me. Looking back at it, he must have suffered a great deal of humiliation for the rest of the school year. It must have been difficult for him, seeing all those kids every day, knowing they were still laughing at him inside.

"The only time we had contact with each other after that

incident was several years later after we had graduated from high school. I had met Guy and dumped Willis. Guy proposed, and we were going to get married the following month. One night very late, I was walking home from a friend's house— she was going to be my maid of honor—when he suddenly appeared out of nowhere. He threw me down on the ground beside some thick bushes and gagged my mouth with a cloth. He didn't say anything at all while he was raping me. When he finished, he stood over me and said, 'Thought I'd help myself to a little dessert before your wedding night.' I never saw him again after that, but I remember those words as if he had said them yesterday."

"So, he's Percy's father?"

"I went to the doctor because I was feeling a little queasy a few days before Guy and I were married. That's when I found out I was pregnant by a month. Yes, he's Percy's father."

"And there's no chance that either Willis or Guy is Percy's father?"

"No. Willis and I hadn't had sex for a few months before I broke it off with him. And Guy and I waited until we were married."

"And you think this guy took revenge on you by killing everyone you brought into your life."

"The thought entered my head just a few days ago, but not seriously. But when you gave me the list of names just now and asked me who would want to harm me, his name stood out."

"Whose name?"

She took the paper and turned it over. Without saying anything, she then pointed at a name.

"Branch York?"

The guy who had saved Eddie's life.

Chapter 28
THE BIG HURT

EDDIE RETURNED TO HIS OFFICE TO SEE HOW his father was doing and to spend some time with him. *Spend time with him,* he thought. How ironic. He was going to spend some time with the very man who'd left his mother and him to their own devices in Brooklyn—penniless.

Was it out of curiosity, wanting to dig deeper into Lincoln's psyche to better know what made him tick? After all, besides what the old man had told him about his life yesterday, Eddie really didn't know him. Or was he going to spend time with him out of obligation? Funny word, *obligation.* What obligation did he have toward the man who'd been in his life for only nine years? Hell, he'd known Bruno for longer than that, and in his own way, Bruno had been more of a father figure than Lincoln. Lincoln had abandoned Eddie's mother and him, albeit to save their lives, but abandoned them nonetheless. Had that been his only option? Eddie could think of a half dozen other things he could have done without breaking up the family. But that was easy for Eddie to think; he hadn't been in that situation, so he'd never know. What he did know for sure was that Lincoln Wade had put them in that situation himself—by his drinking and gambling—where abandonment had become an option. He also knew that it was going to take an enormous amount of willpower to forgive him. He wasn't sure he had it in him.

After all was said and done, maybe Eddie simply wanted to know more about the life Lincoln had led all those years apart from him. Yes, he'd worked for the mob and killed people for a living, but there were twenty-six years to account for. Never once in all that time had he reached out to his son and wife. He must have had some opportunities. If he couldn't cross the border, there was a telephone; he could have called. He could have even sent a telegram. "Hi! It's me. I'm in a bad situation, but I want you to know that I love you both. I'm trying to get to you. Until then, I'll send some money."

Nothing.

For twenty-six years—nothing.

Instead of spending some time with him, maybe Eddie should just take him back to rue Sherbrooke where he found him and dump him there.

But he didn't take him to rue Sherbrooke where he found him. Instead, he took him out to eat at the local greasy spoon, where they had bowls of chili and soda crackers and talked about the gangsters in Montreal and about who was going to win the Stanley Cup this year.

After an hour went by, they returned to the office. Eddie showed him where the cat food was, got his gun, and then when the sun was setting, he got into his car and left the old man to his own devices. He left him with a full bottle of Canadian Club for company.

He drove north to Cartierville and then turned east onto boulevard Gouin to Roxboro. The house was off the road, with its rear facing the Black River. Eddie switched his headlights off as he made the turn into the long driveway and stopped a distance away. It was a gray stone structure typical of houses in the nineteenth century, and it looked derelict. Two dormer windows jutted out on the roof, which was in need of repair. The land on which it sat was mostly dirt and weeds. He got out of the car with a flashlight and walked toward the house. The night always seemed darker in the country than in the city. A car sat on the east side of the house. Only one light was on in one of the dormer windows.

Branch York was home and in his bedroom.

Eddie walked to the side of the house where the car was and laid a hand on the hood. It was cold. Branch had been home for a while. He went to the side door, grabbed the doorknob, and turned it slowly. It was unlocked. He pushed the door open a few inches and listened. He could hear a muffled voice coming from upstairs. He flipped the switch on the flashlight and shined it inside. It was the kitchen. He stepped in and carefully went to the other side of the room, following the voice. There was a staircase leading upstairs just around the corner to the right. There had been a door separating the kitchen, but it had been taken off, maybe years before. He went to the bottom of the stairs and stopped. The voice was loud enough to hear clearly.

"You know, Chanel took my life away from me, and now I'm taking hers away, little by little. There were some things I never told you, old buddy."

Was he talking to himself or someone else?

"I started with Guy Dupont, and then I waited a long time. I'm a patient guy, you know. And sure enough, Thornton Hill came on the scene. Maybe you didn't know, but Hill was an asshole. He had been beating on her, so I really did her a favor. And then I waited for the next one. Like I said, I'm a very patient guy. Chanel always had to have someone in her life, except for me, so the next one to go was Luc Legrand. I'll have to tell you, I was surprised by him. I missed him for quite some time. I bet you hadn't known about him yourself, eh? I followed them around until the stars were aligned just right, and I shot him dead in front of his house. But even before that, I was surprised again. You had come back into her life. I have to tell you, Willis, I hadn't seen that one coming. You really knocked me for a loop."

Willis? He's alive.

"Did you know that Chanel had been screwing that Legrand character while she was married to you? I don't think you did. She even did it when you went missing and hired that jackass of a private dick to find you. You couldn't have known about that. I forgot to tell you about Eddie Wade. I was following him around one day, trying to figure out a good place to put a bullet between his eyes. He was trying to find you, and I couldn't let that happen. I didn't want to screw it up like I did a few weeks ago when I fired into his office window and missed. Anyway, just when I had him, Chanel's weird-ass kid pops up out of nowhere with a gun. I wanted to kill Wade myself, so I jumped out and clobbered the kid a good one. So now, I've got to take care of Wade again.

"I really don't want to kill you, Willis. I really don't. We've been good friends for a very long time, but you've got to understand. Chanel's got to be punished. She humiliated me in front of all the other kids outside school. You weren't there, but you heard about it. You even told her that it was unfair of her to have done so. She's got to pay for that, don't you think, Willis? I'm really sorry, my friend. Sorry I have to kill you. You shouldn't have hooked up with her again."

There was a long moment of silence.

What was he doing? Was Willis really there with him, or was Branch truly insane and talking to himself?

"You hungry, Willis? Just nod your head if you are. OK. Fine. I'll go downstairs, see what's in the icebox—fix you some grub, as they say in the western movies. I won't kill you tonight. I want to get Wade first, but when I do, I promise you won't feel a thing. I promise you, Willis. That's the least

I can do for a best friend, don't you think? I hope you can understand the position I'm in, the position Chanel put me in. Anyway, I won't go down that road again. You know the story as well as I do by now. I'll just go and get you some food. I'll be right back, kiddo."

Eddie could hear Branch's shoes on the floorboards above him. The footfalls were slow and heavy but steady and firm. Eddie backed up quickly and quietly a few feet and went into the kitchen. He set his flashlight down and then took off his overcoat and hat and set them on the floor. Branch was coming down the stairs. The steps were straining under his weight. It was pitch dark. He'd have to reach for the light switch inside the doorframe of the kitchen.

Eddie waited.

The steps continued to creak and whine as Branch descended. The noise was amplified by the silence of the house. It sounded as if all of Montreal could hear it miles away. Branch reached the landing, a few feet from the doorless doorframe leading into the kitchen. Eddie could see nothing but pitch blackness; there were only sounds.

He waited.

He heard the rustling of clothes, the scraping of shoes on the floor, and a hand searching the wall for the light switch. Blackness. Suddenly, the kitchen lit up brighter than a military spotlight. Eddie found himself standing about three feet away from him. He stepped forward and threw a vicious left hook to Branch's right jaw that took him by surprise, jarring and shaking him off his feet, and then he followed up with a straight right that landed partly on his nose and partly on his upper lip, knocking him backward out of the kitchen to the bottom of the stairs. *Whop-whop!* The combination was so fast that Eddie was certain Branch had no idea what had hit him. He lay spread-eagle on his back, out cold. It had been more than a decade since Eddie put on the gloves with an opponent; he wasn't exactly wearing gloves, but he still had it—the big hurt.

Eddie reached down, grasping his clothes, and turned him on his stomach. He undid his tie and used it to bind his hands behind his back. Then he went back into the kitchen, opened a few drawers, and found some heavy twine. He returned to Branch and bound his ankles with it. Branch York wasn't going anywhere.

Then he went upstairs. He recognized Willis from his picture. He was sitting on a chair with his hands tied behind him. There was a gag in his mouth. Eddie undid it.

"Let me make a wild guess," Eddie said. "You must be Willis Steele."

"Who are you?"

"Your wife hired me to find you. She's a little pissed at you right now, but I think I can smooth that over for you."

Eddie stepped behind Willis to untie his hands and arms.

"Where is he?" Willis was agitated and looked terrified. "He's going to kill me!"

"Branch's killing days are over, so you don't have to worry."

"He's a murderer. He killed—"

"I know," Eddie said, standing in front of him again. "I heard it all. What I don't know is how he got you here."

Willis stood up and stretched, glancing at the stairs, still looking afraid.

"Don't worry. He's sleeping it off. I tied him up securely; he's not going anywhere."

"I can't believe it. We were friends. Then he turned into a monster."

"How'd he get you here?"

"We went out drinking one night—must be weeks ago. I lost all track of time. He said that he wanted to show me something in his house. When we got here, he pulled a gun on me. He wanted to know if Chanel had cash lying around the house. Jewelry too. I told him she kept them in the safe. He wanted to go to our house late that night and take them. If I didn't do as he said, he said he'd kill both Chanel and Percy, shoot them dead. So, I did as he asked. He waited outside in his car. Then we drove to his house. I've been in this room tied up ever since."

"Chanel and Percy are fine, but they think you stole the jewels and money and took off on them."

"That was what Branch wanted them to believe. To punish Chanel. I would never have done that, not to them. But Branch threatened to kill them. He would have too. I'm sure of that. What choice did I have?"

"Not much," Eddie said. "Branch didn't give you much of a choice."

Then his father's image flashed in his head.

What choice did he have?

Chapter 29
TO EVERYTHING
THERE IS A SEASON

SATURDAY NIGHT AT THE LION'S DEN WAS always crowded. It was the one night that rowdy drinkers during the rest of the week would bring their wives, snatching a semblance of respectability. The results were fewer fistfights, and usually no one was thrown out by the seat of their pants. Bruno, the owner, would rely on his nephew, Benedict, to take up the slack behind the bar. It was never Ben or Bennie. Some of the patrons would at times call him Benjamin for the fun of it, trying to get his attention, but they were always unsuccessful. His name was just Benedict, which meant "blessed" in Latin. Fourteen popes had had that name. So had four antipopes. So had that traitor to the American Revolution, that short, stubby, rounded "horse jockey" with a bovine face and a wild military appetite, who had been run out of Quebec City by the British, holding onto his shattered leg and bruised ego. But Bruno's nephew was different; he was a plumber by trade, and by all accounts, he wasn't particularly religious and knew little of Quebec's history. He just fixed water pipes and unplugged toilets during the week and served drinks on Saturday nights.

Eddie Wade and Jake Asher of the *Gazette* sat at a small, square wooden table far in the back. Eddie was puffing away on his pipe, while Jake was blowing smoke rings with his stogie. The late edition of the paper and two Molsons sat between them. "Shake, Rattle, and Roll" was playing on the jukebox, and Bruno and Benedict were behind the bar fixing drinks and going crazy. But they worked well as a team.

"Jesus, Eddie," Jake said, fingering the paper. "I really feel sorry for him."

"Who? Branch York?"

In the background, Bruno shouted over the voices, "Hâtez-vous, s'il vous plaît! Last call! Get 'em while you can!"

"Him, too, but no, I was referring to the kid, Percy. That was a lot for him to go through—you know, being arrested and accused of killing his own father, not to mention the others. The kid is unstable. He has limited resources up here," he said, pointing a finger at his head, "if you know what I mean. If there's too much pressure on him, he could lose it completely and maybe do something really violent. I've seen it happen before. It's just like they explode, and all of a sudden there's bodies lying everywhere. The whole situation could make him a real killer this time. After all, he's Branch York's son. He's got killer blood in him."

"You don't even know Percy, so how in the hell would you know what he'd do? Just because he's related to York doesn't mean he's going to go on some rampage and start killing people."

"You're not talking to some cub reporter, Eddie. I've been doing this same job for decades. I've seen what people can do when the pressure builds up. It's like a water heater; the pressure builds up over time, and it springs a leak. If the tank doesn't get repaired, the pressure continues, and before you know, the whole thing becomes a bomb." He paused a moment then added, "I'm just saying."

"Why do you feel sorry for York?"

"Same reasoning, only more so. Here you have this guy who carries a grudge around with him for—what, twenty years or more? Then he starts knocking off everyone who Chanel hooks up with. One—then after five years—two, three, and almost four, if you count Willis Steele. Almost five if you include yourself. A normal mind wouldn't think like that. A normal mind would forget the grudge and go on with his life. But not him. His head wasn't wired right from the beginning. There's something mixed up inside. You gotta feel sorry for someone like that. It's got to be a huge burden for him."

"Would you feel the same way if he'd murdered your wife?"

"Now, that's disgusting, Eddie." He took a pull from his cigar and gulped down some of his beer. "Frankly," he continued, wiping his mouth with his hand, "I'd probably strangle the bastard, but I'd still feel sorry for him while I did it."

"The hell you say!"

"I knew you wouldn't agree with that," Jake said, pointing the tip of his cigar at Eddie. "You've been hanging around the seedy side of life for too long. You let it color your disposition. You've become too hard, too unsympathetic to the vicissitudes that people experience in life."

"What about you? You've been writing about crime since Moses was a babe. What about your disposition?"

"That's different. I can go to a crime scene where a wife had just slit her husband's throat, you know, blood all over the place, and then go home and have a nice plate of spaghetti and meatballs, followed up by some grand-pères with two scoops of vanilla ice cream, a big Perfecto, a cuppa joe, and a pousse-café, and never blink an eye. That's on account of I've learned to—what's the fancy word they use nowadays? Oh, yeah, I've learned to com-part-ment-al-ize. In case—"

"You're full of—"

"In case you're unfamiliar with that word," he said, leaning into Eddie, "it means I can leave my work at work when I go home, so I'm not always thinking about it, and hence not screwing up my disposition."

"Jake, you're so full of—"

"You should try it sometime. That way you can see someone else's point of view more clearly."

Eddie took a swig of his beer and relit his pipe. Trying to have a rational discussion with Jake Asher was sometimes like trying to have a coherent talk with a hungry fox about why it would be unfair to raid the hen house. But maybe he had a point. Nevertheless ...

"Shit!"

Jake took the cigar out of his mouth.

"What?"

"You're full of shit, Jake, but I like you anyway."

"That's very kind of you to say. I think the feeling is mutual, but I'm not quite sure. Ask me next week."

"Besides, you did a great job with the article," Eddie said, tapping the paper with his fingers.

Branch York made the front page with Jake's byline. He had freely confessed to murdering Guy Dupont, Thornton Hill, and Luc Legrand and to the attempted murders of Willis Steele and Eddie. The police, with the help of Willis, had found Chanel's money and jewelry in Branch's house.

"I kind of wish York had held out and not confessed though. I would have gotten some more articles out of the case. Now, there's just going to be the sentencing. If they're going to hang him, that's another article. Maybe another one interviewing relatives, if he has any besides the kid." He grabbed his beer. "There wouldn't have been an article, Eddie, if it weren't for you, so here's a toast—wait! We should have your old man here for it. Where is he?"

"Lying down on my couch. He wasn't feeling well when I left. I think he drank too much."

"OK, I'll toast you without him." Lifting his glass, he said, "Here's to the man who restored justice to a little piece of the planet and let a few people sleep better at night."

Eddie, embarrassed by the attention—if only from Jake—raised his glass and clinked it against the other.

"Bottom's up!" he said.

They both bottomed up.

"Hâtez-vous, s'il vous plaît!" Bruno yelled again. "Last call! I'm turning off the poison in ten minutes!"

"On that note," Jake said, getting to his feet and wiping his mouth with his sleeve, "I've got to get back to the office. I had someone take over the police desk for me, but he's got to leave by two, so I must skedaddle. It's been a pleasure as always, my friend."

After Jake left, Eddie continued to sit there. He should have been happy about solving the case and rescuing Willis Steele before he had been murdered, but he wasn't. He was satisfied, if that was the right word, with the outcome, but something else was bothering him.

It was his father.

What was he going to do with him? More importantly, how should he relate to him now?

Of course, Lincoln Wade was Eddie's biological father. To Eddie, though, he was a stranger who had appeared out of nowhere. What did he want? If Eddie were to believe him, he had wanted to clear the air, set things right. He'd done that, hadn't he? What now? Eddie had gone over this already, and he didn't want to do it again. He didn't dispute that he was his father. He had known too much about Eddie and his mother. But was Eddie to believe everything else he said? He could have concocted this story about being with Murder Incorporated and not free to leave and go to Montreal.

Maybe that had been one big lie to cover up the real reason he abandoned his family. Maybe he'd been simply a hopeless drunk who couldn't handle the responsibilities of being a husband and father. Maybe he'd decided to worm himself into Eddie's life with his sob story of dying and use it to get Eddie's sympathy—and then hit him up for money. It wasn't far-fetched. Gamblers and drunks do and say anything to get what they want. Eddie had to have a plan.

He tamped the ash down in his pipe and relit it.

Tomorrow, he'd take him out for breakfast. When they finished, he'd tell him that he had to leave, that he was on his own. He could return to St. Paul or any other place he wanted to go. Eddie would even pay for the one-way ticket. Hell, he could stay in Montreal if he wanted and live on the streets, but Eddie was finished with him. He didn't want to see him again. His father's reaction would tell the story. Eddie was good enough at reading people to know what was behind Lincoln Wade's intentions.

Then he'd know.

"Hâtez-vous, s'il vous plaît! Last call! One minute, and that's all she wrote!"

Eddie left the Lion's Den and walked the short distance to his office. The lights were off. His father would be sleeping. Eddie decided not to wait until tomorrow; he'd tell him now. He unlocked the door and turned the light on. Lincoln was sound asleep on the couch where he had left him. He took his coat and hat off and put them on the coatrack. He cleared his throat loudly enough for his father to hear. He didn't budge. Apparently, it was going to take more than that to wake him. An opened bottle of Canadian Club was on the floor next to the couch. More than half of it was gone.

Eddie placed his pipe in an ashtray on this desk and then walked over to him. He stood over the man. He still couldn't believe that after twenty-six years, his father suddenly reappeared in his life. This was the man, a drunken gambler, whose seed had been planted that brought forth an only son. And after nine years, he disappeared on a nondescript evening in Brooklyn. Eddie felt his throat tighten. His eyes were becoming glassy. He felt hatred in his heart. His mother was dead, and this was the vile man who was responsible, this sorry excuse for a husband and father, this pile of shit lying in front of him, sleeping off another drunk—on *his* couch, wearing *his* clothes. *Goddammit,* he thought, *goddammit. I want you out of my life for good.*

He reached down and jostled his shoulder.

"Wake up, Lincoln."

He jostled him again.

"Goddammit, I said wake up!" he shouted, his body trembling with fire and loathing.

He didn't move.

Eddie leaned down and stared at his chest for a full minute. Then he reached for his wrist and felt for his pulse. He shifted his hand to his neck and felt for his carotid artery. Nothing—no pulse. He slipped his hand away and stared into the face of his father for a long moment.

Then he knelt down beside the couch and gently placed the side of his face on his father's chest and wept.

Epilogue
THE BEGINNING

Two months later.

THE ADIRONDACK MOUNTAINS IN UPPER STATE New York formed a roughly circular dome about one hundred sixty miles in diameter and about a mile above sea level. Humans had lived in the region since the Paleo-Indian period shortly after the last ice age. Legend had it that the word *Adirondack* came from the Mohawk word *Haderondah*, meaning eaters of trees. A few centuries ago, a French missionary priest had explained that the word was used by the Iroquoians as a disparaging term for the Algonquians, who had foregone agriculture and at times were forced to eat tree bark to survive the harsh winters. It wasn't until 1837 that the mountain range had been officially christened Adirondack by a pioneering American geologist named Ebenezer Emmons.

There are more than one hundred native tree species in the Adirondacks, including fir, maple, shadbush, birch, hickory, chestnut, dogwood, hawthorn, beech, ash, oak, elm, aspen, cottonwood, sycamore, poplar, pine, spruce, ironwood, sweet gum, and even sour gum. Collectively, they provide cover, food, and homes for wildlife; they provide shade for the shrubs, wildflowers, ferns, and moss on the forest floor; they host mushrooms and insects; and the decaying plant material from them enrich the soil below. They are the mosaic heartbeat of living organisms that form nature's communities that make up the Adirondacks.

Additionally, there are more than fifty species of mammals and more than a hundred species of aves that live in these mountains and surrounding wetlands and lakes—from subterranean moles to massive moose. White-tailed deer, black bears, coyotes, squirrels, chipmunks, bobcats, red and gray foxes, porcupines, raccoons, beavers, and weasels all take from the trees and give what they can in return.

Both within the forest and above it, you'll find bluebirds, chickadees, sparrows, robins, finches, redheaded woodpeckers, thrushes, kestrels, bald eagles, red-tailed and red-shouldered hawks, peregrine falcons, the occasional osprey, great horned owls, barred owls, great blue herons, Canada geese, common loons, and wild turkeys. If you hike on the many mountain trails, you're bound to run into a ruffed grouse or two. You may not see them because of their excellent camouflage, but if they sense danger, you'll definitely hear their loud, drumming wings beating vigorously.

Eddie Wade felt at home here more than any other place on the face of the earth.

———

Yesterday, he'd arranged with Bruno to watch his cats. That morning, he packed a suitcase, got into his car, and drove to Côte-des-Neiges to pick up Josette. Four hours later, he was picking up the keys to the cabin he'd rented from Birdie Doyle, who owned and operated Birdie's Tavern on Lake George in the heart of the Adirondacks. Birdie had moved out of the cabin five years earlier when her husband died and bought a small house nearer to the tavern. She had been renting it out, mostly to hunters, ever since. She had had enough of rustic living. This was the fourth straight year Eddie had rented it from her. After picking up the keys while Josette stretched her legs outside, they purchased some groceries and supplies at a small bait shop down the street from the tavern.

The cabin was located across the road from the tavern and about a mile deep into the dense forest, accessible by a single dirt road wide enough for only one vehicle. By today's standards, the cabin was primitive. Built of stone and logs, there was no electricity; nor was there plumbing. But it had a large fireplace, and it was spotlessly clean. It did have many modern conveniences, if they didn't have be plugged in. There was a double bed, a large dresser with four drawers, two rocking chairs (padded both on the seat and the back), a picnic table with benches on either side, a good supply of sheets and pillowcases, blankets galore, plates and cups without any chips in them, cutlery, pots and pans with cooking utensils, as well as a kerosene refrigerator and several kerosene lanterns—all contained in one room. During his time in the war, Eddie had done with far less.

"I've never been this far away from civilization before," Josette said, eyeing the inside of the cabin skeptically. "Are there bears here?"

"I don't think there are any inside here, but you could have a peek under the bed. They mostly like to live in the forest— big black ones! If we're lucky, we may get to see a few of them before we leave."

"Very funny."

"They're more afraid of us than we are of them. They usually keep to themselves, except if there's food left out. But just in case one gets any crazy notions, look over there above the fireplace," he said, pointing. A Winchester 94 lever-action repeating hunting rifle and a Parker break-open style, side-by-side double-barrel shotgun sat in a rack. "Birdie has plenty of ammo in that dresser there. She also keeps a handgun there too. She used to hunt a lot, but now she just goes to the grocery store."

After they unpacked their clothes and put them neatly in the dresser, they ate lunch outside on the porch. They had picked up some sandwiches, potato chips, and Cokes at the bait shop. They sat on a porch swing with red cushions.

"It's so peaceful out here," Josette said and then took a big swig of her Coke.

A couple of ornery blue jays were jeering at them from one of the surrounding trees. They made whistling and gurgling sounds, clearly upset by the intruders.

"It's a whole different world. I've been coming here now for a few years to unwind and recharge my batteries. Makes a difference." He took a bite of his sandwich.

Suddenly, a loud screeching sound echoed from above.

"What was that?" Josette asked, looking up at the tops of the trees.

"Sounds like a hawk, probably looking for a mate ... or something to kill. Maybe it's just scolding us for trespassing on its territory. Or all of the above."

"Wow! You don't hear that in the city. I have to tell you, I was a little unsure of all this when we first arrived, but now I'm beginning to really enjoy it. We should go for a walk in the woods when we're finished."

"Sounds good to me, but aren't you afraid we'll run into Smokey the Bear?"

"He's friendly enough. It's the others I'm worried about. You'll bring a gun, won't you?"

"We won't be going hunting, but I did bring my own .45, if that's any comfort for you."

"It is."

They cleaned up after finishing their lunch. Eddie made sure they hadn't left any crumbs on the porch. Not entirely leaving his city habits behind, he locked up the cabin and the car. They followed a hunting trail that started from behind the cabin. The trees at that point in the forest were mostly oak, ash, and pine, with some birch and spruce now and again. In parts of the forest, the foliage let in little sunlight. It was warm with little breeze. They had to constantly brush aside the insects from their faces with their hands. The terrain was at a slight incline, so after an hour or so, Josette was a little out of breath. They sat down beneath a small dogwood tree to rest, surprising a couple of chipmunks who ran off and quickly disappeared.

"I can't believe how beautiful it is here," Josette said. "I ought to get out more."

"I thought you liked the bakery."

"I do, but I'm not sure I want to do that the rest of my life. The work is fine, but it's the same thing day after day. Frankly, I don't know if I have the staying power to last another thirty years. I've worked in the shop since I was ten years old. I started with just cleaning up the place, but by the time I was fourteen, I was actually baking. I know every operation with my eyes closed."

"What would you do if you didn't do that?"

There was a long pause before she answered.

"You'll laugh at me."

"Why would I do that?"

"Because you'll think it's the stupidest thing you've ever heard."

"Try me."

She turned her head and stared at him.

"If you so much as giggle," she said, pointing a finger at him, "I'll haul off and punch you a good one."

"Just don't hit me in the nose. It's already been broken twice before."

"I was thinking lately ... not too seriously ... well, just a little, I guess ... about what it would be like to be an ... investigator like you. I mean a private investigator."

"You'd make a good one. You're bright, and your instincts are sharp. Yep, you'd make a good one."

"Wow! That wasn't what I was expecting to hear from you. You really think so, or are you just placating me, hoping you'll luck out tonight under the sheets?"

"Well, there's that too, but I do think you've got what it takes, and there are too few female investigators as it is. I think you should give it some serious consideration."

She said she would.

With another hour's hike back, they decided to return to the cabin. They preferred to hold hands, but with all the bugs, they needed both to keep them out of their eyes, mouths, and ears. As they made their way down the trail, Eddie was as content as he had ever been. Certainly, he never approached this state in the city. Maybe he'd consider making two trips here instead of the usual one each year. Spring and fall were good times of the year. Being with Josette gave him more incentive.

As they approached the clearing where the cabin stood, Eddie noticed something that hadn't been there before. He walked carefully around the cabin, looking at the ground. Josette watched him.

"What are you looking at?"

He squatted down on one knee.

"These shoe prints. They weren't here when we left."

Josette stared down at them too. It had rained the previous day.

"They're sunken a bit," she said. She looked around the front of the cabin and to the sides. "They're all around."

"See what I told you? You'd make a good investigator."

"Only good?"

"For now. What else can you tell me about them?"

"They're not ours. We're wearing boots." She pointed. "See? Those are ours."

"Good. So, while we were on our little hike in the woods, someone was here checking out the place. Look at them carefully again. What do they tell you?"

Josette squatted down and examined them. After a long moment, she answered him.

"By the size of them, I'd say they belonged to a man."

"Maybe a woman was wearing a man's shoes, or maybe she had big feet, and they belonged to her."

"Where's the evidence for that?"

"Conjecture. I'm just exploring ideas."

Eddie got up and slowly walked around the cabin again, taking a second look at the prints. Josette followed behind. Then they walked down the road for about a quarter of a mile.

"Whoever it was walked down the road and then had a good look around."

"Maybe he was just looking for the owner and then left."

"If that was the case, chances are he would have driven here instead of walking. And then there's the timing. He waits until we leave, and then he has a good look around the cabin. I don't think he went inside, because there wasn't any dirt on the porch."

"That's a hypothesis but a good one."

Eddie smiled at that, but he was a little worried. His gun was in the small of his back with his shirt covering it. Instinctively, his right hand went to it and rubbed against it, giving him a sense of comfort.

Off in the distance, a barred owl hooted.

⸺◈⸺

For the first night there, they had decided to have supper at a restaurant in town instead of cooking for themselves.

They had hamburgers and french fries in a hole-in-the-wall that was open only six months of the year, catering to out-of-towners there on vacation. On their way back, they picked up some beer at the bait shop. They spent that evening on the porch, drinking beer and talking. Josette shared many of Eddie's interests, so their conversation was spirited with a lot of exaggerated gestures and laughter. Eddie found out for the first time that Josette could go toe to toe with him on just about any subject. He liked that. A lot.

When the conversation started to wind down, Josette asked him about his time in the army. That was the last thing Eddie wanted to talk about, but he did anyway, because that was part of his past; if the relationship was going to work, he couldn't keep anything from her. Secrets tended to make a relationship crumble at its foundation.

At three o'clock in the morning, they were sleeping soundly, their bodies keeping each other warm. It was still cold at night in June in the Adirondacks, even though it could be hot in the daytime. At six minutes after the hour, Josette suddenly jumped up, disturbing Eddie's sleep.

"What is it?" he said sleepily. "A bad dream?"

"I thought I heard something outside. I know I did."

"We're in the middle of the woods," he said, rubbing his eyes. "Nocturnal creatures. They hunt at night for food. It's probably a hedgehog or a raccoon. Maybe a red fox or skunk." He yawned and stretched his arms. *Or a bear,* he thought, but kept it to himself. "You should try to go back to sleep. We're gonna have a busy day tomorrow." He rolled over.

"It didn't sound like an animal. It sounded more like a person's footsteps on the porch. I wasn't dreaming that. I was already awake."

That got his attention.

"You sure?" he asked over his shoulder.

"Yes!" she said. The word sounded like a whispered hiss.

"OK, I'll have a look. Go back to sleep."

He got out of bed, threw on a T-shirt, and slipped into his pants and boots, lacing them up only halfway. He reached under his pillow for his .45 and then grabbed the flashlight off the table. He unlocked the door and then opened it slowly, standing in the middle of the doorframe, listening for a few minutes. All he heard were the crickets.

He already had his night vision, and the moon was peeking through the tops of the trees, so he wouldn't need the flashlight if it wasn't absolutely necessary. He stepped onto the porch, which creaked under his weight. He took four long steps before reaching the ground. An owl hooted. He slowly walked around the cabin, stopping every so often to listen. In about five minutes, he was back where he started. The cool night air, the smells of dirt and trees, the stillness of the forest, and the anxiety of unknown danger reminded him of Germany during the war. His .45 semiautomatic hung at his side; he grasped it tightly, remembering the shoe prints he'd seen earlier. *Come out, come out wherever you are,* he thought. *Whoever you are.*

But there was no one.

Nothing.

⸺⟨◆⟩⸺

They had gotten up early the next day, having had little sleep after the incident the previous night. Eddie had built a fire in the pit beside the cabin and made some coffee for them as well as some bacon and eggs. As they were nearly finished cleaning up inside, Josette mentioned Percy.

"I found out from my parents last month that Chanel told Percy who his real father is." She reached up to put the clean plates and cups back in the cupboard. "I forgot to tell you."

"How did he take it?" He was sitting in a rocking chair, going through a tacklebox.

"They didn't say, but it mustn't have been too bad," she said over her shoulder.

"Why do you say that?"

She turned around, facing him. "Apparently he started the process of changing his last name to York."

Eddie stopped what he was doing and looked up at her.

"You gotta be kidding."

"I wish I were."

"He doesn't even know Branch York. Guy was the only father he knew."

"And he'd always been a good father to him."

"Why would he want the last name of a homicidal maniac? It doesn't make sense."

"I'll have to ask him that sometime."

"Jesus, Mary, and Joseph," Eddie said.

After they finished cleaning up, Eddie put the fishing rods and tackle—they went with the cabin, compliments of Birdie Doyle—in the car. They drove to the bait shop. Inside, Eddie reached into a cooler and pulled out a Styrofoam cup, handing it to Josette.

"What's this?"

"Look inside."

Josette took the lid off.

"Yuck! What do we want with worms?"

"Bait! We've got to have something to catch fish with."

"Poor little things."

"Why don't you pay for this up front. I want to have a look around before we leave."

Josette took the worms to the cash register. She dug into her pants for a dollar bill.

"Going fishing, dearie?" The clerk was a stout elderly woman in her sixties with short gray hair. "They're real hungry this time of the morning."

"It's my first time fishing."

"Well, then, good luck to you! You put those worms on your hook real good now. You'll catch a ton of fish!"

Josette got her change and waited for Eddie by the door. She glanced out the window. A few pickups went by on the road, part of the local traffic. Then a Greyhound bus roared by going south—last stop, Port Authority Bus Terminal in Manhattan. She leaned a little to the left for a better look when she saw someone walking down the road. He was wearing a light blue jacket and black pants. She could only see him from behind, but she watched him carefully until he was out of sight. Eddie came up behind her.

"Let's go. If we're going to have trout or bass for dinner tonight, we've got to a shake a leg. We've got to drop our lines while they're still biting." Noticing she had a strange look on her face, he asked, "What's wrong?"

"Nothing. I just thought I saw someone I knew."

"Here? Who would you know here?"

"That's just it. I don't know anyone here. Maybe I was just imagining it."

"Probably. OK, let's boogie-woogie! We've got a date with destiny out on the lake. The fish are waiting for their breakfast!"

———— ✦ ————

"I can't do it!"

"What do you mean you can't do it? Sure you can. I just showed you how. You just take the worm and slide it on the hook."

"But it's alive! It's wiggling."

"That's the whole point. You want a live worm to attract the fish. Wiggling is good."

"Yuck! I can't do it to the poor thing."

"But it's a worm! If a fish doesn't eat it, some furry creature

273

will. Worms are used to it!" Eddie laughed, shook his head, baited her hook, and threw the line out. "Keep your eyes on the bobber—that little red and white thing there," he said, pointing at it. "When it goes down, that means you caught a fish. Just reel it in. The fish is going to be wiggling like crazy. You going to have a problem with that too?"

She just narrowed her eyes at him. He winked at her and then threw his own line in the water.

After a few minutes of silence, Eddie decided to tell her about his father, leaving no details out. They had a long talk about him. He wanted her to know about his past, both good and bad. Several times, he had to remind her to keep her voice down so as not to chase the fish away. When they exhausted that topic, they stopped talking. Eddie poured them some coffee from the thermos jug. They sat and watched their bobbers and drank coffee.

Lincoln Wade, Eddie thought. He had both his name and his blood. Like Percy would with his father. But did it matter? Eddie was nothing like his father. Or was he? Maybe not now, but what about when he grew older—five years down the line, or ten? Would he get married, have a child, and then abandon them as Lincoln had? Was it in his blood? Was that the future he had to look forward to?

"Eddie! Eddie!"

Eddie was jarred out of his thoughts.

"What?"

"My bobber disappeared. I can't find it."

"That means you caught a fish. Reel it in slowly. Keep the tip of the pole down; give it some play. Slowly now. Good. Here it comes; I can see it. It's a good one! Slowly now. I'll get the net under it." And that's what he did. He scooped it up out of the water and into the boat. "It's a bass—four or five pounds. We'll eat well tonight!"

"Look at it. It's alive! It's ... it's flipping all over the place."

"Lake George has a great reputation of having live fish here. They don't allow dead ones."

"We can't eat that. It's alive!"

They fished for another hour and caught three more good-sized bass. Having more than they could eat, Eddie suggested they give half of them to Birdie after they scaled and filleted them. Eddie rowed the boat back to shore, while Josette sat in front. In spite of herself, she was very pleased at her performance. As they approached the dock, Eddie noticed Josette staring at something intently.

"What is it? You're staring daggers at something."

"It's that man again, the one I thought I saw across the road from the bait shop. See? There!" she said, pointing. "He's wearing the same clothes."

Eddie stopped rowing and looked, holding a hand above his eyes to shade the glare.

"All I see are those people there getting onto the pontoon boat."

"He's gone now, but I know that was the same person. I'm not imagining it."

"Maybe he's just someone who works around here. That's why you keep seeing him. Maybe he just looks like someone you know."

"Yeah, I guess you're right."

Yeah maybe, Eddie thought, but he wasn't so sure.

———◦(◦)◦———

Eddie had done the honors when they returned to the cabin. He showed Josette how to scale and fillet the fish; at least that was what he had intended to do. When he cut off the head of the first fish, she ran into the cabin and didn't come out until she was certain he was finished.

In late afternoon, he had fried the bass in oil after a light coat of flour and eggs. While they were frying, he fixed a lettuce and tomato salad and opened a can of pork and beans, adding more than a little maple syrup to it. The fish was crispy on the outside, and the meat was tender on the inside. Josette seemed not to have an issue with that. After they had eaten, they cleaned up, making sure no food was left out for the bears and raccoons.

They each had taken a bucket bath (Josette's first ever) and put on some fresh clothes. Then they drove down to Birdie's Tavern to spend a few hours relaxing. At that time of year, the days were long. The sun wouldn't be setting until nine or so, so Eddie brought his binoculars with him to show Josette the beautiful scenery across Lake George that she might have missed when she was busy watching her bobber.

Birdie was thrilled to receive the filleted bass and insisted on paying them. Eddie wouldn't hear of it. He introduced Josette to her, and after a minute, the two conversed as if they had been long-lost friends. Eddie got a kick out of that. Josette fit right in.

The trip to the Adirondacks had been a success so far. He and Josette had done more talking in two days than they had in a week in the city. They were getting to know each other better. They both liked what they were learning about each other. Was marriage in the cards? Eddie thought so. But they were at a crossroads; if they wanted children, they couldn't wait too much longer. The clock was ticking away, at least for Josette.

They ordered drinks from Birdie—who insisted they were on the house—and took them to the back on the patio. They sat down at a table near the railing and looked across the big lake that was like a sheet of glass, with the evening sun shining on it, turning it several different colors. Of course, there were other people there as well, but the table they'd found was off by itself.

"It's so beautiful here, Eddie," Josette said. "And so peaceful. I'm glad we came."

"It's nice to get out of the city once in a while. It gives you a different perspective on life."

"It certainly does. I know I'm going to have a difficult time going back to the bakery."

Eddie stared at her for a moment.

"How serious were you about looking into this investigator thing?"

"If you had asked me a week ago, I would have said not too, but now I'd say very."

"You know, the job isn't like what you read about in dime-store novels."

"Well, that's good, because I don't read dime-store novels."

"It would be a big change in your life. If you're serious, we could talk more about it. You'd have to partner up with someone and be an apprentice before you could get a license."

"Oh, might you know someone I could do that with?"

"Yeah, as it happens, I know a guy in Mile End."

"Is he good to work with?"

"He's a little rough around the edges, but I guess he's a pretty good guy."

Something caught his attention across the lake. He picked up his binoculars and looked.

"Wow! There's a pair of great blue herons." He gave the binoculars to Josette. She took them and adjusted the lens.

"They're just gorgeous! Now that's something you don't see in Montreal."

She continued to look through the binoculars, following the shoreline to her right, viewing the lakeshore properties, oohing and aahing as she did. She continued along the shoreline until she got to the patio of the bar next door to Birdie's, a fair distance away. Then she stopped. It was about as crowded as the one they were at, with people laughing and having a good time. They could hear rock 'n' roll music playing off in the distance.

"Oh, my God," she said. There was a tremor in her voice—and fear.

"What?" Eddie asked.

She continued to stare through the binoculars and didn't answer.

Eddie reached for the binoculars and put them up to his eyes. He adjusted the lens and slowly looked to the left and right, in the direction she'd been looking. All he saw were people—locals and vacationers—enjoying themselves. Then he moved the binoculars over a few inches farther to the right and stopped. Someone was sitting alone; his head was turned in their direction, as if he were staring at them—a twisted expression on his face.

"Christ almighty," he said. "It's him."

Printed in the United States
by Baker & Taylor Publisher Services